A TREATISE OF AIR

ALSO BY CL JARVIS

The Edinburgh Doctrines series

The Doctrines of Fire

A Treatise of Air

A TREATISE OF AIR

THE EDINBURGH DOCTRINES SERIES
BOOK TWO

CL JARVIS

PEWTER LYNX PRESS

First published in 2023 by Pewter Lynx Press

ISBN 978-1-7392644-3-7

To past and future mariners.

I

Without coin or chemistry, it would be a long autumn.

"Did ye know George Stephens is a phlogiston-wielder?"

Elizabeth Fulhame set her needlework on her lap.

"He is?"

"Aye, he's trained with Dr Black almost since he arrived in Edinburgh," Thomas explained. "Dr Black himself suggested we practice together."

He knew as soon as the information was absorbed that he'd receive no sympathy from his wife. Elizabeth adopted a position of beseeching the heavens.

"How is it that men manage to communicate so little information between each other? I've seen you with George more days than not—"

"That's an exaggeration!"

"Only slightly. And every time you're together I see your lips moving, and I can hear words coming out of both your mouths...I don't know how you can avoid talking about anything of import."

Thomas shrugged. "The topic of phlogiston never came up."

Elizabeth stabbed her needle through the linen. "When I go to the Grassmarket and find myself matching pace with another woman, by the time we cross the market I'll have learned about her youngest son's persistent cough, the disappointing state of her marital relations, and the rudeness of her goat."

"Ye'll have much in common with her, then," Thomas noted with a smirk.

There was a pause. Thomas put his elbow on his knee and leaned forward. The silence thickened.

Elizabeth almost managed to conceal a smile. "Aye. It wasn't your over-sized wealth or over-sized intellect I married you for."

"So what was it?" prompted Thomas, not looking away.

"Your massive, prodigious, over-sized...confidence."

"Hah!"

"Dr Black's trained George in phlogiston-wielding these past few years?"

"He's also good at proculopathy, I hear."

"So you haven't even spoken to George himself about this? What are you saving your words for, boy?"

"George left Edinburgh to visit his family. Didn't I tell ye? He won't be back for a couple of weeks, I imagine."

"Oh, so you do occasionally communicate pertinent facts about your lives?"

Thomas rose from his chair, stretching, and wandered over to the window. A grey pall was settling over the city, and he could barely see the other side of the street. After a moment he wiped the condensation off the glass with his sleeve. Elizabeth pretended not to notice.

"I think this gown is too far gone to be repaired," Elizabeth commented. "I tried to stitch the tear, but the striped pattern means the imperfection is still noticeable."

"I'm sure no one will notice," Thomas muttered, watching a peddler round the corner onto Cowgate.

"It tore right at the hip," Elizabeth said. "The worst place for it. It's fine for conducting my experiments in, but..." She waited to see if Thomas paid enough attention to her wardrobe to understand the problem. When it became obvious he didn't, she continued. "But this was my last 'good' dress."

Thomas sighed and dragged himself away from the window. "We have a few months until the Season resumes. Plenty of time to get some more fabric."

Elizabeth nodded. Left unsaid was that any money saved for a new dress would mean less money to replenish her chemical supplies. She was down to her last clippings of zinc, which would only last two or three experiments at a stretch. But that was the arrangement she'd come to with Thomas: her chemistry experiments couldn't come at the expense of anything else.

"This morning's letter was from Lottie, aye?" Thomas asked.

"Yes." Elizabeth traced her thumb over the fold of paper.

"How's she keeping?"

"She says they're expecting their second child in February," Elizabeth replied. She was glad Thomas hadn't asked about the contents of her cousin's letter as soon as she'd read it—giving her time to digest her cousin's news and savour the familiar handwriting. After its journey across the country the vellum smelled mostly of horses, fusty stables and mud-covered leather, but when she broke open the seal Elizabeth inhaled it anyway and imagined she could briefly detect Lottie's familiar smell.

"That's good, is it not?" Thomas leaned across the table, catching the tiniest hesitation in his wife's voice. "I'm sure her man is hoping for more lusty weans to help around the place."

In the hollow of Thomas' cheeks were the finest network of pox scars, barely visible. From whispers between family members and the other women in Meath, Elizabeth suspected those scars explained why their marriage had produced no children. Any comments on Thomas' childhood illness were usually paired with pitying glances her way.

"She's happy, as is he, I'm sure," Elizabeth said.

She thought of Lottie's exact words: *A happy event coming sooner than expected. With God's blessing Don will make it work—next year the mill will be in full operation and completed its maiden orders. Love you always, cuz.*

"I suppose it's the usual set of pecuniary concerns. It will be a while before Don brings in a profit." If he brings in one at all, she thought darkly.

Thomas hummed and returned to his pile of books. It wasn't that he didn't appreciate the precarious nature of Lottie and Don's enterprise, but his sense of concern didn't seep as far into his marrow as it did with Elizabeth. "Well, if Don can't make money on textiles in Lanark, he won't be able to make money on anything. He struck me as having at least a modicum of sense in his box."

It takes more than innate goodness to succeed in these industries, Elizabeth wanted to say, before deciding it wasn't worth the energy.

"Unlike this humble servant," Thomas continued. "Don shouldn't have trouble getting a loan to tide him over until fortune is ready to smile."

"Lottie didn't think that would be a good idea, love."

"Why not?" Thomas looked up from his book. "Don's one of the rare breed of men I'd trust not to squander a loan. It's not something I'd advise everybody pursue, mind. But the extra cash'll alleviate their immediate business stress and carry them beyond the survival state."

Thomas had met Don once back in Ireland, before they'd

became in-laws. If Elizabeth's memory served, they'd spoken for all of twenty minutes on a stroll into town. Most of that conversation being about the weather. But Thomas had the blithe ability to decide he'd got the measure of a man based upon scant impressions and his wife relaying her correspondence.

Not that she disagreed with his assessment, technically. Maybe she was overcautious.

"I'll tell her the erstwhile, soon-to-be Dr Fulhame says she shouldn't fret." Elizabeth's mouth quirked. "That he prescribes money for the alleviation of the survival state."

They needed to call on Dr Black within the hour, the success of that visit depended on them acting as a harmonious unit.

2

Elizabeth's money concerns would be smoothed considerably once her husband secured next term's laboratory assistantship.

"Dr Black said he'd discuss future work with you in August, didn't he?" she asked as they made their way to the chemistry professor in question. The walk from the old high school yards took them past the college, eerily quiet in at the height of summer.

"True. But it's only the start of August, and he was traveling last week..."

She shouldn't fret. Black seemed content with the work Thomas put in over the summer, saying there'd probably be more work for him once term resumed. But 'probably' was a loaded word to an academic: it could mean anything between 'a certainty' and 'I'm too polite to tell you it's impossible.'

"It was about this time last year George said Dr Black sat down to discuss tutoring arrangements," Thomas added. "I'm not going to tiptoe around the topic, love."

Well, that was her worry.

She'd promised herself she would never treat her husband

like a son. Her own family dynamics had soured her on that concept.

Dr Joseph Black occupied a lavish colonnaded Nicolson Street townhouse, which he'd moved into a few years ago. The peach wallpaper of the parlour accentuated the extensive fossil collection he displayed on sideboards along two walls. The room had a faint musty, chemical smell that must come off his robes when he returned from the college, because Elizabeth couldn't imagine him dirtying his parlour with chemical experiments.

That didn't mean he abandoned all thoughts of natural philosophy at home, though.

"Dr Black," Elizabeth began. "How bright do you think you could make your phlogistonic light shine?"

Black set down his broadsheet. "A gentleman should never outshine a lady. That would be churlish and ungallant." His dark eyes gleamed like obsidian.

Black appeared ethereal at the best of times. His clothing was of similar vivacity: ranging in hue from drab academic black to elegant dinner party black, with occasional forays into practical outdoors black when he went walking or riding.

Fortunately, Black's demeanour was more charming than his appearance.

"So it's up to me to prove the principle?" Elizabeth's eyebrows rose a centimetre further. "That hardly seems more gallant."

She pushed her sleeves past her elbows. After a moment a white candle flame seemed to flicker in her palm.

"Ah, light should come more from the sympathetic nervous system..." Black leaned forward, then stopped himself. "It's more aetherial than phlogistonic, but you need a little bit of phlogiston to keep it acting like a flame."

"Of course." Phlogiston burned. A strike of aether could render a man unconscious or kill him.

Learning all of this was a slow process. Black never hesitated to correct her husband's technique with a finger into the muscular tissue or ligaments to help him access and control an aspect of his body no one naturally thought about. Elizabeth depended either on watching Black instruct Thomas—a rare occurrence, since most of his instruction took place in private between classes—or hope that Thomas would spare a few hours to repeat the exercises—a more common outcome, but since Thomas wasn't great at explaining things, almost useless.

Much as she wanted to complain, there weren't many alternatives. She estimated there were fewer than thirty phlogiston wielders in Britain, most of them natural philosophers who treated it as an intellectual exercise.

Still, she was in on the secret, so it made sense to persist. After a few splutters, an orb of brightness formed between her fingers. Taking Black's advice, it required more focus on her nervous system than musculature to keep the light bobbing in her palm.

"It's interesting," Black agreed, now matching her glare with a light of his own. "It takes up less energy than expelling the same quantity of phlogiston, so I imagine one could exceed the brightness of a hundred candles. Maybe more."

She'd certainly save pennies on tallow candles this winter, though holding her hand up to see would get tiring after a few minutes. Not to mention the difficulties of single-handed sewing, cooking and cleaning.

"How are your own philosophical investigations coming along?" Black asked after a pause.

"I haven't done much since we last spoke," Elizabeth replied, shaking her head. "Other affairs caught up with me."

Black nodded.

This wasn't true. But only a couple of weeks passed since Black last raised the subject, and Elizabeth thought too much interest would come across as unladylike. Black cautioned her to be careful with ether distillation ("the fumes will ignite at the merest brush of a flame...") and perhaps just let her husband do the distillation for her. Elizabeth nodded politely, thanked the professor, then ran the distillations herself as soon as she got home. Black had a habit of remembering little conversational snippets like that, so if she told him about the results of the ether experiment he might bring Thomas into the discussion, exposing her disobedience.

The husband in question chose this moment to stomp into Black's parlour. Distracted, Elizabeth's light flickered. She refocussed.

Thomas glanced at the twin display but didn't say anything.

"That didn't take long," Black commented, closing his hand. "I take it you found everything you needed in the library?"

"Of course, I figured out the standard writing style after reading a couple of case studies. Seemed simple enough."

Elizabeth looked at Black, but his expression didn't change.

"Quite so."

Thomas fixed his wife with a look. Elizabeth smoothed her dress and rose.

"Oh, before you leave." Black rose and disappeared into his study, emerging with a letter. "I didn't want to distract you from your reading Thomas, but I seek a small favour from you."

"Hmm?" Thomas looked intrigued, Elizabeth pretended to study the classical fresco above her host's fireplace. Black's tone indicated he required something more involved than delivering a note or running an errand. But not, crucially, offer an assistantship.

"Both you and Mrs Fulhame have some understanding of textile weaving?"

10

He addressed the question to Thomas.

"Aye, my brother's been in and out of the trade; Elizabeth's family runs a mill."

"Good, you might recognise the dye in the samples I've received." Black handed the letter to Thomas. Elizabeth could see several thumb-sized swatches of red fabric attached to the second page.

"Madder red," Thomas said, scrutinising the swatches. "Common plant-extract dye, certainly produced in Ireland. Rather nice specimens ye have here, Doctor, the dye usually fades after washing."

"Unless..." Elizabeth interrupted, having peered at the contents of the letter. "It isn't claiming to be madder red dye at all..."

There was a pause as Thomas scanned through the letter in response to his wife's gentle hint.

"It's turkey red? I don't usually see examples of this up close. There was the Lord Provost's frockcoat with the gold trimming he wore to the senate meeting...would have had to put my face halfway up his arse to get as close as this, though."

Elizabeth gave Black a strained smile, hoping to convey an apology for her husband's wit. She felt a shimmer of envy that Thomas had admired a garment made with turkey red: she couldn't recall getting that close to someone wearing one. She would surely remember if she had—when you turning away from the luscious, vibrant red all other reds faded to dullness. No other reds would hold its brightness.

She eased herself back from this reverie. "You received correspondence from as far afield as Turkey, Dr Black? That must be a first."

"No," said Black. "This letter came from Holland, where a Frenchman by the name of Philippe Moreau is readying to depart for Scotland with the procedure for manufacturing turkey red."

Thomas let out a low whistle. "He probably shouldn't tarry long—I don't imagine the French or Turkish authorities will be happy he fled with an industrial secret this valuable."

"No," Black said. "I rather imagine they won't be. I received the letter yesterday afternoon, so I expect Moreau will be a few days behind."

Britain had hungered for the secrets of turkey red manufacture since Elizabeth was a child. Despite offering thousands of pounds in monetary rewards for the process, the handful of Rouen mills controlling the world's supply of dye weren't induced to share.

"And he intends to sell the secret to the Scottish Board of Manufactures?" Elizabeth gathered that was his intention from the content of the letter she'd read. "You're sure this isn't another forgery or poor mimic?" Given the financial rewards at stake, plenty of aspiring philosophers claim mastery of the turkey red recipe, but they were invariably poor imitations.

"That's why the letter was forwarded to me," Black said. "I tested one of the samples—" Elizabeth noticed a gap in the strip of red, "—and it survived a couple of washes and a bleaching attempt without ill-effects."

"It's smart of the Board to bring in a genuine natural philosopher for guidance."

"I've consulted for the Board for several years now," Black said, taking back his letter. "They receive a lot of bleaching and agricultural proposals. It's up to me and a few colleagues to evaluate their scientific merit and make recommendations *vis-a-vis* their general adoption. As you can imagine, the Board is excited by the prospect of turkey red dyeing on our shores."

"It'll be a nice project for ye, Doctor," Thomas commented. "Rewarding."

"A little more agreeable than the current batch of proposals concerning fish guts as fertiliser," Black agreed, ignoring Thomas' naked pecuniary allusion. "But if Monsieur Moreau arrives within the next couple of days I'll need someone to greet him for me in Leith. I have patient visits and consultancy work tomorrow I can't extract myself from at short notice. Since you speak some French, Thomas..."

"I'd be delighted," Thomas said. "Not a problem, dear Doctor."

"I hope it won't inconvenience you, much," Black continued. "I don't think there has been bad weather in the Channel or unfavourable wind that could delay him."

Elizabeth could hear the lilt in her husband's voice. Was it too much to hope he'd hold his tongue on the topic of personal renumeration for this? Granted, it wasn't clear *how* he could be rewarded for escorting a Frenchman up the hill from Leith to Edinburgh, but Thomas tended to believe staking involvement in a lucrative industrial venture from the get-go was the best way to get something from nothing. She squeezed her husband's arm.

"It's very kind of you to entrust such a task to us, Dr Black," she said.

She made a show of stepping towards the door then tapping her husband's arm in belated remembrance of a small fact.

"Oh Thomas, you were going to...?"

"Ahh yes, so I was!" Thomas played along. "I can't remember if I asked ye about continuing with my assistantship during the winter term..."

There was an art to the ask. They didn't want to seem pushy about getting a commitment from Black. Nor presumptuous of the outcome. Having Elizabeth feed the reminder to her husband allowed him to blame the nagging on her.

"Of course, I hadn't forgotten." Black's well-practised

tones hid whether he'd forgotten the matter or not. "I'm updating my account book later this week, perhaps on Friday. After that I'll be better-placed to think about the assistant-ships I need this term. Though I caution the business with Monsieur Moreau might encroach upon my time."

3

"Do ye think our friend will give us the common courtesy of looking French?" Thomas asked, lowering his voice so the other tavern patrons couldn't hear.

"What would that even entail?" Elizabeth shot back.

It was now several hours into their afternoon in Leith. Thomas' good-natured prodding of every dockhand they passed finally yielded the information that a ship from Rotterdam was expected to arrive late that evening.

The pair passed the time walking up and down the sands until the wind picked up and they decided to continue their wait in a tavern. Elizabeth now regarded that decision as premature: the sun would be over the horizon shortly, and then they'd be stuck here until the ship—yet to appear on the horizon—docked. Not that they could see through the fogged-up windows.

"Well, by starting a fight with the first honest John Bull he comes across." Thomas did the drinking for the both of them, and though he was being responsible with his cups under Elizabeth's watchful eye, she knew he'd be tipsy in an hour.

The King's Wark crouched at the shore edge, looking out

over the Water of Leith bridge and the waterfront buildings. Inside, low-beamed joists threatened the hats of the tallest patrons. The Fulhames were lucky to find two rickety stools in the corner. The draught from the door swinging to and fro was enough to give Elizabeth a respite from the fungal body odour surrounding them.

"Poor Monsieur," Elizabeth muttered to herself. "Almost as unfortunate as being Irish."

She'd wasted one afternoon in their previous lodgings enduring a Tory student from London, who lectured her about how the Irish were good-for-nothing wastrels blighting Edinburgh with their uncouth ways, but how she was a charming exception to this rule. He'd drunk a whole pot of her good tea.

"The urinal of the gods indeed."

Elizabeth hadn't noticed how rainy Ireland was until she heard the east coast Scots joking about it. At least in Ireland the rain fell vertically; in Edinburgh it tended to come at you from surprise angles.

"This garçon must be really desperate to seek help from the English at a time like this," Thomas mused.

"Well, the war left our government slightly less bankrupt than the French, so I suppose it makes sense."

"Fine point, lass. Fine point."

Elizabeth's knees bumped against her husband in a bid to avoid jostling the party on the other side of her. In response, Thomas hooked his foot around her heel.

"Do the Leith races begin next week?" Wondered Elizabeth.

"I think it's two weeks from now," Thomas said, surveying the drinkers. "I suppose some people could be here for it."

The Leith horse races brought every opportunistic vendor, circus performer and hustler to town. Many arrived early to negotiate better rates with the coffeehouses they performed in.

Edinburgh wasn't spared the swell of visitors; it made August a maddening time to reside in the city.

A commotion on the front made its way above the noise of the tavern. Imagining it to be a street brawl, Elizabeth didn't bother to look out the window. Thomas craned his neck and tapped Elizabeth's arm. "Bottom's up, my dear. Looks like our ship."

"That's not a ship; that's a speck on the horizon. I'm not rushing the consumption of this piss-weak ale for *that*."

It was already dark the time the Fulhames assembled on the dock to meet Moreau. The breeze had died down, but Elizabeth still hugged her shawl to the chest. Several unaccompanied women loitered on the edges of the crowds and against the building walls, no doubt hoping to make coin on an impulsive sailor.

Their target was easy to single out from the crowd, because he moved from the dock with the confusion of one not used to travel, unaware his naivety radiated off him like steam off a horse.

"Monsieur Moreau?" Thomas elbowed his way to the man, who was clutching several portmanteau and carriers. "I've come to greet ye on behalf of Dr Joseph Black from the university. Regrettably he had business elsewhere..."

Their target was reed-thin, with scraggly blond hair more out of his queue than in. The dampness of the ocean had sunk into his clothes, making them heavy and itchy to look at. He was closer to Black's age than Elizabeth's, but with none of the latter's poise.

"You are from the university?" Moreau asked, in passable English. He didn't notice Elizabeth standing next to Thomas.

"Correct. Dr Black is expecting ye and we'll happily bring ye to him."

Moreau coughed and shuffled his feet.

Seeing his hesitation, Elizabeth stepped forward.

"It's a delight to make your acquaintance, Monsieur. This is my husband Thomas Fulhame, a medical student at the university." She hoped this domestic tableaux would reduce the poor man's fear that they'd come to abduct him off the boat.

Indeed, it did seem to provide some comfort, because Moreau finally broke into a grin.

"Enchante, Mrs Fulhame. It is so kind of you to welcome me."

"Yes, no problem," Thomas beckoned and helped Moreau through the dissipating crowds. "We'll get ye in a carriage in no time."

The frown returned. "Dr Black stays...very far away?"

"It's only a mile and a half," Elizabeth said, pointing into the darkness. "A very quick journey by carriage."

"Oh, no—I must apologise. I will stay in a tavern tonight. Tomorrow I will call upon Dr Black." Moreau began warming up to his excuses. "I am very tired and hungry, and I would not wish to trouble Dr Black at such a late hour. Please."

"It won't be an inconvenience at all, Dr Black is expecting you," Elizabeth said. She thought quickly. "I'm sure he can prepare supper."

Moreau's face wrinkled. For a moment she hoped it was a sign of his indecision relenting, but a few seconds later she realised it was his reluctance scrunching in on itself to form an immobile core.

"I really could not..." Moreau shuffled his feet.

"We were asked to..." Thomas began.

"No! You are very kind to offer, monsieur."

Thomas looked ready to storm off in frustration. Suddenly a revelation hit Elizabeth so hard she had to stop herself from smacking her forehead. Of course!

"Sweetheart, didn't Dr Black pen a letter of introduction for us?"

They'd been so caught up in hunting down Moreau on the dock the letter had clean slipped their minds. Black had scrawled the note without much care while the Fulhames waited in his parlour, but his wax seal and signature should calm Moreau's suspicions they were imposters attempting to rob him blind.

"He did! How thoughtless of us to forget..."

Moreau's wariness lifted an inch as Thomas patted his coat pocket.

He kept patting.

Then his hands started moving across his body.

"It was in your waistcoat pocket was it not?" Thomas had checked on Black's letter in the tavern while fumbling for loose pennies to buy his wife a second drink.

Thomas dug into the pockets of his breeches, waistcoat and greatcoat. His hands came out with lint, quill feathers and blackened pennies...but no paper.

"I must have dropped it..." Thomas' cheery countenance dulled.

She looked around, hoping for a flash of white floating along the ground, but there was nothing.

Moreau bit his lip.

"I apologise, monsieur. We had a letter from Dr Black, but it, well..."

This was somehow worse than forgetting about the letter entirely. She could hear the humiliation creep into her husband's voice, but to Moreau this encounter must appear more suspicious by the minute. Would she trust her husband if he greeted her like this on the dock in a foreign port?

Elizabeth thought about protesting the loss of Black's letter was accidental, but she decided against it. Short of grabbing Moreau by both arms and hauling him to a carriage, they weren't going to convince him to move. This man had no reason to trust them, and the more they insisted he come with them, the more stubborn he got.

"I think I will find supper now," Moreau said quietly. "If you please."

Thomas swallowed a belch. "Well, the King's Wark seemed a reputable place. Our dinner was very cheap wasn't it, Eliza?"

Moreau didn't wait for her to nod. "That building, you say?" he asked, following Thomas' gaze.

"That's the one." If they knew where he went, it would be easier to find him in the morning.

"Well, thank you again for your kindness, I do not wish to detain you." With that, Moreau marched off.

The Fulhames could only stare.

"Damn," Elizabeth muttered.

"My breath doesn't smell too strongly of drink, does it?" Thomas asked, looming into her face.

"Ack! Watch yersel'."

"Sorry. I imagine we should try to speak with Dr Black before he turns in for the evening."

They watched Moreau vanished into the crowded tavern.

"Yes. Not that he'll want to deal with this mess in the morning, but I'm not sure we can induce Moreau from the dockside by ourselves tonight." A few minutes ago she's allowed herself to believe she was a simple carriage ride away from home. But without the Frenchman it wasn't justifiable. Now she flexed her toes and braced herself for a long walk uphill.

* * *

Interlude
Edinburgh—December 1767

20

Black's dinner guests knew something was afoot by the way the corners of their host's mouth kept fluttering upwards.

It was a peculiar sight, because the candles in Black's modest College Wynd apartment frequently flickered from draughts under the door, or the rigadoon lessons conducted two floors above, so the host's smiling features distorted in the shadows.

However, the company needed to wait until the third guest, James Hutton, arrived before Black explained what was behind his unusual display of amusement.

At least Hutton—a rumpled, balding man about Black's age—wasn't too late this time. Black observed Hutton was the type to obsess over the accuracy of his clocks multiple times a day...then forget to check them before departing for dinner.

"You know Finney Dillon?" Black asked, suspecting the answer was yes and hoping to remind Hutton of the fact.

"Of course!" Hutton sounded a little breathy, but tipped his hat brim. "The October Poker Club wasn't it? A pleasure to get re-acquainted, sir."

Dillon made equivalent polite noises back, much to Black's relief. He was also close to Black's age—a bit younger, if Black had estimated correctly—with a youthful leanness and arresting dark features. He often came across as aloof in company; Black could sympathise with his reserve, so tried not to introduce him to too many new acquaintances at a time.

Bringing Hutton and Dillon together and hoping for friendship was a gamble: Hutton had a tendency to take up more space than his scrawny frame would suggest; Dillon preferred to keep himself still.

"You again?" Hutton asked genially to the final guest, the Earl of Hopetoun, who seemed ready to deploy the same witticism. The Earl, with the face of a gardener, had a refreshing bluffness to his manner. If he thought Black's lodgings disappointing, he never uttered that sentiment or flashed as much

21

as a sarcastic eye tilt towards the upstairs dancing school. The Earl and Hutton could spend all evening talking about soil and rocks, while as far as Black was concerned, an hour's stay on the topic was more than sufficient.

Black was glad Dillon and Hutton greeted each other warmly, because it nagged at him that ten minutes ago his introduction of the Earl to Dillon hadn't gone as smoothly as he would have liked. When Dillon arrived the Earl was perfectly civil to him, but there was an absence of...warmth, perhaps? Black thought the Earl already socially acquainted with Dillon—they moved in similar Edinburgh circles, after all —and they both had lively, curious personalities.

As dinner host, it made Black anxious when the Earl continued his conversation with Black as if another guest hadn't arrived, but he managed to draw Dillon into their discussion of recent Town Council business without acrimony. Maybe he'd presumed an existing connection where on hadn't existed. Or perhaps Dillon was intimidated: it often slipped Black's mind how much clout the Earl wielded in Edinburgh.

"Have I missed something?" Hutton asked, tearing open his coat and setting himself down at Black's table. "Why is everything looking at each other so peculiarly?"

"We were waiting for your arrival, Dr Hutton," the Earl said. "When hopefully Dr Black will unveil what amusement he's keeping from us."

Black bade the Earl and Dillon join Hutton at the table. He nodded to the servant peering in from the adjacent room.

"You are all men of a philosophical bent," Black began, still fighting to control his smile. He jerked his head up. "Tell me what you make of that."

On the ceiling of Black's dining room rested an inflated ball, roughly head-sized. It appeared made of knotted intestine, and a foot of string dangled from its knot.

"A curious ornament, even by your standard, Joseph," Hutton remarked, scraping his chair back so he could better regard the object.

"But Dr Black hinted that this display concerns natural philosophy," the Earl of Hopetoun said slowly. "So I suspect there is more here than meets the eye."

"How have you affixed it to the ceiling?" Dillon asked. "Did you use hot wax?"

Black finally relinquished control of his smile. "A very astute question. Perhaps you gentlemen can discern for yourselves."

Despite the object being nearly above Dillon's seat, neither Dillon nor the Earl were the type of men who stood on chairs, so after a brief fuss Hutton moved his closer.

"Watch that string..."

Yet when Dillon took hold of the trailing string to keep it away from Hutton, the ball floated away from the ceiling.

"There's no wax or nail keeping it affixed..."

"Well of course there wouldn't be a nail, it's pig gut is it not?"

"Quite right, your lordship."

Black pressed his fingertips to his mouth. "Now humour me Mr Dillon, and release the string."

The ball sprung back up to the ceiling.

"This has the intriguing flavour of a parlour trick," muttered the Earl. "Were it not for the fact we're in the dining room."

"It's probably just weighted string attached to the top of the ball through a small hole in the ceiling," Hutton said, still standing on the chair.

"Well, that's an easy enough hypothesis to test," Black replied. His mouth was still partially concealed by his hand, but his eyes glinted.

Dillon obligingly pulled on the string again, and drew the

ball in. Hutton waved his hands above it. He patted the ceiling. Then he patted the top of the ball.

"I don't understand, Joseph. There doesn't appear to be any string."

Dillon cautiously pulled the ball down to head height.

Hutton got down from the chair. The Earl of Hopetoun carefully touched the ball.

"This is intriguing, Dr Black. I don't think I've ever seen the like. What phenomena could account for this?"

Hutton glanced around the room with a suddenly excited air. "Joseph, it is...?" He wiggled his fingers.

"Is it what?" Dillon asked, frowning.

Hutton trailed off and looked at Black. The Earl of Hopetoun's face became suddenly—aggressively—neutral.

"Dr Hutton wonders if it's witchcraft," Black said, after a pause. The men all chuckled, but only three of them knew Black wasn't quite joking. "I can assure you that the solution to this mystery rests in the world of nature."

"What's inside the ball?" Dillon asked, jerking the string back and forth. If he'd noticed the change in atmosphere following Hutton's half-asked question, he didn't dwell upon it.

Black's smile peaked. "Inflammable air. The gas Henry Cavendish collected from metals dissolved in acid, which he discovered was less dense than air, but infinitely more flammable."

"Though if I recall his papers, his method of demonstrating the density was less elegant than this," Hutton said. Now that the mystery seemed resolved, he kept glancing around the room, no doubt wondering where Black's manservant with the food was.

"Very clever, Dr Black," the Earl said, relaxing. "Did the savant Cavendish suggest any use for his new gas?"

4

Two steps into the King's Wark, and the Fulhames collided with trouble.

"Alors! You returned!" Moreau sprung from his chair, positioned an arm's reach away from the door. "Oh, my good friends!"

"Dr Black presents his compliments," Thomas began, handing him a signed letter. "He'll be delighted to receive ye at eleven o'clock..."

"Oh..." repeated Moreau. Now even Thomas couldn't miss his distress. He appeared on the verge of tears. "Such misery has befallen me. I am ruined."

Elizabeth had plenty of misgivings about leaving an obvious Frenchman alone in Leith overnight. That Moreau was still alive and unharmed allayed only some of her worries.

The other patrons were staring, some with a markedly hostile set to their mouths. This time Moreau let himself be guided out the front door towards the hired carriage.

"The papers. Ugh, I am such a fool."

"The papers?" Thomas and Elizabeth echoed. She felt her own panic simmer and bubble.

"All gone."

Thomas brought the man to a standstill. "What happened, friend?"

"Errr..." Moreau shot an agitated glance at Elizabeth and blushed a ferocious crimson. "I could not possibly..."

"I'll tell you what," Elizabeth said brightly. "I'll go and tell the carriage driver to wait a few minutes longer."

She didn't need to sneak back in to earshot, because it was painfully apparent what had transpired.

"...and he fucked a whore who stole his turkey red papers while he was sleeping." Thomas explained to Black a few hours later. "Woke up the next morning. No sign of the whore. No sign of his papers."

"I see," was all Black said.

Although a gentleman scholar very much of the university milieu, Elizabeth sensed that Black did see.

"The Monsieur had the good sense to conceal some of his money in diverse locations, so she didn't empty out his funds completely," Thomas continued. "But it's still a very unfortunate occurrence."

"It's our fault for losing your letter," Elizabeth blurted out. "I'm sorry, Dr Black. We should have insisted he accompany us back to Edinburgh."

"Knowing a little of Monsieur Moreau," Black said with sigh, "I understand him given to passionate, obstinate convictions that he is not easily swayed from. I don't think you would have had much success convincing him to go against his initial inclinations."

"What would a whore want with his private papers? I'm surprised the good women of Leith docks can read. Maybe she needed kindling." Thomas rocked back in his chair.

While Black wasn't immune to Thomas' attempts at

levity, this time his frown only deepened. "Yes, it's peculiar. I noticed Monsieur Moreau retained some papers in his valise—albeit a few letters of introduction or friendly notes."

Elizabeth didn't like this one bit. "You think the turkey red process was deliberately stolen, Dr Black?"

"It's a possibility," Black admitted. "It's a valuable process, after all. However, I'd advise against fanciful speculations: a lot of rogues prey on unwary visitors to Leith, and spy profit in any documents bearing a fine wax seal. If there is any more I need from you I'll be in touch. In the meantime I'll confer with Monsieur Moreau and attempt to reconstruct the procedure as best we can. He'll stay with me a few days until I can figure out what to do with him."

As soon as they left Black's study, the Fulhames simultaneously clutched each others' arms.

"The papers were stolen," Elizabeth exclaimed via unspoken proculopathic connection just as Thomas told her: *"We're going to get the papers back."*

In their five years of marriage, Thomas' attempts to teach his wife proculopathy—the art of manipulating atmospheric aether to drive communication by thought alone—was the thing that came closest to rupturing their union. Despite learning the skill from the most eloquent teacher available, Thomas' explanations were pitifully vague. Elizabeth got so frustrated she locked herself in their bedchamber and refused to come out until she'd made sense of it, reasoning that no tutoring was better than incorrect instruction. Then she got a terrible nosebleed and Thomas had to pick the lock to get in because she was too dizzy to stand.

Two minutes with Dr Black and her proculopathic abilities were deemed immaculate.

"Sweetheart, what?" Elizabeth merely sought validation

from her husband to assuage her of guilt, because a determined thief was outside their control. Proculopathy avoided her embarrassment being aired to a wider audience.

Thomas ushered her down the hallway. *"Imagine how relieved Dr Black and the Board of Manufactures will be if we return the papers to them. I know he's acting sanguine, but that's because he thinks a recovery is hopeless."*

"The esteemed doctor may have a point..." Assuming this was more than an opportunistic blackmail attempt, anyone with the foresight and resources to steal Moreau's turkey red procedure probably planned to keep their stolen goods secure. After all, only a select few in London and Edinburgh knew of Moreau's mission.

"Well, there's some obvious avenues of enquiry," Thomas said, rapping on the parlour door and entering without giving the Frenchman inside enough time to respond.

Moreau had recovered some of his composure since this morning, though there was a bleak stillness as he sat on the settee reading last week's broadsheet. Having thrown his lot in with the British at the expense of his countrymen, the man had few good options available to him.

"What can ye tell us about the doxie who robbed ye, Monsieur Moreau?" Thomas asked.

It took several beats for Moreau to translate that question in his head.

"What did the woman look like?" Elizabeth tried, hoping he wouldn't be overcome with blushing again. Some men were cute when they blushed. Moreau wasn't one of them.

"As tall as me, brown eyes and thick brown hair. Very confident, err, how-you-say, amiable..."

"Did she have any distinguishing features?" Thomas asked. Monsieur Moreau was of average height. Most women would be about as tall as him.

"She had the most splendid...errr..." Moreau froze in the

middle of an expansive hand gesture at chest height and wilted. "Perhaps, a scar on her thigh also."

"How much did you pay for this...service?" Elizabeth found herself wondering.

"Three guineas for the night."

That put her in a class of whoredom above the street-walkers and bulk-mongers.

"Was there anything else ye recall? Her manner of speaking? Her accent? Her name?"

Moreau avoided eye contact. "I cannot...recall. It was very loud in that tavern."

"How old was she?"

"Errr..."

A creak in the stairwell indicated Black was returning from his study to attend to his forlorn houseguest, so the Fulhames questioning ended there.

"Big-breasted brunette wench with a hidden scar, the search should be a breeze," Thomas muttered sarcastically once they cleared the threshold. "She'll stand out like a sore thumb in Leith."

How many whores sold themselves in the Leith taverns and alleyways? Let alone unblemished ones?

"The papers are as good as lost," sighed Elizabeth, descending the front steps into the hum of Nicholson Street. She held out her arm slightly; Thomas linked his through it a moment later.

"It's worth returning to Leith while memories are fresh," he said after a few paces. "Or at least, ye can trust they'll be reliably refreshed by coin."

Elizabeth could deploy a number of wifely silences, confident even on a crowded daytime street their nuances came across. This time, it was the silence of irritated disagreement.

"Come on love, my appointment diary is about as full as my purse. There's no harm in running our own inquiries."

"Is Monsieur Moreau even being forthright with us about the identity of the whore? Could he really recall so little about the woman's appearance?"

"He was probably tired and a little disorientated," Thomas said. "Ye know how it is."

Elizabeth, who tended to remember a lot of useless details about people's appearance, did *not* in fact know how it is.

Thomas cleared his throat in a way that indicated his opinion was set. "A few hours' search cannot hurt."

"Aye, I imagine you'll take to the search with great diligence," Elizabeth muttered back.

Thomas placed his hand over his heart in mock outrage. "I am as virtuous as *Joseph Andrews*, my dear. How could ye doubt me?"

She figured it was better to let her husband go than have him wear holes in her rugs and eardrums. "Well, don't let the business become...too expensive."

5

It cost Thomas two shillings to get the tavern keeper to answer his questions with more than a shrug.

"Doesn't sound like one of the local girls," was all he said, slipping the coins into his pocket.

Thomas was already sick of his clever idea. "Well, where can I find the girls to ask them about their friend?"

He wasted another hour trying to incite more than a scowl, snort or curse from the prostitutes up and about at ten o'clock on a Wednesday morning.

Squinting, Thomas looked out over the Firth. The harbour pier curved from the shore like a sickle, silhouetted against the glare of the silvery North Sea.

The morning wasn't a great time for questioning Leith's night life, but Elizabeth insisted he wrap up the business well in advance of nightfall.

"Who's askin'?" one surly woman demanded, spitting tobacco juice at Thomas' feet. Her face was caked with lead powder, but as she briefly met Thomas' eye he noticed the makeup couldn't conceal a black eye and cut lip.

Probably from a disappointed cull or bully, Thomas

thought. Beaten if they're suspected of theft, beaten when they don't steal enough from their marks.

"My client was very *distressed* by the loss of his property," Thomas began. "He will be deeply grateful to secure the papers."

The woman spat in the dirt again. If the allusion to compensation registered, it wasn't tempting enough.

"Well...if yer memory is refreshed, please let me know." Thomas pointed along the docks, to indicate the direction he'd walk in. The penny-bunting went back to ignoring him before he'd got two paces.

Whatever jokes he made to his wife, Thomas felt more pity for these ladies of pleasure than desire. The docks belonged to transient men: sailors anchored for a few days, knowing months or years would pass before they called at Leith again. If they survived their journeys. Women only sold themselves in the harbour when they had nowhere else to go.

No one claimed knowledge of the whore, and none of the women Thomas spied matched Moreau's description.

"What's the point in stealing papers when ye aren't trying to blackmail?" Thomas wondered. A lifted pocket-watch or necklace could be resold in an hour. There was no such market for industrial dyeing processes.

Maybe the blackmailer called upon Black while Thomas was kicking pebbles into the harbour, and this was all a colossal waste of time.

A murmuring nearby caught his attention. Thomas turned to study the nearest berthed galley, straining his peripheral vision as casually as possible.

Several unshaven men congregated across the street, watching him with folded arms. He thought one of them was carrying ale flasks into the King's Wark a few minutes ago. The rest looked like dockhands. Although he was the target of their observation, they were still conferring among themselves—

deciding on a plan of action unlikely to involve warm smiles and free ale.

Thomas fingered his purse, flipping the solitary coins inside. Offering these dirty pennies and shillings would be as much of an insult as throwing a punch.

He should have noticed he'd outstayed his welcome ten minutes ago. Unfortunately, the quickest way out of Leith was back the way he'd come, past the hostile dockhands.

He'd been to Leith a few times with George and his friends for a weekend billiard game or horse-race, but this side of the docks was warren of warehouses, half-repaired sloops and shacks. Thomas could try slipping away, but the last thing he wanted to do was provoke the hostile dockhands by sprinting into a blocked alleyway.

Nothing for it.

Keeping his hands loosely at his side—lest they think he was clutching a weapon—Thomas turned around with a jaunty 'oh look at the time!' air and began walking. Ignoring the dockhands was as much a cue for a fight as glaring at them.

His observers detached from the wall, hands conspicuously unfolded.

Thomas waited until he was almost parallel with the men before breaking into a pelt. No point trying to say anything: Thomas recognised menacing intent. Wisecracks or feigned innocence was a waste of his breath, better saved for flight.

The men took off after him. Despite his diminutive stature, Thomas could move his legs. His lungs sputtered with exertion, but the noises behind him receded once he'd crossed the bridge.

As expected, the chase was half-hearted. The men had identified Thomas as a foolish interlocutor on their territory, but he clearly held no valuables worth theft. If they couldn't catch him and leave him bloodied on the dockside, it wasn't worth a pursuit as far as Leith Junction.

George could probably have tossed all four dockhands in the harbour without breaking a sweat, but Thomas knew his limitations. Besides, there was no glory to be found in a street fight.

"We're aren't anything to those people," Thomas complained that afternoon, once he was safely home and got his breath back. He hadn't dawdled. "Neither scary nor rich enough to induce cooperation. For all we know Moreau is misremembering her hair colour or forgot she's missing an eye..."

Elizabeth did an admirable job of not looking smug.

"It's surprising that no one offered to sell me back the stolen papers, is it not?"

His wife shrugged.

"We don't know with certainty that the woman *was* an agent of Venus. Maybe she was a bored noblewoman..."

"...Whose wealthy husband travelled to the colonies leaving her bereft of companionship, causing her to fall upon vice to gain the vicarious thrill of desirability. Aye, I think I've read that book."

"Or otherwise willing to engage in ad hoc selling of virtue. In which case, how would we ever find her?"

Having made the flippant remark about a salacious novel, Thomas' mind kept dragging him back to the concept of a 'book.' He tried to slow his thoughts.

Elizabeth however was warming to her thesis. "It's unlikely a second visit to Leith will endear you further to the women there, so we have no way of identifying the whore in question." In Thomas' absence, she'd come to another dissuading realisation. "Unfortunately, in a few days I think Dr Black will have recreated Moreau's turkey red process and our part to play in the affair draws to a close."

"But what if he cannot?" Thomas rocked on his heels.

"Why would the honourable monsieur care if he lost the papers in the first place, were his knowledge of the turkey red process worth a grubby penny?"

Elizabeth squinted in bemusement. "He worked on the turkey red process though, love. That's what he said in the letter Dr Black showed us."

Thomas retreated to the window. "I suspect Moreau may have...garnished the truth."

"Garnished?"

"Or embroidered."

"Perhaps he took the bleached homespun truth and dyed it a more pleasing shade, if we are searching for the most appropriate metaphor."

Elizabeth thought on it for a moment.

"I'm thinking about the exact wording of his letter to Dr Black," she said slowly. "Moreau said he worked in the mill where turkey red dye was created, but he didn't claim involvement in *producing* the dye."

They were realising what Black had probably deduced and was concealing: Moreau lifted the dye papers without fully understanding what they detailed. He was banking on the British textile manufacturers understanding the shorthand.

Thomas' mood lightened at the realisation. "Poor luck for Dr Black."

Elizabeth might have had the opportunity to make a smug remark had Thomas not been seized with another idea, finally realising why he'd fixated on books.

"Actually honey, I think Dr Duncan might be able to help us..."

"Thomas, no!" Elizabeth's wince was unfeigned.

"Or rather, he told us about a speaker at the Beggar's Benison, the gentleman wrote a guide to Edinburgh's ladies of pleasure. Dr Duncan said the man's cataloguing was 'most rigorous.'"

"Of course he did."

Knowing of Dr Andrew Duncan's proud involvement in the Beggar's Benison, a society devoted to the celebration of the sexual arts, Elizabeth had expressed her displeasure at Thomas' decision to complete his medical dissertation under the man's guidance. Thomas tried to explain there was more to Dr Duncan than that—his medical theories were startlingly original, and he was actually one of the better physicians in Edinburgh—but it was a point of disagreement always threatening to erupt.

"The intrepid explorer goes by the pen-name 'Ranger,' but from how Dr Duncan spoke about the man it seems he knows his real identity."

"And Dr Duncan spends his time discussing puerile amorous topics with the scholars of the university?" Elizabeth was quick to reheat her grievances.

"No, this was casual conversation as we were walking back from the Dispensary." Thomas paused to absorb his wife's glare. "Honestly my love, it's a refreshing change when Dr Duncan starts off on his Beggar's Benison exploits. He spent my entire round at the Dispensary that day desiccating my ears with medical jurisprudence and a legal case he was consulting on. As far as I can tell, whichever side utters the most Latin gibberish wins the court case."

Elizabeth redirected her glare to the windowsill, an indication she considered further expressions of disdain pointless. "Well, if you believe the man a reliable source of information on the condition of Edinburgh's finest ladies' inner thighs, I suppose it is cheaper than bribing half of Leith."

* * *

Thomas didn't consider himself an unusually optimistic person, though he knew his breezy outlook often rankled George.

"Are you always this cheerful?" George would gripe, as if cheerfulness was a moral failing.

"Yep," Thomas would boast in response, taking advantage of the fact he was winding his more cautious and melancholic friend up.

Though as he was ushered into Duncan's spacious Adam Square townhouse, Thomas had to admit the process of retrieving Moreau's papers was dividing into tasks of infinite complexity.

"Come in, good sir. The more the merrier!"

It was then Thomas noticed Duncan's parlour already occupied by the dark, sombre mass that was Sandy Monro *secundus*, professor of anatomy. Thomas nodded bluntly and received a brief nod in return, Monro allowing that he knew of Thomas Fulhame.

"Greetings, professor," was all Thomas said. Monro didn't think much of him: he preferred quiet, intense students like George Stephens.

"Sit yourself down." Duncan bustled into the room. "What's your poison, Mr Fulhame?"

Despite being one of the younger faculty members, Duncan moved through the world in a kind of sideways crouch, which made him appear several decades older than forty.

"Nothing for me right now." Monro frowned in the background, judging Thomas' decision to snub the host's hospitality. Unless Monro was preparing to depart—and given his resolute clinking of his teaspoon in cup that seemed unlikely —Thomas must bring up the purpose of his visit in front of Monro.

"Dr Monro and I were just discussing Harrison's paper at

the London Society on comparative avian anatomy. It caused quite a stir, I wonder if you heard about it?"

"Um, no sir..." As a longstanding host of the Beggar's Benison, and one of Edinburgh's most celebrated medical mind, Duncan often swayed across the line between propriety and indecency. The Beggars Benison were celebrants and enthusiastic proportions of various natural acts the clergy warned against. Ecclesiastical disapproval never dissuaded Duncan, in fact it seemed to encourage him. However, Duncan possessed the vexing habit of being censorious when one needed him to be saucy, and obscene when one needed him to be respectable. Were Thomas to bring up the guide to Edinburgh's prostitutes now, he risked being upbraided.

"It does one good to keep up to date with the scientific papers from London," Monro sniffed. "Even when you're preoccupied Mr Fulhame—as you no doubt are—with the drafting of your dissertation."

"I am serving as President of the Physical Society," Thomas protested, too frustrated by the sudden obstacles to his task to mind his words.

When telling him about the guide the other week, Duncan said he owned a copy and either had or intended to make a presentation to the Beggars about it ("Is about time Edinburgh's ladies of pleasure were given the same attention as those in London..."). This meant it probably sat with the rest of his Beggar's paperwork in his study.

"Indeed, I heard of your election." Delivered in the tones one would admit they heard a dead pigeon was blocking their chimney.

The sensible, prudent course of action would be to take his leave and return when Duncan was unoccupied. However, it was three o'clock and Duncan would be busy in a few hours with society business. Probably Horticultural Society or Gymnastics tonight: it'd explain his restrained mood.

What if Duncan was busy tomorrow as well? Besides, it looked bad if Thomas departed now. Not that he cared what Monro thought...but he'd probably make a snide remark Thomas couldn't invent a witty response to. Duncan would merely think him an time-wasting idiot.

Not to mention the earful his wife would give him when he told her he needed to call upon Duncan *again*...

"As I matter of fact Dr Duncan, I wanted to make use of yer library, which I hope won't be too major an intrusion."

No one knew why a man as humourless as Monro enjoyed the company of Duncan. Nearly every other faculty member —barring Black, perhaps—avoided prolonged contact with Duncan off the college grounds.

"Not in the slightest. What fruits of knowledge do you seek?"

"Err, yer case notes on puerperal fever at the Infirmary. From the um, last epidemic?"

Duncan blinked. "Of course. I thought you'd already read them."

"Um, but I don't think I read them all." Thomas hoped the slight redness of his cheeks came across as nervousness rather than deceit. "Or I lost a page of my notes."

"Alright Mr Fulhame. You know your way upstairs."

As Thomas closed the door behind him, he could hear Duncan and Monro resume their earnest discussion. "Well, it was very *presumptuous* of Dr Harrison..."

Duncan's first floor library was opposite his study.

Checking the coast was clear of servants, Thomas slipped into Duncan's private study. He knew roughly where Duncan kept his Beggars' accounts.

Sure enough, in the top drawer was a copy of the *Rangers' Guide* and assorted letters. If you didn't stop the read them you'd mistake it for the dry contents of any physician's correspondence. Thomas skimmed through the pile as fast as he could, looking for a flash of the word 'Ranger'.

Downstairs, a door slammed. Duncan's cheerful whistling filled the stairwell.

Thinking quickly, Thomas grabbed a couple of items to hand and rushed out the room, giving him time to slow down and meet Duncan halfway down the hallway.

"Ah professor—ye don't mind me borrowing yer inkwell? The one in yer library has dried up." Thomas smiled with good cheer, as if it was natural he'd seek out an inkwell without consulting his host, and there was nothing wrong with him entering Duncan's private study to do so. He patted his chest, hoping the papers he'd stuffed into his waistcoat hadn't bunched.

"Of course not. I thought I refilled it an hour ago. You found the case notes alright, Thomas?"

"Right where I left them," Thomas said blithely, hoping Duncan wasn't about to accompany him into the library. "Or thereabouts." He paused. "I'll pour out the ink I need and bring the rest back to yer study, shall I?"

"Good man. I wanted Dr Monro to see the paper I received last year from the Philosophical Society in Dublin." Duncan continued on his way. "It seems Dr Harrison is rather late to the game with his comparative study...or a plagiarist."

6

The man behind the 'Ranger' pseudonym lived in the charming village of Duddingston, nestled at the base of Arthur's Seat a short walk from Edinburgh. Thomas was familiar enough with the village and its inn, so finding the abode of James Tytler proved quick work.

The countryside stirred mixed emotions in Thomas. At times he yearned for the simplicity of rural life: growing up it was the only existence he knew. But the simplicity could turn to brutality: you *had* to live simply and be self-reliant, or else your family starved. Life in overcrowded Edinburgh brought complexities he didn't know how to handle: having grown up in the centre of Navan, Elizabeth was slightly better equipped to deal with their new surroundings than him. Passing a well as he trudged through Duddingston's heart, Thomas reflected how strange it was to rely on others for water: with only a handful of wells inside Edinburgh city walls, you needed to pay your local water carrier a penny to deliver your water every morning.

A few enquiries brought Thomas to a homily, if dilapidated, cottage at the end of a narrow lane. The cottage itself was barely visible behind a twirling veil of cloths and laundry hung around the garden. The air was filled with the scent of lye and soda. A few upturned washtubs leant against the cottage wall, drying in the sun. With such a domestic sensibility to the place, Thomas expected the squeals of playing children, but the house was silent. Only a half-opened front door indicated someone was home. When Thomas knocked, it took an age for the occupant to respond, even though the cottage was hardly bigger than the Fulhames apartment.

When he came to the door, Tytler was an unassuming man with wispy hair and a jagged nose and chin. He looked like the kind of downtrodden clerk Writers to the Signet would throw discarded paper at. He beckoned Thomas into a cluttered side room. This appeared to be his own living quarters, and Thomas realised his assumption that Tytler was married to the washerwoman was erroneous.

Papers were strewn around Tytler's lodging space; made crispy by dried beer stains.

One sheet located at the forefront of Tytler's makeshift desk—a upturned bathtub—caught Thomas' attention. Unlike the surrounding scribblings, its lettering was particularly handsome and well-spaced, giving the impression Tytler put a lot of consideration into drafting it.

Most of the sheet was devoted to a sketch of a large balloon, every patch of fabric and rope rendered in careful detail.

"You are familiar with the hot air balloon launch in Versailles last year?" Tytler asked, sidling up to Thomas' shoulder. "Quite extraordinary."

"Indeed," agreed Thomas, only vaguely aware of what Tytler spoke about. But a light came on in the man's eyes, and his curtain of reticence temporarily rose.

"I wanted to write about it for the latest edition of the

Encyclopaedia Britannica." Tytler waved his hand across the desk. "When I began, it was just another topic to study and summarise. But the more I read the more excited I became. Flying through the air like a bird! Wouldn't it be wonderful? To think that man can achieve that miracle with hot air and gases."

Thomas made another polite noise. Tytler hung beside him, licking his lips.

"You said you were a man of natural philosophy, Mr Fulhame? Have pneumatic chemistry experiments occupied much of your time?"

"Next to none," Thomas cheerfully replied, hoping to nip this distracting line of enquiry in the bud. "Dr Black is the foremost expert in such matters."

"Oh, Dr Black! You are on familiar terms with him?"

"Yes, I'd be delighted to make an introduction," Thomas said, stepping away from the diagrams. He recognised Tytler entertained him out of hopes he'd further his own hobby horse, though if that secured his cooperation Thomas had no problem with it.

This goodwill gesture performed, Thomas decided to get to business. "I'm needing yer assistance to track down a good lady of Leith."

Despite keeping his voice as low as possible, Tytler still flinched and hurriedly looked around the deserted cottage.

Thomas slid a guinea onto the table, but Tytler recoiled in affront at the bribe.

"Some of my friends have familiarity with these types of ladies," he said cagily after a pause. "Perhaps I have heard of this cat."

Thomas described the woman from Moreau's recollection. As expected, a flicker of recognition passed Tytler's face when he mentioned the scar.

Tytler rose and started rifling through the piles of paper

stuffed onto his bookshelf. He pulled out a few sheets from under two heft encyclopaedias.

"Sounds familiar..." he muttered. "Ah, yes. Lydia. Thought she resided in the Cowgate, though."

Looking at the table, Thomas realised his guinea had vanished.

"I looked through a copy of the Edinburgh guide, and don't recall her."

"No, she disappeared just before the first edition was published." Tytler seemed determined to maintain the charade that he wasn't the one who wrote and published it. Thomas was fine indulging him if it meant the information came. "Found a wealthy keeper, which wasn't hugely surprising. Beautiful, talented woman. She seemed intent on that securing that outcome."

"And she had a scar then?"

"It was claimed her mother spilled boiling water on her when she was a baby," Tytler said. "Nothing particularly tragic or interesting."

It sounded like the mystery was solved. "So Miss Lydia is still in Edinburgh?"

Tytler's mouth twisted, as if he'd chewed a lemon. "No one keeps track of former whores, Mr Fulhame. Not unless they're *internationally* fascinating and scandalous. If she's back on the game it appears her lover discarded her. Probably tired of her sharp tongue."

"Was it known who her keeper was, sir?"

Tyler's eyebrows rose. He was perhaps surprised Thomas didn't already know.

"Yes, on that the rumours were consistent..."

* * *

"Sir Phineas 'Finney' Dillon," sighed Black. "His involvement does not surprise me."

Elizabeth held her breath. Black over-enunciated every syllable, and made a show of focussing on his correspondence.

"But was does *surprise* me..." Black continued, regarding the pair critically. "Is that you would pursue this matter after I expressly advised you leave it be." His queue swished between his shoulder-blades, putting Elizabeth to mind of a disgruntled feline tail.

"That process is worth thousands of pounds—to Scotland —how could ye let it vanish?" Thomas appeared stung by the rebuke.

Black tutted. "There is a league of noble scoundrels, pardon my crude expression, like Sir Finney who engage in these sorts of games. If he had the means to deduce Monsieur Moreau was coming to Leith with the turkey red process, he had the means to acquire it. I despise that calibre of men, but it's pointless dragging yourself into their affairs."

"But..."

"I took you into my service Mr Fulhame," Black continued, hardening his voice, "because I valued your keen mind and ability to follow directions..."

Elizabeth tried not to wince.

"...While I can say without ego that my association and support is beneficial to you at the start of your physician career, it goes without saying—though I suppose since I'm saying it now I was mistaken in assuming so—that there is an obverse relationship where my reputation is now connected to you. I do not wish rumours to reach me of my laboratory assistants meddling in business that skirts the law. We have already discussed how some of your *jocular* remarks could be misinterpreted by gentleman unfamiliar with your humours, and you assured me of your heightened caution."

"*Don't say anything,*" Elizabeth silently begged Thomas,

recognising her husband's preparation to mount an indignant defence. Thomas audibly inhaled and exhaled, but clamped his lips shut.

If Black noted that Thomas was on the brink of saying something inflammatory, he neither encouraged nor discouraged it. "I am in the process of conferring with Monsieur Moreau to see what can be salvaged from his memory. I am confident that despite the brazen theft, the Board of Manufacturers will still end up with a more efficient turkey red dyeing process at the end of this. I therefore won't need your assistance with laboratory work this week." Black eyed the couple. "Please be patient, Mr and Mrs Fulhame."

"We're sorry," Elizabeth said, hoping mollification could stem the damage.

"Understand that I'm not blaming you in any way for the theft," Black said, the rigid control over his syllables loosening. "There is little one can do to prevent Sir Finney seizing what he covets."

"I grant you full liberty to explode with outrage the minute we are back in our apartment," Elizabeth said, patting Thomas' forearm. *"But please restrain yourself until that point."*

Thomas gave a tight-lipped smirk. He waited in the centre of their living room with an exaggerated stillness, until Elizabeth sank into the settee and gestured she was ready.

"Avoid skirting the law? Does Dr Black forget what he did to the Brunonians?"

When the Fulhames arrived in Edinburgh, their first impression of extramural lecturer Dr John Brown was a colourful personality who attracted students to his lecturers because of the entertainment provided hearing his provocative medical theories. They failed to realise the depth of his animosity towards his former teacher William Cullen, nor the fact that Brown's experiments with phlogiston-conduction inadvertently killed a several student volunteers. Cullen and Black—though mostly Cullen—eventually took matters into their own hands and decided to put a stop to Brown's teachings. However, by then Brown had already set a larger plan of revenge into motion.

While the professors involved remained coy about their role in an explosion in Monro's anatomy theatre and destruction of the Brunonians' Grassmarket headquarters the same night, the professors' semi-willing accomplice George Stephens had no such reticence.

"I think Dr Black meant to distinguish between illegal acts he condones and those he doesn't. A refined philosopher such as himself deals in nuances ordinary mortals cannot grasp."

"Hypocrite," muttered Thomas.

* * *

Interlude
Edinburgh—December 1779

Unveiling her knowledge of phlogiston-wielding to Joseph Black was one of the most awkward experiences of Elizabeth's life.

By this point she was socially acquainted with the famous chemistry professor: Black had taken tea at their lodgings, he'd invited the married students to bring their wives to dinner at his spacious Nicholson Street home. Thomas bragged he'd attained a measure of friendship with Dr Black.

But as Elizabeth was led by a servant into Black's parlour, she was reminded she'd had scant interactions with the man that weren't heavily curated by social requirements.

"Good afternoon, Mrs Fulhame." Black rose, kissed her hand, and fixed on the books she clutched to her abdomen. "I

CL JARVIS

see you are keeping better account of your Thomas' circulating library acquisitions than the gentleman himself."

The man cut an impressive figure. Even at leisure he glided through his surroundings like a knife through silk. The silver buttons on his jacket gleamed like stars. While not ostentatious, everything about his appearance suggested a rigorous attention to detail.

"Quite..." Elizabeth had stacked the lies in careful order within her head. *Oh, I was happening on my way to the Grassmarket anyway...Pardon? You said Thomas had another week to consult your chemical treatises? Gosh, I hadn't realised... Maybe I am confusing these books with another set he'd borrowed from Professor Duncan.* But Black didn't ask questions or seem surprised by her interference. Maybe he dealt with a lot of over-anxious wives.

"You can leave the books on that table, madam. Myself or Morris will carry them upstairs later." Although courteous, his smile was slightly bland.

Elizabeth hesitated, annoyed with herself. Of course she would have interrupted this celebrated professor in the middle of some important task: letters to answer, another visitor expected upon the hour, a dinner invitation across town. She'd rehearsed what she would say to Black a million times— muttered into the silence when Thomas was in class. But faced with the sudden pressure of time, she wasn't sure her speech was appropriate.

Black saw her hesitation. "Can I offer you tea, madam?"

What an uppity, coarse rube he must think me! A nobody from Ireland, making an ill-disguised attempt to ingratiate herself with a world-renown philosopher. Elizabeth's cheeks began to scald. She was rapidly losing control of the situation.

All sorts of other doubts weaselled their way forward. *What if he's disgusted to see a woman practicing these philosoph-*

ical arts? What if Thomas was lying when he said Dr Black willingly taught him these secrets?

An exchange with Thomas bubbled from the bottom of her mind as she stood in front of this man. Thomas was talking her through the things he claimed Dr Black could do with phlogiston and aether in the days after she'd learned such things were possible. Crucially, that since aether was an integral part of the animal nervous system, an aethereal strike could disrupt a person's consciousness. Fatally.

"The thing is..." Thomas had said as he compulsively folded a scrap of parchment onto itself. "The way Dr Black talked about it...I think he may have killed someone using that technique."

"Sweetheart, he's a physician," Elizabeth scoffed. "Of course he'll speak with knowledge about the passage of life. It's his bread and butter."

Now, as she stood fumbling for words, Elizabeth wondered if she'd been too quick to dismiss her husband. Black's expression faded into unreadability. There was a certain *edge* to his bearing, an inner confidence, she'd seen in former soldiers.

"I...I...wanted to show you something, Dr Black," Elizabeth managed. This wasn't anything close to the speech she'd prepared, or the order of events she wished to proceed through. She'd intended to start by indicating her familiarity with the theoretical framework of phlogiston-wielding, then having convinced Black of her intellectual capability she'd move to a demonstration. This all hinged upon her having more than a minute to speak with the doctor.

Panicking, she thrust her arm towards the stunned professor and started flicking her fingertips against her palm.

If she'd practiced her now-discarded speech a million times, she'd practised this gesture a million times more. The ignition of fire. But her index fingernail slipped across her slick palm. Her fingers couldn't gain traction. There was no fire.

An eternity passed. But it was only a few seconds during which Black went from concerned alarm ("What nervous fit is this strange woman falling in to?") to confusion ("What is wrong with her hand?") to a widening of the eyes and brief parting of lips in an uncontrolled moment of shocked recognition.

By this point Elizabeth was on the verge of tears. She felt little and foolish. Her impotent finger flicks were getting wilder and more ineffectual. She'd studied theoretical texts until she understood them better than Thomas. She'd mastered the technique on her own when he received hours of personalised tutoring from an expert. And here she was failing for the stupidest reasons: nerves.

"If you concentrate on the scapula, that is your shoulder blade," Black said quickly. "I find it helps direct the phlogiston."

Elizabeth stared. The flash of shock had vanished from Black's face, his dark eyes now focussed on her with unnerving intensity.

"No, pause for a second. Please, madam. Take a few breaths. You're too tense for the phlogiston wielding right now." Black moved forwards, stooping slightly to maintain eye contact with Elizabeth, who wanted to shrink into the floor. "You're getting frustrated—I understand, it's all right—and your muscles need to be relaxed for this to work."

The last time Elizabeth cried was aged sixteen, following a stupid argument with Lottie about a boy (not Thomas, and Lottie's harsh assessment of the boy in question proved apt within days anyway). Alone in her bedchamber, Elizabeth sobbed into her handkerchief until it dripped with phlegm, then stole her sisters' handkerchiefs to repeat the humiliating exercise. She berated herself all the while that sixteen was too old to be snivelling like a baby, and from now she should avoid all situations that made her cry.

She was dangerously close to breaking this non-crying streak. Only now she wasn't sure if her eyes prickled through humiliation or gratitude.

"Your husband taught you this?" Black asked, looking at Elizabeth like she was that pitiful dribbling sixteen year old once more.

Elizabeth worried about explaining Thomas' full involvement, given the techniques were supposed to be kept secret, but there was no recrimination in Black's voice. She nodded.

"Right, madam...Mrs Fulhame...exhale as you focus on your scapula. Press it down, then relax all other muscles. Let your fingers loosen, and..."

A microscopic flash of light appeared in her palm. For a moment Elizabeth feared it was hidden by her thumb, but then Black stepped back and nodded.

"Hmm, that's interesting. Most wielders default to phlogistonic fire. It's the easier system to access, or at least it can be controlled in a more instinctive way. It seemed you defaulted to aetherial light."

Would that explain why she had so much trouble picking up the technique from Thomas? Elizabeth was struggling to pull herself out of this childlike state, in this case coming down from the exuberance that came when she pleased her father.

Black did look impressed. "Nicely demonstrated, Mrs Fulhame." He was probably saying that to make her feel less embarrassed for her abortive initial attempts, but Elizabeth couldn't detect patronising or insincerity. "Elizabeth, is it? Or do you go by Betsy or Eliza?"

"No, Dr Black. Elizabeth is fine."

7

With Thomas sulking in textbooks, the most productive thing Elizabeth could do was take a stroll.

She set off on her usual short route, the walk she took when short of time or avoiding the mental exertion of deciding where to go. Turn down the hill from High School Yards, plunge into the mercantile artery into Edinburgh that was the dim Cowgate, hoist her skirts an inch to avoid the worst of the ooze collecting there. Elizabeth followed the incline down and out.

After a few hundred metres she emerged from the grimy valley, through the city gates. To her right, the sharp edge of Salisbury Crags, to her left the gently cultivated gardens of the Canongate. Given the fetid, cramped conditions within the city walls, these gardens seemed indolent in their sprawl.

She still smarted from Black's reprimand. Her pride had sustained a wound, that much she knew. It hurt because while she knew Black contained a temper—everyone did—she never thought she'd bare its brunt.

"So what if Sir Finney is an opportunistic thief or greedy dilettante?" she asked, trying to run through a more successful version of this morning's conversation. Imagining Black's brow crease in reluctant concession to her arguments didn't prove satisfying. "How difficult can it be to ask him for the papers back?"

"Is that yerself, Elizabeth?" So much for orchestrating a one-woman argument in private. Looking up, she found her neighbour Emmeline and elderly mother taking a careful stroll back into town.

"Good afternoon, ladies."

Emmeline huffed to a stop, looking pleased. She was the kind of woman who could feed a four-hour conversation from the verbal equivalent of a fish and a loaf of bread.

"You and yer man were out when we called this morning, wasn't she Ma?" Emmeline patted her panniers. "In fact I think I forget to leave this on the table to deliver later..."

"Oh, you really shouldn't have..." Emmeline withdrew what looked at first glance to be silver coins and pushed them into Elizabeth's hand.

"It's no' a bother, m'dear. Pip has plenty to spare."

Elizabeth thumbed through the metal scraps. Copper, zinc, a shining iron nail.

"Well, I have a bit of time tonight if..."

"Please, the little ones were so excited to write their names. I couldn't get them to stop—they were copying them onto the walls. Twisted their ears and made them scrub them off..."

"That was a pity. I'd be interested to see if they were copying them correctly."

"Right, right." Emmeline looked chastised. Elizabeth knew she loathed her own illiteracy, and wanted better for her bairns. But schooling would keep the children away from home too long, so the ad hoc tutoring Elizabeth provided in the evenings had to do. Demanding renumeration from a family in worse condition than her own was too cruel, but

Emmeline's husband did a lot of joinery and so had ready access to metal scraps.

"It's so hard to find iron nails not rusted through..." Elizabeth said quickly. "You have my utmost gratitude."

"I'll say it again Elizabeth, jist ask..."

"I know, I know..."

Elizabeth studied Emmeline and her mother. The family had lived in Edinburgh all their lives; if she recalled correctly Ma MacBride was born in the Cowgate. It might be worth asking...

"I don't wish to trouble you Emmeline, but there is something you might be able to help me with..."

Emmeline puffed up with pride, relishing the opportunity to feel useful.

"...do you know anything about a Sir Finney Dillon? I believe he was well-known in Edinburgh several years ago."

On the one hand, Black claimed he wasn't surprised Sir Finney was involved in the theft of Moreau's turkey red process. But hadn't immediately suspected the aristocrat played a part, nor did he want to pursue the matter further. The dynamics were confusing.

"Name rings a bell doesn't it, Ma?" Emmeline scratched her neck and appealed to her mother, who clung onto her arm and worked her lower jaw.

"Good-for-nothing rake," Ma MacBride said with finality.

"Ooo, he was that one, was he?" Emmeline's recollection stirred. "Made a fortune here selling sherry. Was slippery as a jellied eel. I nearly tripped into him once outside the Stag's Head Inn, didn't I?" It always surprised Elizabeth how much of Emmeline's memories were stored with her mother, who never appeared interested in keep her daughter's facts. Her own bond with her mother involved preserving very separate spheres of recollections. When Ma MacBride didn't contradict her, Emmeline continued. "We all said he was stooping to conquer in Edinburgh. He went off to Parliament, didn't he? Maybe not. We always knew he'd rather be slithering round Court and doing whatever they do at the opera."

"You'd think the purpose of attending the opera was to listen to the opera..." Elizabeth said, though she knew for nobles the opera and theatre was all about being *seen*. Her mind was elsewhere, anyway. "He made his fortune selling wine?"

"It was wine, wasn't it Ma?"

"Sherry, port, claret." Ma MacBride said with disdain. "All that French stuff."

There was only so long Elizabeth could pursue this line of enquiry with the MacBride women without it seeming unusual. Anyway, the pair maintained that same line: Dillon was a successful wine merchant who returned to London to acquire even more obscene quantities of wealth.

So what to make of his coveting interest in Moreau's turkey red?

Elizabeth sat down at the kitchen table, shoving her husband's piles of books into the opposite corner.

She relaxed as soon as she began the familiar process of rearranging her glassware and bottles of chemicals. She tipped out the clippings of magnesium from a old beer bottle and set them on a handkerchief. She could almost pour out the correct volume of nitromuriate solution by eye, but measured it carefully all the same, taking pleasure in reaching the correct volume in almost one pour.

This wasn't an onerous or particularly interesting experiment. She'd run a similar reaction last week; this time she was reducing the magnesium with sulphur instead of phosphorous. She smoothed her pile of silk squares under her palm.

Once the magnesium dissolved in the nitromuriate solution, she dipped a silk square in, let it dry then fumigated it with sulphur gas. The sulphur should precipitate the metal back out, leaving a silvery sheen on the cloth.

If she was lucky. The phosphorous experiment produced nothing more than a red-brown stain, and Elizabeth suspected today's silk awaited the same fate. Still, she had to perform this experiment, for completeness.

Her hands moved through the procedure of her own accord. The reaction glassware was possibly the most expensive thing she owned, even though she'd bartered it second-hand from a glassblower in exchange for assistance with his wife's sewing projects. It was the size of a toddler, comprising three stacked compartments connected by valves to control the flow of gas and liquids. To Elizabeth it was a thing of beauty.

Her husband lacked her sense of romanticism. When she first told him, Thomas shrugged at her ideas to create a metallic dyeing process. "Doesn't sound probable," he'd said. "Dissolving metals in acid then reducing them out back into solid form is one the easiest chemical transformations—if it could imprint metals on cloth somebody would have done it already."

"Well, it was probably enough for them to make metallic threads. This is a more accessible method of achieving the same ends," Elizabeth had insisted. "I can use my own coins for the supplies."

That was what convinced Thomas to let his wife pursue this hobby.

Elizabeth had heard the insults slapped on Princess Dashkova, the Russian princess who'd spent part of her exile in Edinburgh, for daring to take an interest in gentlemanly pursuits and disregard proper feminine behaviour. Not content to simply serve tea and cakes at her scientific salons, Dashkova was known for wading into the discussions and debating the men as equals. The thought of this woman brow-beating Edinburgh's smartest minds provided titillation across every strata of Edinburgh society. She was also a self-taught phlogiston-wielder, who never cared how that might be perceived. While it appeared the Russian princess wasn't hurt by the slurs...Elizabeth knew she would be, in her place.

Elizabeth touched the side of the flask with the back of her hand, feeling its warmth as the metal dissolved to nothing.

Lottie always supported her cousin's hobby horse. "Let us know when you've mastered the dyeing—I'm sure Don will try the process in our factory," she wrote. Lottie knew very little about the chemical processes at play in her husband's business, but her encouragement of Elizabeth always felt genuine. If she found a reliable dyeing process she was sure Don would give her an audience, though she might have to rope Thomas in to make her case convincing.

By the time she'd worked out the tension in her mind through soothing repetition, Elizabeth felt confident in her ideas.

Fortunately, her husband was in need of a distraction as her.

Whatever Black knew of Dillon's character and motivations, it was more than the Fulhames did. And Elizabeth doubted she could prompt him to action while knowing so little.

Thomas was hunched over his Practice of Physic notes when Elizabeth joined him in the bedchamber. He glanced up briefly as she settled herself onto the corner of the bed.

Then he looked at his wife more closely. "Sweetheart, I spy a distant look on yer fair countenance. While not dissimilar from the look ye give when pretending to ignore me, such dreamy eyes usually presage...a complex enterprise of persuasion."

"And if that were the case?"

"Well, I would wonder if it is me ye intend to persuade? Ye can't possibly agree with Dr Black's decision to let the theft go."

"It's an interesting dilemma, faced with two men who seek competing courses of action, both adamant in their convictions. The question might come down to which man I think easier to persuade..."

Thomas flopped onto the bed beside his wife. "Spare me the unflattering assessment, wifey."

"I know you too well." Elizabeth permitted herself a smile. "But I think the more pertinent question is of the overall morality and greater issues at stake."

"So it's harder to persuade Dr Black to change his mind... but more important we succeed."

Elizabeth hoped Black wouldn't be vindictive enough to fire Thomas from the assistantship, but she knew there was a ruthless side to the man. Suspending Thomas from laboratory duties for the next week at least was warning enough.

"Do you suppose Dr Black has a personal history with this Finney Dillon? I thought he reacted a little strongly to his name."

"Ye think." Thomas flung his legs over the bed and put his arms behind his head.

It made the situation more complicated. If Black objected to involving himself with the thievery of Sir Finney, it would be harder to overcome than an objection to interference against thieves on principle.

"Its hard to imagine Dr Black being scared of anyone, even a rich bastard."

"I don't know if it was fear, though..." Elizabeth struggled to parse through her fresh memories of the conversation. Black concealed his emotions well.

"Reluctance, disdain, Whatever repulsive force it may be, I suppose."

"We need Dr Black's assistance," Elizabeth said. He was the only one of the professors who offered her anything close to respect. Right now, he was contemplating cutting off her husband's assistantship.

"Well, we need Monsieur Moreau's assistance," Thomas pointed out. He was still thinking of the financial prize.

"And you saw how he treated us at the Shore. It's only because Dr Black's name was on our lips that he gave us the time of day to begin with." To Elizabeth it was obvious: if Black offered support, Moreau would follow. Despite Black's claim of powerlessness, Elizabeth couldn't see how they'd successfully outmanoeuvre Dillon if Black wasn't on their side. Not to mention the disastrous financial consequences.

Elizabeth tapped her vermilion-stained fingers against the bed frame.

"Sweetheart, did this James Tytler strike you as particularly ashamed of his inclinations?"

Thomas frowned. "He made no more than a cursory attempt to deny his penning of the guide, if that's what ye mean."

Elizabeth tried re-ordering her thoughts to make her meaning clearer. "It's just that some men plagued with such vices will adopt—through guilt or denial—a front of stringent intolerance to such worldly evils."

"Decrying whores from the pulpit in the morning, then seeking their embrace in the evening?" Thomas shrugged. "No. Tytler did not seem particularly ashamed of his cataloguing activities, nor did he utter any hypocritical statements."

"Would you say that he seems a man quite comfortable with the world of sin and vice?" Elizabeth persisted.

Comprehension started to dawn for Thomas. "Ahh, ye think he might be able to help us where the luminaries of the town will not?"

8

If Tytler was surprised find Thomas and Elizabeth Fulhame at his cottage door, he did not show it. The man seemed to exist in a permanent state of wariness, aware he lacked the social graces to navigate complicated situations.

Elizabeth thought her presence might act as a 'honey pot' for the libidinous Tytler, but if anything he seemed startled by a strange woman, and avoided looking at her. She tried to keep a reassuring distance, but between the piles of laundry, books and dusty junk, she couldn't move very far.

Since Tytler knew the name 'Dillon', Elizabeth supposed he might know something of his dealings in the city that the other professors either did not know or would not share with her.

"I came across his name when collecting subscriptions for the Encyclopaedia," Tytler explained, easing himself onto a stool in the corner. "He is known as a man of wealth and commercial ambition, but I can say little of his character."

"Is he known as a ruthless businessman?" Elizabeth asked.

Tytler stared out the grimy window. "No more vicious or underhand than the average merchant of his standing."

Not the answer she wanted to hear.

"He instructed his mistress to steal proprietary information from a potential rival."

Tytler shrugged. "I cannot tell you whether that is in-keeping or unusual behaviour for the gentleman."

What it would take to prompt Black into action against Dillon? Exposing a pattern of unseemly behaviour? Rumours of more vicious tactics attributable to his name? She must convince him Dillon was more than an indolent rake of means.

"But have there been other individuals he's crossed?" Men —even rich ones—didn't wake up one morning and decide to use their mistress to seduce a merchant and steal his papers. It took a certain amount of practice to pull off such a theft, especially with only a few days to prepare.

Tytler made a show of wracking his brains. "Maybe the McNaulty family, but in the end their fall from grace was due to the cruel hand of Lady Fortune."

"What happened?"

"Oh, the McNaultys specialised in wine importation, an area that stoked curiosity in Sir Finney. This was some years ago, right after he arrived from London. He wanted to enter a partnership with Alasdair McNaulty—I've no idea about the specifics, but there was some advantage Sir Finney perceived regarding importation fees or warehouse storage. McNaulty got cold feet late in the negotiations and threatened to dissolve the partnership, putting Sir Finney in a difficult spot.

"I can't remember what happened next, I wasn't living in Edinburgh at the time. But some years later I found a woman at Mrs Sweet's house rumoured to be McNaulty's eldest daughter, though she took great pains to hide her identity. It was quite shocking."

"That's a fall from grace and a half," Thomas said with an awkward chuckle. "What happened to the family?"

"Like I said, I was in Ayrshire with my family while this played out, and I'm not sure anyone knew for certain. Perhaps I was told and forgot. I had no occasion to revisit the incident in my mind until you enquired."

"Dr Black and associates keep themselves appraised of these kind of goings-on," Elizabeth whispered to her husband. "Dr Black in particular would be alert for bad behaviour connected to Sir Finney."

"The McNaultys aren't well-known in Edinburgh," Thomas replied. "And it doesn't sound like the initial deal took place here."

"We wouldn't know the turkey red process was stolen by Sir Finney were it not for Tytler identifying the thief as his paramour. But if you recall it took us several days of stumbling to unearth that fact, and we need to uncover evidence of any even more malicious crime in a shorter period of time."

"That's why we need Tytler's assistance. He can get into a few places we cannot."

Elizabeth turned back to Tytler, sat fiddling with the edge of his grimy tablecloth. "You said McNaulty's daughter worked in Mrs Sweet's brothel?"

"Oh, I doubt she's still alive," Tytler replied matter-of-factly. "She was in her early thirties at the time, though she pretended she was far younger. It was clear her value was on the wane even then. If she didn't escape the game, the pox, bottle or an angry bull would have got her."

Elizabeth winced. Even Thomas swallowed in dismay.

"It's not that Dr Black would recoil at the testament of a whore on principle...but I think we need more solid evidence to convince him."

Elizabeth fixed Tytler with her brightest smile. He flinched like he'd glanced into the sun. "In the course of your Encyclopaedia editing Mr Tytler, you must have made use of many resources within this city."

"The Advocate's Library?" Tytler asked, catching her meaning quicker than she expected. "Yes, they let me use the visitor's desk to consult their collection."

"Examining criminal cases and legal texts?" Thomas asked, repressing a shudder.

"Hmm? A few. The Advocate's Library takes in a copy of everything registered at Stationary's Hall in London—their catalogue is commendably broad." For a moment, furtive Tytler was replaced with a dreaming scholar, floating through a sea of books towards enlightenment. Then he shook the fantasy clear. "If there was some resistance or objection to Sir Finney's treatment of the McNaultys it would appear in the local court records at least."

All Elizabeth knew about the Advocate's Library was its subscription fees were exorbitant, priced to prevent admittance of shabby individuals such as herself or Thomas. If their new friend possessed a work-around, they'd use it.

* * *

While Tytler conducted his enquiries, the Fulhames waited in Balfour's Coffeehouse, a crowded establishment a stone's throw from the Advocate's Library, set in the shadow of St Giles.

Elizabeth fell into a tetchy mood, because Thomas drank half of her capuchin under the guise of 'sampling it' and refused to buy his own.

"It's something of a womanly drink is it not?"

"Because it contains large quantities of milk? If that was a barrier to masculine enjoyment, no male bairn would pass nursing age..."

"Friends!" Jogging over to their table, exuberance brightening his face, Tytler looked like a different man. That he held an addiction to whoring was apparent; but it concealed an equally-gripping addiction to the second greatest vice of the age: empiricism.

He only carried a notebook—he wasn't allowed to take any documents off the premises—but it was filled with fresh scrawling.

"Success?" Thomas asked, his hands finally withdrawing from Elizabeth's capuchin cup.

"In the expected places...and a few less so."

Tytler settled down at the table and ordered a glass of wine.

"The McNaulty-Dillon partnership *was* contested by the McNaulty family, who considered it unlawful and wished for it to be dissolved. However, Dillon argued this was opportunistic *ex post facto* regret, and the courts upheld him against McNaulty's widow."

"His widow?"

"Yes, it came back to me that Alasdair McNaulty passed away after the partnership went through—I was perhaps confusing him with another businessman in my memory when you asked for my recollections—so I explored the other library catalogue to refresh myself on the circumstances."

He took a drag of wine and continued. "I'm surprised a bigger deal wasn't made of it, but when I say McNaulty passed away after the partnership was finalised...the tragedy occurred within days."

He pushed his notebook to the Fulhames. Elizabeth read the copied extract.

In a letter postmarked 12th November 1766, the deceased instructed his lawyer, the Honorable Daniel Knight, to proceed with the partnership under the Defendant's proposed terms (see Evidence D).

On the night of the 13th November 1766, the prosecution confirmed Alasdair McNaulty was waylaid by robbers in the vicinity of Greyfriars Kirk and succumbed to his injuries within hours. His stolen effects were never recovered.

"That's all?" Thomas asked.

"I don't think his murderers were ever apprehended," Tytler said. "You can imagine how sensational *that* trial and execution would have been. The fact there's no record of it suggests it never occurred.

"It's a pity, truth be told. I think the widow McNaulty and her wretched daughter would have acquired some public sympathy ahead of their own criminal case had details of the slaying being aired through a trial."

Elizabeth found herself agreeing. The botched mugging of Alasdair McNaulty wasn't enough to scandalise Edinburgh by itself. But right now, one sordid detail stuck out like a sore thumb.

"I would hate to be accused of womanish paranoia and fancifulness at such a crucial juncture..." Elizabeth began. "But does the order of these events not strike you as curious? Alasdair McNulty capitulated to Sir Finney days before he died."

Tytler smacked his lips. "A botched robbery where no thieves were caught? The Town Guards should have dragged *someone* to the gallows for the murder of a man like this McNaulty fellow. But if he was on the cusp of agreeing to Sir Finney's terms, then why..."

"But what if he didn't change his mind? After all, the way that account is worded, his lawyer received McNulty's direction by letter." Elizabeth wished she could see the full trial record for herself and she didn't have to trust Tytler on this.

Thomas whistled. "That's a level of evil beyond what Sir Finney currently stands accused of. Killing a business rival and planting a falsified document?"

"It's safe to conclude he benefited from the deal?"

"Aye. Sold the merged company a few years' later and at a tidy profit. There's some accounts of McNaulty's widow and daughter contesting the sale in court. I haven't had time to read through the whole proceedings..."

"Though given his daughter was dying in a brothel a few years' later, I imagine the case didn't work out in their favour."

"I know little of law," Tytler said. "Though I presume Sir Finney...knows a lot more law."

"What do ye think, madam?" Thomas asked. "Does this constitute proof of wrong?"

Elizabeth frowned at Tytler's scrawls. "On it's own...probably not. However, it could lead to Dr Black pursuing his own enquiry using resources unavailable to us."

"Surely this revelation is enough to shake him?"

"I think at this precise hour, Dr Black is genuinely uncertain about whether or not to act against the man. But if he comes to the decision at this damning juncture against action, he will set himself up so that dissuasion from his decision is nigh-impossible."

"...because if he excuses such obvious immoral behaviour, he's excusing most of the future immoral behaviour emanating from Sir Finney?"

"Precisely. He's signalling he doesn't want to be confronted with the atrocious reality of his former friend's actions."

"So we better hope we've nudged him in the right direction?"

Elizabeth nodded.

* * *

St Giles Square was crowded with foot traffic as they departed the Coffeehouse.

Nevertheless, someone watched them leave.

* * *

Interlude
Navan, Ireland—Spring 1766

At first Elizabeth thought the noise came from a stray cat or goat outside their house. She couldn't imagines the cries originated from a human, much less anyone she knew.

She was too young to know of company shares, stakeholders, or financial forecasts; why the wholesale price of cloth in Amsterdam mattered in Navan, why storms in the Bahamas led to tempests on the London Stock Exchange, why men furrowed their brows and ruined their lives over money and goods that did not yet exist.

All she knew was when she crept downstairs to the parlour, she found her mother kneeling on the floor in front of her father, clasping his wrists, entreating him. Her father was doubled over almost to his knees, as if seized by a stomach upset.

"I can't..." he was was whispering, over and over again.

"You must tell the children why you intend to go through with it then," her mother snapped. "Answering every question they have. Because I will not be the one who sits them down, looks them in the eye and tells them that their father..."

"Tell me what?" Elizabeth asked, hugging the door frame.

Her father's head shot up, a hand rising to cover his mouth. Her mother looked at the Turkish rug.

"It's nothing, angel," her father said after a long pause. "Your mother and I have important things to discuss. You and your sisters need to stay in the nursery this morning—we'll call you down when we're finished."

Elizabeth dawdled in the doorway, wondering if she could

plead with her father to tell her more. But the scene made her uneasy, and the smile couldn't stay on her face. Her father's face was red, she wondered if he'd fallen in nettles. Her mother's face was pale and sharp. Elizabeth sung loudly as she clomped up the stairs, letting her parents know it didn't matter that they weren't sharing this important thing with her —she intended to have a good time anyway.

In less than a month that house—with its Turkish rugs that went on forever, and the wide bannisters suitable for knotting ribbons around—would be sold, and her father would never be the same again.

* * *

The only fight Elizabeth got into as a child happened just after she turned nine. She was sewing on the damp front steps of their lodgings, trying her damnedest to ignore what the other children were saying.

"Well *my* mother said the baby died."

"No, my aunt Carol said she was making up the pregnancy for attention..."

"Liar! My mother was in the street and heard her crying. Said it was only to be expected, with all the misery put upon that poor woman."

"That's my mother you're talking about you useless gobermouth!" Elizabeth yelled, hurling the needlework to her feet and charging the ringleader. They'd ignored her furious expression, the silent curses she'd projected towards them. She had to act.

Stupid Eoife with her stupid curly blonde hair and smug expression. Always thought she knew everything; that she was better than everyone else.

Elizabeth took a handful of that curly hair and tugged.

Eoife screamed.

With hindsight Elizabeth didn't do a good job of fighting. She'd been kept under tight watch growing up by a succession of housekeepers and nurses, who never let Elizabeth or her sisters manage more than a vindictive pinch of each other. Elizabeth had little concept of how boys or men fought, only that they were encouraged to practice. It seemed rather unfair.

Eoife fought back, swatting at Elizabeth's face. "You sloppy bob tail!"

Elizabeth didn't know what that insult meant—neither did Eoife, probably—but it drove her fury hotter. Mimicking the cat fights she'd seen, Elizabeth set her fingernails into Eoife's cheeks.

It was at that point an adult broke up the squabbling pair, both wailing that they were the wronged party and the other girl started it.

However, when Elizabeth's mother sat her down in the kitchen and demanded to know what she was doing behaving like that, Elizabeth pressed her wobbling lips together and stared at her knees.

"I can't believe it—I can only hope the devil possessed my daughter, because she knows better than to scrap like a boy."

It was only a week since Elizabeth's mother had taken to bed clutching her stomach, and the older sisters ran to get a midwife.

"She's early..." Lottie whispered. The younger siblings were ignored as the midwife and family friends rushed to console Elizabeth's mother, who'd turned an eerie grey.

"The baby isn't due for another two months," Elizabeth said gravely, though the import of her words and what was happening didn't sink in until much later.

Her friends and the physicians tried to force her mother to rest in bed, but she was up and about within days.

"Life's for the living," she said, sweeping the floor with

such force the broom bristles snapped. "No use moping about."

A week after that, despite her stoicism, her mother was still the prime object of gossip in Navan.

Elizabeth was still too confused about what had happened —she thought she'd be getting a brother, but then was told her brother had been called to heaven instead—and scared of what would happen if she admitted to her mother the reason for the fight. She could only bite the inside of her cheeks and hope for a swift punishment.

As an adult looking back on her mother's miscarriage, Elizabeth wondered whether it hurt her father as much as her mother. If her mother refused to speak of the lost child, there was an even deeper silence from her father, who went days without leaving their shabby lodgings. Sometimes he'd refuse to leave the bedroom. It seemed that all his pain and grief blurred into one: the loss of his livelihood, his house, his unborn child.

9

A terse note from Black arrived before Elizabeth had time to brew her morning tea. After a brief deliberation, she removed the kettle from the fire. This was a summons.

Thomas wasn't at his brightest this early in the day, so she withheld speculation as they rushed across town. Unusually, Thomas didn't have much to say either.

"He can't down-play a murder," Elizabeth whispered, more to herself than Thomas. "He can't ignore this."

Neither of the Fulhames had the courage to tell Black their findings in person. With minimal coaching from his wife, Thomas had written a report outlining Tytler's findings and the suspicion it cast on Dillon and delivered it to the professor as late as he dared. Black's reply came less than eight hours later.

"If you have business today you should cancel it, Thomas," Black said before they'd even got through the door.

"They're here?" queried a voice from Black's study.

Seated in front of the dining room fire was the venerable William Cullen himself, thinner than she'd seen him several months ago, but still bright and alert. Despite the heavy physic wig falling past his shoulders, he appeared unperturbed by the warm August weather.

"Thomas, madam," Cullen offered in greeting.

As Elizabeth understood it, four years ago Cullen resolutely opposed the idea of women wielding phlogiston. He apparently thought it abhorrent, though not just out of concern for the delicate wombs and humours of the average female, even though he cited this as an excuse. This was until Princess Dashkova—a Russian noble serving an exile in Edinburgh—learned how to wield phlogiston. Miraculously, her womb didn't fall out, nor did she deteriorate into hysterics, forcing Cullen to conclude the princess was as capable of wielding phlogiston as his male students, if not more adept.

But Dashkova's bravery and skill actually made it harder for Elizabeth to gain Cullen's approval. For in the face of this humbling challenge to his dogma, Cullen sought to justify to himself why he held those erroneous views in the first place. The solution he settled upon was that it was fine for Princess Dashkova to wield phlogiston, because she was a high-class woman of exceptional breeding and intellect. So obviously Cullen's only concern was with *common* women wielding phlogiston, because they didn't understand half of what they were doing. Unfortunately, Elizabeth was as common as they came.

No one in her social circle confessed to slipping Cullen her secret. It seemed anathema to Black's character, and Thomas swore on the bible that he knew better than to brag to the Professor of the Practice of Physic about his wife's talents.

It mattered not. Cullen knew Elizabeth wielded phlogiston. And he disapproved.

The old professor remained civil enough to her, only pursing his lips or folding his arms when the topic came up, which happened rarely. All the sarcastic retorts Elizabeth wanted to make about the agreeable suitability of common *men* for phlogiston-wielding were wrestled into the back corners of her mind, never to be uttered.

"Sir Finney, eh?" Cullen said, tapping his physician cane against his chair leg. "Took me aback to hear his name after so long."

Moreau perched awkwardly at the far end of the dining table, misery radiating off him. When he boarded his Leith-bound ship he probably assumed his fortune would be assured by now. Elizabeth couldn't mock him: her husband believed much the same.

"I knew him before he assumed his titles," Black explained. "He came up from London shortly after Dr Cullen and I cleared the dark chymists out of Edinburgh. A number of wealthy men made the same migration, hoping to capitalise on the Scottish power vacuum. I believe Dillon's family owned land in Essex.

"Anyway, we became moderately close. He sought my advice on Scottish investments, and it was clear he held an appreciation for modern science. That's rare among men of his calibre: rich merchants usually view science as a tool to enrich themselves, they only care about what it can do for them. I trusted only a handful of friends enough to tell them about phlogiston-wielding, and Dillon was one. My reasoning was that despite his affluence, since he was English he wouldn't be connected with the dark chymist families. He wasn't a threat in that sense...I simply misjudged his character. He departed Edinburgh to join Westminster politics some years ago. We haven't spoken since."

Elizabeth tried to focus on what wasn't being said. "You are surprised he murdered a business rival?"

Cullen cleared his throat. Elizabeth had watched his dubious expression solidify as Black spoke, warning the conversation was about to veer off course.

"Why doesn't Mrs Fulhame wait in the adjourning room while we discuss these concerning developments?"

Elizabeth looked at Black. Black looked at Thomas.

"She's fine to stay here, doctors," he said, with more meekness than Elizabeth would have liked.

"Perhaps Dr Black did not mention that I helped uncover evidence of Sir Finney's murderous deeds," Elizabeth said. "I assure you my role is more than ornamental."

Attention returned to Thomas. Cullen clicked his tongue.

It would be nice if someone adopted a vigorous defence of my usefulness, Elizabeth thought. Black would avoid any defence of her that made Thomas look weak or indecisive. If Cullen decided to push the matter, he could probably shame Thomas into dismissing her from the room.

"It's not a pleasant topic for a lady to hear," Cullen said gruffly.

"Your concern for my wellbeing is touching, Dr Cullen," Elizabeth sweetly voiced the most charitable interpretation of Cullen's behaviour. "But since I've already contended with Sir Finney's awful actions when working with my husband and Mr Tytler, I suspect the damage is already done."

Cullen gave Thomas a dirty look, implying negligence on his part for dragging his wife into this sordid mess. Thomas continued to look uneasy, but eventually Cullen shrugged and returned his attention to Black.

"You asked whether I was surprised to learn what Sir Finney is capable of. Well, 'dismayed' might be a more apt descriptor." Black weighed his words carefully. "He's a conceited, self-interested noble who cannot process the word 'no.' That he cares little about other lives was apparent years ago. Based upon what I know, when murder enters the repertoire of a man like Sir Finney, he becomes exponentially more dangerous."

A lot of rich men committed despicable acts in the service

of personal interests. Elizabeth supposed most had lines they wouldn't cross, murdering rivals being one.

"Tytler, you say?" Cullen rubbed his knuckles against his chin. "That name rings a bell. Was he a student here by any chance?"

"Perhaps. He's two-score and change," Elizabeth said dubiously.

Cullen waved a hand. "Decades, months, days—at my age they're all equidistant, madam." With Tytler's age established, he probed deeper into his memory. "Ahh, I think I remember the boy in my chemistry class. Average scholar, but not in a particularly endearing way. Had the heart of a mouse. Never completed his medical degree: he dropped out when he had enough knowledge to set up shop as an apothecary."

"The mediocre and good of Scotland all pass through the Edinburgh medical school, trying to secure the facsimile of its lustre," Thomas noted, deftly excluding himself from that appraisal.

The Fulhames filled Cullen in on Tytler's services rendered as delicately as possible. Cullen flushed when he understood it all, but it was more indignation than modesty.

"I would not be surprised if that...guide...is as fanciful a rendering as Tytler's other notions. How could he afford so many ladies of pleasure?"

Elizabeth quietly wondered the same thing, since the Guide helpfully listed the ladies' prices, many running to five or ten guineas. Tytler's Encyclopaedia editing business must be more lucrative than it appeared.

"I apologise if my initial reaction to news of his involvement was petulant," Black said, picking through the conversation like a wading bird. "I assumed Sir Finney meant the theft as a personal insult to me, residual churlishness if you will. Under that assumption, ignoring his bait was the most prudent course of action. I'm concerned now that a broader motivation exists."

"Do ye know what that might be?" Thomas asked.

Black set his saucer down. "It's been years since I was privy to the inner thoughts of Sir Dillon. I don't even know what business he's maintained in Edinburgh. But you're welcome to speak with my friend Mr Smith tonight at the Oyster Club—he's likely informed of Sir Dillon's ongoing activities."

* * *

Interlude
Navan, Ireland—June 1772

Elizabeth first noticed how oblivious people could be at twelve years old.

It was a pleasant afternoon in the family shop. To Lottie and Elizabeth, helping customers was still more of a game than an obligation, and they chattered furiously.

"Those gents and ladies aren't paying attention half the time to what they buy," Elizabeth had whispered to her cousin. "You could show them a dirty rag and as long as you were telling them it was the finest indian muslin, popular in Versailles, they'd nod and agree they should buy it."

"No, that's an exaggeration!" Lottie giggled. This was her first week helping in the storefront, while Elizabeth considered herself a seasoned hand at selling fabrics. A few nights' ago, a violent storm had brought down a beam at the family warehouse, and Elizabeth's parents were overseeing emergency repairs. When her father admitted that Elizabeth could take care of the shop provided Lottie or her sisters were there too, she had to nod and smile like she was a responsible adolescent who could be trusted with such tasks. But once alone she'd squealed and jumped up and down.

"It's not!"

"It is!"

Lottie was always the optimistic, hopeful one. Elizabeth sighed and looked around. "Well, I'll prove it to you."

"Bessie! You wouldn't dare sell a customer a dirty rag— your father would whip you."

A fair point. Elizabeth bit her lower lip.

"Alright, so we won't try to trick the customers into buying something they don't want..." She kept looking around the shop for props or inspiration. But she kept coming back to Lottie, watching her with wide-eyed anticipation of gentle mischief.

By the time both girls reached adulthood, Elizabeth thought they looked more like sisters than cousins. But in childhood they were fairly different. Lottie shot up in height that spring, leaving Elizabeth a head shorter than her. Lottie's hair was light blonde—it would darken with age—while Elizabeth was a brunette. Today, Elizabeth wore a pale blue gown, and Lottie wore vibrant yellow stripes. To a twelve year old, this seemed a world of difference.

And so she devised a plan. The next customer would enter the shop and see only Lottie behind the counter. She'd begin serving him, carrying on a conversation about the weather, the upcoming market day, etc. But at some point she'd duck below the counter to pick up her scissors...

...And up would pop Elizabeth, who'd continue the conversation her cousin had been conducting as if nothing was amiss.

"That's so silly!"

"Just don't giggle or laugh. Then of course they'll know you're playing a prank. Can you be serious about this?"

As an adult, Elizabeth sometimes wished she possessed the self-assurance she had for the world at twelve.

The young Lottie was eventually induced to agree she'd take the exercise seriously.

The switch went undetected. When the customer—a furniture-maker looking for swatches for his wife—left the shop, Elizabeth looked down to see bite marks covering Lottie's wrist and hand from restraining her laughter.

"I can't believe he didn't notice!"

Elizabeth pretended she wasn't as excited as Lottie.

"I told you."

"Yes, but he has bad eyesight, you heard him say he'd left his spectacles at home."

So the cousins repeated the prank on the next customer— the wife of the parish priest. She didn't notice the switch either.

As the day progressed Elizabeth and Lottie became bolder. Elizabeth affected a Dublin accent. Lottie twisted her hair into an elaborate pile while Elizabeth left hers in a simple braid. Lottie donned a vivid pink bonnet.

Nobody noticed, because at the same time the cousins were getting better at redirecting their customer's attention: focussing them on the rolls of fabric, or on calculating prices in their heads, or recalling what other Navan citizens were doing. "Did you see Mrs Donal just now in the lane? She and her youngest were here before you arrived..."

By the end of it, neither Lottie nor Elizabeth were giggling. In fact, Lottie quietly suggested they give the game a rest. Elizabeth agreed just as fast.

* * *

The Fulhames found the smartest man in Edinburgh trying to eat his napkin.

Adam Smith grunted when he saw Thomas, and ignored

Elizabeth. He then tugged the napkin from his mouth, licking the mutton from it.

The fifty year old moral philosopher had a face of folded edges and the movements of a vulture. Smiling was something he required a few hours' notice to perform. His gravelly Scots accent flowed underneath the simmer of conversation in the cramped oyster cellar bar; guttural consonants popping and twisting.

The Oyster Club met in a side-room of Deacon's dingy cellar. Such philosophical gatherings weren't for ladies, but Thomas contrived to bring Elizabeth to the main room for a plate of oysters in the hope they could draw the learned philosopher out for a few words.

Smith currently sat at the central table, engaging in polite chatter with a man she couldn't tell if he knew or not.

Elizabeth hoped they'd engineer their own conversation sooner rather than later. A gentlemen in the corner was stroking his accordion in a menacing fashion, and as soon as he scared off the woman flirting with the fiddle player two tables over, they would likely unleash song. The Oyster Club itself would convene in a few minutes.

Smith gave his napkin a disgusted look, as if it morphed from a foodstuff into textiles to spite him. "It's George, isn't it?"

"No, I'm Thomas Fulhame," Thomas said with unusual patience. "But it's of no concern. We wondered what you knew of Sir Finney Dillon's present business dealings through your tax commissioner work."

The presence of a woman was spooking Smith, but at that moment Black appeared, like a silent shadow hovering over the table.

"Not much of interest," Smith explained, talking directly to Black as if he were the only audience member. "He appears to have paid his Scottish taxes and import dues, or done me the courtesy of pretending to...which is more than most."

"Does he have any interest in the textile trade?" Elizabeth asked, raising her voice. The threatening hum of a bow across strings built in the corner.

In some ways, a philosopher who ignored women was preferable to one who scorned them. Smith pretended Black asked him the question.

"It's funny you should ask that...word reached me he was elected to the British Linen Company Board of Trustees a few weeks ago."

"They organise and support linen manufacturing in Scotland?" Elizabeth knew this from her father's discussions. The company called itself 'British' as a patriotic gesture, but its interests primarily focused on the west coast of Scotland where the founders originated.

"They're entirely mercantile banking now, madam," Smith said, giving Elizabeth the briefest glance before returning to Black. "Have been for the best part of a decade."

Elizabeth fought to conceal annoyance at her slip up. Still, it was useful to know the theft of the turkey red papers was connected to Dillon's movement into the textile trade.

Black's watched the proceedings without consternation. "It makes sense Sir Finney would get involved with the British Linen Company given he has the money to throw around, though I'm not sure he has the expertise."

"I don't know much more about his business interest," Smith said. "He spends most of his time in London, which is where his main holdings are."

It struck Elizabeth as a little strange that a man with no footprint in Scotland would want to join a Scottish-based linen bank, especially if Smith didn't think he operated a textile mill here. She leaned forward.

"What benefit would Sir Finney have from becoming a British Linen Company trustee?"

"Very little, besides from ego gratification," Smith said, fiddling with his napkin. "Possibly the board was short of members—him and Archibald McIntyre were elected at the same meeting."

Black no longer watched the proceedings. His attention was distracted by the singer and musicians yelling at a barmaid.

Someone hailed Black and Smith from the back room. The professor raised his hand, index finger raised.

One minute left.

"Who's Archibald McIntyre?" Elizabeth asked.

"Nobody of note, only..." Smith began. Then he froze.

"Pardon?" Thomas asked, frowning. Smith muttered rapidly under his breath.

Black's attention snapped back to his friend.

"Adam?"

Smith's eyes darted back and forth as if totalling an invisible ledger, fingers flicking through the air.

The tallow candles on their table bulged and sputtered. Elizabeth thought the tavern door must have let in a gust of air, but it remained closed.

"Adam," Black said sharply.

Smith blinked, then slowed his shuffling of the imaginary papers in front of him.

"Doug Stewart sits on the Holland Timber Associates board," he announced with a flourish.

There was a confused silence.

"We were talking about Mr Archibald McIntyre...?" Thomas said slowly.

"Yes, yes..." Smith sounded annoyed that he had to guide the table through what must be an obvious causal process to him. "And Dillon sits with Dougie on the Holland Timber Associates board."

Elizabeth and Thomas looked to Black, whose expression turned a good deal more opaque. It was never a good sign when Black's expression because this unreadable.

"This Mr Stewart is also involved with the British Linen Company?" Elizabeth hazarded.

"It was Emmanuel Turner's marriage to Sophie Lawrence last summer that convinced me," Smith continued, now speaking in earnest to Black. "At the time I thought it was about offloading shares in his glassblowing business, but now it's obvious..."

Thomas looked helplessly at Elizabeth, who could only shrug and indicate he take his cues from Black.

"...And after Hamish Goodfellow's outburst in Lloyd's Coffeehouse in March..."

Black's eyes narrowed.

"...You'd think the fifty guineas from Henry to Peter was sloppy book-keeping, but..."

"Professor Black?" Thomas finally ventured, knowing Smith's fragmented thought process would only accelerate from here.

"What he's saying," Black enunciated each word, glaring at Thomas. "Is Finney Dillon—through the recent marriage of his widowed sister, his friendships and mutual business connections, has now acquired a majority stake in the British Linen Company board of trustees. He has six allies on the ten-man board."

"So he can do what he pleases," Elizabeth said heavily.

"As it pertains to funding other textile mills, deciding on their trade partners and controlling company mergers," Smith added.

Not only had Sir Finney just stolen a lucrative dyeing process, but he had gained the power to crush any Scottish competitors.

"Adam, we need to rejoin the gathering; the others are

starting the discussion," Black said sharply, though he was also trying to be heard over the instrumental groaning.

"Right..." Smith didn't bother to acknowledge the Fulhames as he rose. As Black turned to close the meeting room room door she thought he looked directly at her, but his expression was impossible to fathom. A second later the door slammed shut.

IO

It was still a cool predawn light when the Fulhames made their way to Black's laboratory. Elizabeth had been too tense to sleep, and felt the detachment that came with sleep deprivation as she entered the college yards.

The only other individual about at this hour was Cullen, who entered the quad at the same time as the couple.

There wasn't anything to do but fall in step. Cullen tapped his tricorne in curt greeting.

"Did ye hear what Mr Smith deduced last night, Dr Cullen?" Thomas asked deferentially.

"Aye." Cullen jabbed his cane into the dirt. "It appears there's a viper nesting in our city."

"Given the dearth of evidence, you assume Sir Finney is in Edinburgh?" Elizabeth asked.

Cullen shrugged. "I would suppose so. I raised the topic with some friends better informed than Joe and myself. Their understanding is Dillon often attends the final summer masquerade ball."

"The one at the Assembly rooms next week?" Thomas asked.

"He prefers the winter season in London, but tours Scotland in warmer weather. Rumour has it he never stays in Edinburgh for more than a week."

Well, this seemed like valuable information. It wasn't as if they could call upon Sir Dillon for tea.

"I wish you hadn't dragged your poor wife into this," Cullen said, tutting.

Not again.

"It's not common knowledge, Dr Cullen, but I actually have reasonable familiarity with the subject in hand. My family are textile dyers and weavers, you see. I helped in my father's business since I was old enough to count." Elizabeth continued to speak, trying to give the appearance of addressing Cullen while avoiding full eye contact. It was easy to maintain a facade of feminine charm that way. "Indeed, I have lately pursued my own chemical experiments into metallic textile dyes."

She hesitated, wondering if she'd said too much.

Cullen leaned closer. "Experiments, madam?"

"Yes, genuine chemical experiments based on simple dissolution and precipitation of various metals onto textiles. Did you know Dr Cullen that some of the nitro salts only reduce metal back into solid form in the presence of light?"

Instantly she knew she'd said the wrong thing. In trying to ignore Dr Cullen's sarcastic inflection and prove herself, she'd stumbled onto a topic where Cullen undoubtably knew more than her. He was a chemistry professor before he assumed the Practice of Physic role, after all.

"'Only' is a rather strong qualifier, Mrs Fulhame. It implies a degree of certainty natural philosophers are careful to avoid."

"Well it happens to be true," Elizabeth retorted. "I ran the experiment on an overcast day and thought it failed because the metal didn't precipitate onto the silk cloth. It was only when the sun came out that the silver sheen appeared."

They'd reached the door of the laboratory building. Cullen came to a halt and leaned on his cane. He looked like a parody of a professor at the lectern. "And did you rerun the experiment on a sunny day, madam? You assume the weather outside your dwellings influenced the speed of the reaction, but maybe if you ran that experiment today the same delay would occur? Or did you even run a second experiment on the same day to check you applied the metallic solution correctly the first time?" There was condescension in Cullen's voice Elizabeth doubted he used on his students.

"It was self-evident that light prompted the reaction," Elizabeth said, mustering all her polite firmness. "If you had been in the room, you would understand why I drew that conclusion." She stopped herself from challenging Cullen to come see the experiment for himself, because she was down to the last spoonfuls of the acidic solution and didn't know when they could afford to buy more.

"And yet unfortunately I wasn't, madam. So I will have to take the word of a lady, which I usually presume is honourable." But not reliable.

Elizabeth couldn't do more than bare a fake smile and keep quiet. Regretfully, this kind of condescending treatment plagued most aspects of life. Her brother-in-law ignored her suggestions on how to negotiate a better lease of his mill property, despite the fact she'd been in her room when her father navigated similar discussions. In his first week as a student, Thomas rebuffed her warnings that he'd wrongly annotated his anatomy lecture sketches, and it wasn't until Monro pointed out his mistake that he corrected them.

There's the reason I don't want to play natural philosophers at their own game, she thought. I need a dissertation's worth of experiments to convince them of anything.

She entered the building with feigned courtesy to Cullen, who didn't seem to notice he offended her. She was halfway into the laboratory when Black caught up with her. He must have been standing just inside the door.

"If you're interested in philosophic enquiries, perhaps I can introduce you to Mrs Monro-MacDonald," Black said in a low voice. "She's the older sister of Professor Monro. A very intelligent woman with a flair for cultivating roses. Mrs Monro-MacDonald hosts a gathering for women like yourself with an interest in natural philosophy. I don't think any of them have dyeing or textile projects, but they do kitchen and gardening experimentation."

'They do?" Elizabeth perked up.

"Yes, a few of the ladies have consulted with me on such topics," Black smiled ruefully, as if the interest of intelligent, beautiful society woman was just another unfortunate activity natural philosophers like himself must endure.

If Black was talking about the woman Elizabeth thought he was, Monro-MacDonald was the wife of an influential clan chieftain, putting her near the top of Edinburgh society.

"I can make the appropriate introductions," Black added, seeing her hesitate. "Mrs Monro-MacDonald will happily accept my recommendation. I think the ladies meet in the third Saturday of the month."

That was coming up soon.

Elizabeth's mind accelerated, eager to distract itself from Cullen's cutting remarks. Perhaps this was just what she needed?

"I didn't realise you were investigating light-sensitive reactions," Black said, glancing back to the doorway where Cullen remained in earnest conversation with Thomas. "Perhaps I can look in my papers for similar studies on the matter?"

"Oh, you don't need to do that Dr Black," Elizabeth said,

laughing lightly. "I fear I overstated my findings. I meant my remark to Dr Cullen as a curious observation, nothing more."

The natural philosophy world of men was a rigid, cut-throat place. Why appease the likes of Cullen, when they'd never take her seriously anyway?

"By the way..." She cast around for a suitable change of subject. "While I understand you and Sir Finney had a falling out a few years prior, I don't recall you mentioning what caused the rift. Why don't you fill us in on the particulars?"

* * *

Interlude
Edinburgh—January 1771

Black and Smith sat at the table opposite each other, separated by swathes of vellum and leather-bound ledgers. Several were crusted in mould, and Black fought the urge to wipe his fingers every time he touched the pages.

Smith didn't seem to care about the state of the materials, he'd been humming that jaunty, tuneless melody for the past hour. Instead, Black tried to focus on the ticking of the clock in the corner.

The company directors had been more helpful and agreeable than he'd feared. It was probably the presence of Smith and his curt assurance that he *wasn't* there to conduct a formal audit of behalf of the Customs House that spooked them the most.

"Did you look through that pile?" Black pointed to a stack of small ledgers occupying the middle ground of the table.

"The records from 1768? Aye." Smith barely glanced up. His own notebook was rapidly filling up with microscopic scrawls.

"It's the records from September '70 we really need. That's

the earliest Dillon could have met with the committee. Are they in that pile, do you think?" Black pointed to another pile, the paper greasy and stained.

Smith set his quill down. He put his head in his hand for a moment.

"Joe, you have all the sympathy in the world from me, you really do—"

"—That's only because you know me!"

"—True...but I doubt we're going to find evidence of fraud. These ledgers are sloppy yes, but they're clean."

"They're filthy," Black muttered, grimacing at the green-grey smudges on his fingers.

"The books aren't cooked, if that's a more palatable metaphor for you."

Smith wasn't known for his emotional astuteness—it wasn't the reason Black valued him as a friend—but there was concern in his eyes as Black tutted to himself.

"You'll recover the loss in a few years, Joe. A lesser man would have thrown all their savings into a venture as alluring as Sir Finney described, where you held back."

"I should have held back more, Adam." Black turned his face away. "Besides, the money isn't the point."

"I know that—but you're distracting me with your fidgeting, and I'm trying to come up with a platitude that will get you to stop."

Black looked around the dusty closet that served as the Bray's Merchant Bank office. His energy—which burned nonstop this week—was running out, quenched by the dull reality.

He must re-focus on contingencies. The Edinburgh winter did its worst in January and February; he should close off his dining room and parlour and do without heating them. It wasn't as if he could afford to entertain guests. Maybe those household cuts would be enough to avoid dismissing any servants.

"I know you said you were too busy for the Board of Manufactures consultancy, but can I persuade you to reconsider my offer?" Smith tidied his pile of ledgers and beat dust off his frayed waistcoat. "The Board are generous with their compensation."

Black stayed silent. They'd tread this argument before. He pointed out—and Smith couldn't disagree—that evaluating scientific proposals took hours. Black hoped to use the next few months to conduct the floating balloon experiments he tried running last year, which were squeezed from his schedule by teaching obligations.

"Even if the Board were meagre with their compensation, it might turn into an inevitability."

Smith clicked his tongue to indicate he wasn't pushing the matter.

"You're the most celebrated chemist in Europe, Joe. You needn't run a single experiment more: your scientific reputation is assured."

Black decided he was ready to turn the subject back to the disagreeable paperwork before them.

"Finney had to know the company was on shaky footing when he told me about the venture last winter. You heard the secretary tell us how the trouble stemmed from the bad weather in the North Sea and the first shipment loss in November."

"All I'm saying is that the company didn't short you. What I'm seeing here," Smith waved at the papers around him, "is a set of underwhelming businessmen who chose to hope blindly that their misfortunes would turn around if they acquired just a little more capital, and a little more time. Many the wreckage of a business I've surveyed suffers from such folly. I would wager some of the other companies you held stocks in paid off similar debts of blind hope with no one any the wiser of how close they came to ruin."

"I understand..." Black trailed off.

Smith dropped another ledger on the floor.

"Have you spoke with Sir Finney lately?" He asked the question with no pretence at neutrality.

"Not since the bank folded." A pause. "There is nothing I wish to say to him."

Word on the town was Sir Finney's fortunates remained undamaged by the collapse of Bray's, despite his close affiliation with them.

Dillon must have discarded his shares in the bank quietly; probably in piecemeal over several months. Not that Black would find proof—Dillon was too smart to capture such manoeuvres on paper—but he imagined his own investment in Bray's was much bandied about by Dillon as proof the company was on firm financial footing and his disinvestments a piece of minor housekeeping.

"If I knew what Sir Finney knew last winter about the loss of their shipments and the volatility on the Amsterdam stock market, I would have notified any business acquaintances about the risk of investing the company at that time, and made sure they understood the potential for the complete loss of their investment." Black set his quill in the inkstand. "But if I were speaking to my friends, I'd have beseeched them not to invest."

The loss of his savings wasn't catastrophic—after a few lean months he should be made right with course fees and a bit more consulting work. It was the realisation Sir Finney had used Black's investment in a shaky mercantile company to bolster his own savings and avoid financial ruin. It was a kind of grief Black felt, which he supposed Smith could sense. The man Black considered a friend had *used* him.

* * *

"We didn't speak after the merchant bank collapse," Black said, tracing his cheekbone with a fingernail. "Sir Finney moved to London a few months' later anyway. There was no public acrimony: he didn't bother to write, and neither did I.

"What hurts is that I thought there was a possibility for reconciliation—I heard Sir Finney asked after me at the Select Society and Poker Club last time he passed through Edinburgh. He wanted to know how I was getting on with the Board of Manufactures work. He framed the questions as if they were a concern for my wellbeing and general household oeconomy. In fact, I now suspect he was manipulating the other Board members into telling them about Moreau's letter."

"It was Simon who squeaked," Cullen commented from across the room. "The man has a *compulsion* to brag that overtakes all common sense. All Sir Finney would have to do was sneeze forcefully enough to rattle his purse, and that would set auld Simon off."

"No doubt." Black's lips thinned in disdain.

II

"I'm still unsure the difference between a masquerade and a ridotto," Elizabeth admitted.

"I believe the pertinent difference is ridottos are tolerated by the Edinburgh Kirk...and masquerades are not," Black said.

Masquerades were often cited by Scottish ministers as a symbol of societal depravity in London and Bath, and attempts to import them into Edinburgh hadn't gone far. Summer ridottos, however, were a common evening entertainment for nobility in the city. That the fashionable gathering was in the form of a masquerade seemed hardly worth commenting on.

Elizabeth was glad her face lay concealed behind a brocaded mask as the sedan chair carrying her and Thomas was deposited outside the Assembly rooms behind Black's. Black made a point of helping her onto the street, then made sure the bored door sentries got a glimpse of his face before he pulled his domino mask over his eyes.

"Good evening, Dr Black..."

Satisfied the Fulhames were here at the behest of Black, the sentries waved them past with barely a glance at their ticket.

They joined a trickle of sable-cloaked revellers in the lofty flag-stone passageway to to the building behind the street. Wall-mounted braziers roared around them.

They'd committed no deceit—their tickets were purchased by Black—but Elizabeth tugged her husband past the haughty Lady Directress welcoming guests where the passageway opened out into the gilded Rooms themselves, fearful she'd sniff out their rustic origins.

She tried not to gawk. The dancing hall was transformed into an orangery, with palms adorning every corner and the pillars wreathed with carnations. The air smelled heady and luxuriant. Small succulents garnished the sideboards, their prickly fur illuminated by a thousand candles.

The couples milling around the dancing floor were beautiful and fearsome in their masquerade costumes. Pale flesh against velvet masks; rosebud lips accentuated with glinting diamond earrings. Visions of bared teeth flashed behind ostrich feathers and oriental fans. The garden was paradise, but its inhabitants were demons.

"Your ticket is for the second and ninth dance," Black said, leading them to a pocket of space in the far corner. "The minuet and a country dance, should you care to take part. I advise you to listen carefully for the numbers, because Lady Don has little patience for stragglers."

Elizabeth glanced across the room to the martinet dowager, draped over the arm of a blond gentlemen twenty years younger. She was all smiles and laughs to the couples as they approached her in greeting, but several oblivious backs received a contemptuous glare.

"You'll keep your voice down in here, won't you love?" Elizabeth straightened her husband's mask. *"I fear these beautiful residents of Edinburgh will tear us to pieces at the hint of an Irish brogue."*

"Don't fret," Thomas said cheerfully, patting her hand. "We'll start looking for Sir Finney after our dance."

That reminded Elizabeth. "Do the Assembly matrons sell tickets without dances, Dr Black?"

"Pardon? Oh, I'm actually accompanying Lady Reid." Black patted the breast pocket where he stowed his ticket. "Her husband has a sore back, though I suspect that's a fiction to recuse himself from public entertainment. We're assigned to dances three and six." Black caught the eye of a gaggle of older ladies, who cooed and waved. "If you'll excuse me, I wouldn't expect Sir Finney to arrive until a fashionably late hour anyway."

Their first minuet survived, the Fulhames retreated to the adjourning tea room. The crowds had thickened since their arrival, but it was a genteel level of crowdedness making it possible for the pair to claim a small table. A miniature carved pineapple on a bed of Amaryllis served as centrepiece.

Thomas slid half an orange across the table.

"Thank you, good sir," Elizabeth said.

"Is the lady also desirous of tea or coffee?"

"She might be persuaded to take tea." The orange helped refresh her, but couldn't reverse the mugginess descending upon the room. In a few hours the press of sweating bodies would be intolerable.

Thomas took off, wiping his brow. The room filled with equally exhausted ladies desiring refreshments, and Elizabeth suspected her husband would be gone a while. She settled in to watching the crowds and listening in on passing conversations.

"It pains me to see a woman so elegant sitting alone," a silky voice behind her said. "May I have this dance?"

When she turned around, Elizabeth thought for a moment she was regarding Black. The man standing behind her was tall and slim, with gunmetal grey hair in tight rolls against his cheeks, features disguised with a vibrant red Venetian domino mask. Elizabeth realised after a moment this couldn't be Black—but the man possessed the most impeccable posture and...poise.

"I'm afraid my ticket is only for the second and ninth dances, my lord," Elizabeth stammered, unsure of the etiquette for this assembly, but remembering the glaring Dowager.

The gentleman laughed. "Oh, you don't have to worry about those silly rules. You're stuck here until the ninth dance? I insist you accompany me." He held out a gloved hand.

Elizabeth had an awful suspicion she knew who this man was, which was confirmed as soon as they stepped onto the ballroom floor.

"I saw you at Leith port the other day, did I not? I didn't mistake you for one of the ladies of the dockside—don't take my remarks the wrong way—but I'm nonetheless surprised to see you here tonight."

"I hear many ladies of the night gild the assembly rooms. They are often better dancers than the lords' mistresses...Sir Finney."

Elizabeth tried to recall if she recognised Sir Finney from their first encounter with Moreau. She'd glanced at the crowd on the docks, keeping an eye for danger, but it was too dark to make out faces. This man could have watched them from a distance and she'd be none the wiser.

"I always find these ridottos so refreshing," Sir Finney mused, guiding her to the top of the forming quadrille set. "I always encounter the most lively people."

"I would be glad to oblige, my lord. I hear *textiles* are the most stimulating topic of conversation this season."

Sir Finney had an easy laugh. "Dr Black isn't too upset about that, is he?"

"He appears more sanguine than I would in his position."

The first chords struck. Sir Finney sank into a bow. "Dr Black has the head of a philosopher, but the heart of a businessman. He understands how the world works."

It didn't surprise Elizabeth that Sir Finney was a confident dancer. He seemed to enjoy the intricate patterns he was making. Elizabeth had to focus on what the correct moves were, but despite what she thought were a couple of obvious stumbles, Sir Finney was always aware of her position and ready to catch her arm.

Talking during the dance was out of the question. There wasn't much she could do but glower at her partner, who smiled wolfishly back.

When the dance was over—onlookers applauded, and several people shot admiring glances at the noble Sir Finney—Elizabeth was escorted back to her table. A pot of tea sat cooling in front of her chair and shawl, but Thomas hadn't materialised.

Sir Finney set Elizabeth back in her chair.

"Sadly such an encounter can't repeat itself, for I will depart Edinburgh on Friday and don't expect to return for a while. It's been an honour to make your acquaintance, Mrs Fulhame. Give my regards to Dr Black."

His back was turned before Elizabeth realised she'd not volunteered her name. She supposed the Irish couple who orbited Dr Black made a small name for themselves in the town.

Too late to question Sir Finney, though. He was promptly swallowed by the sea of dancers.

She wasn't going to let her target escape that easily.

Elizabeth shoved her way back out the crowded side-room,

applying her elbow into stomachs and backs as genteelly as possible. She caught a glimpse of the man's retreating back in the doorway, but two steps forward Elizabeth found her path blocked.

The woman was a few inches shorter than Elizabeth, though her dark hair dwarfed hers. On most woman that quantity of hair would be the telltale indication of a wig or extensions, but in this case it appeared to be natural. Very fine cheekbones accentuated a tiny, unlined mouth and delicate chin. However, the luscious turquoise gown barely covered her...

Ah.

"You must be Lydia," Elizabeth remarked.

"Always a pleasure to make a new acquaintance," the woman said with a smile. "Especially one who does not immediately accuse me of stealing her husband."

"I understand you only steal expensive things," Elizabeth retorted. It had been a long night, and she could feel a blister forming on her big toe.

Lydia's smile grew wider. She had an easy, unaffected charm about her. Or—Elizabeth supposed—she was skilled at cultivating that perception.

"Is it not demeaning to carry out such tasks for Sir Finney?" Elizabeth asked. She would have needed to grit her teeth to endure an evening in Moreau's intimate company, even if said encounter occurred in the royal chambers of Kensington Palace.

"That's the modern world of commerce and survival, is it not?" Lydia replied. "We do unpleasant things in exchange for more pleasant things."

"Since you appear so eager to engage me in conversation..." Elizabeth looked over Lydia's shoulder and found no trace of her quarry. "...Perhaps you can tell me what Sir Finney is doing with the papers you stole."

No use being coy or subtle. Sir Finney's remarks made it

clear he knew the Fulhames and Black sought the dyeing process.

"It's of little concern to me." Lydia shrugged. "I delivered the papers straight to my lord's study—I have more interesting books I can read. What my lord did with them next is his own affairs."

The crowds ebbed around them. The silence between the two women turned stony.

"I am curious as to your costume, my lady," Lydia said.

The evening's theme was The Wonders of Eden. Lydia was clearly dressed as a peacock.

Elizabeth hadn't the means for an ornate costume, but found she could improvise. She wore a black robe with white apron and stomacher. A trailing sash of turquoise almost to her feet was the only adornment.

"I'm a magpie, madam," Elizabeth replied.

The two women locked eyes for a minute. Saying nothing, Lydia bobbed into a perfunctory curtsey and let the tide of dancers sweep her away.

"There ye are, love."

Elizabeth saw a flicker of relief—quickly repressed—on her husband's face as he pushed through the blockade, taking her by the forearm.

"Ye didn't want to stay for the country dance, did ye? Thought not," he concluded before Elizabeth had time to express an opinion on the question. He'd no doubt seen both her conversations, and maybe tried to follow Sir Finney too. No sign of Black. Elizabeth suspected Sir Finney and his mistress were already departed.

Once home, Elizabeth waited until Thomas snuffed out the bedchamber candles before relaying the details of her conversations with Lydia and Sir Finney. Part of the delay was because she didn't know if she wanted to tell her husband what occurred.

"Lydia said she delivered the papers to Sir Finney's study. If they're still on his person we must act soon: he's departing for London on Friday." She was glad the dark bedchamber hid Thomas' expression. He lay unusually still.

* * *

It should have been a simple harmonisation of ideas. Instead, it turned into an argument.

Elizabeth thought they'd be safer meeting at Black's or Cullen's, but Cullen insisted they join his usual afternoon gathering at the Nicholson Tavern.

"I know the tavern owner—he's the honest sort—and he can set us up in a side room."

She supposed Cullen's motivation was that Sir Finney might be watching the professors' homes and be on the alert for sign of a gathering.

Tytler had passed on his apologies to the Fulhames and explained he was busy collecting sponsorship for his balloon project.

"Funny, I didn't recall inviting him," muttered Cullen, brooding into his claret. "I wonder what 'balloon project' is a euphemism for?"

"The way he described it, I think he genuinely wants to fly the first fire balloon in Britain," Thomas replied.

Cullen tilted his head to and fro. "I suppose I'm surprised his hobby horse trumps ingratiating himself with the well-heeled of Edinburgh."

Elizabeth doubted Tytler would pass up a meeting with Black for something as mundane as sexual congress like Cullen insinuated.

"What do you think of his plans, Joe?" Cullen asked.

Black gave an equivocal hand wave. "If his Encyclopaedia entry on the subject is any indication, he had a solid grasp of the dynamics of heated air. But theoretical understanding does not guarantee a smooth transition to application."

"I don't imagine generating the requisite heated gas is trivial."

"No, that's why he fixates on subscriptions."

"Seems stupid to me," Moreau said, shaking his head. "This Tytler wastes his own savings, and that of more poor fools, for a grand vanity project. Even if the balloon gets off the air for five minutes, what does it achieve?"

"We shouldn't all pursue natural philosophy for fortune," Elizabeth objected. "I imagine a great many discoveries had no apparent use at first glance." Men like Dillon looked at the world through the lens of how much money everything could make for them.

"But we should pursue science to make the world a better place, no?" Moreau became animated. "How does an elephant-sized balloon drive agricultural improvements? Or make sick infants healthy?"

"I don't know, maybe a farmer in the balloon could scatter seeds onto his fields, or pick apples from trees." Elizabeth wasn't sure why she was defending Tytler so harshly. She supposed she was still annoyed with Moreau for losing the turkey red process in the first place.

Moreau scoffed. "When we still have horses, ploughs and ladders?"

Elizabeth recognised this argument was going nowhere. "The whole point is that there are uses in the future that exist beyond the confines of our current imagination."

"Those balloons could be used for war, I suppose," Thomas said. "Carrying attackers into fortifications, firing grapeshot from the skies."

The worst thing was that the men around the table nodded thoughtfully at Thomas' comment. Even Moreau declined to offer a rejoinder. It would be nice if some innovation wasn't driven by violence, Elizabeth thought as she returned to her sherry.

"I don't like this," Thomas said, returning to the events at last night's ridotto. "Dillon found out our names, and he knows what we're up to."

Black sighed. "He enjoys the attention, no doubt."

Once they'd regrouped, a still-yawning Black appeared surprised that Elizabeth spoke with Dillon. Black caught rumours Dillon had arrived at the ridotto, but he was on the opposite side of the dance floor from where Elizabeth danced with him, hidden from view.

Black had never met Lydia, so if she was monitoring him to shield her paramour he wouldn't have noticed.

"Where is Sir Finney dwelling?"

"Probably in Moray House. I believe he's stayed there on previous visits to Edinburgh." No one Black talked to claimed knowledge of how long Dillon intended to stay in town, meaning next Friday was the best intelligence they had.

Thomas couldn't hide his frustration that Dillon whisked his wife away when his back was turned. His personal animosity to the man appeared stoked. "If he knows we're trying to recover the turkey red process, would he really tell us it's in his study?"

"There's no reason to suppose that's where it is now," Elizabeth said. "We only know that's where Lydia first delivered it to."

Cullen gave her an approving nod. He's going to set himself the task of educating me in logical reasoning isn't he, thought Elizabeth.

Moreau shuffled uncomfortably on his stool, looking overwhelmed by the crowded tavern. With the wide-eyed stare of a fresh provincial, he clutched his purse in a way more likely to draw the attention of pickpockets than discourage them.

Black steepled his fingers. "From what I recall, Sir Finney

used to spread important documents across multiple buildings. His lawyer might have some, others might be kept in a safe in his office, but he'd never put all his valuable records in the same place. He said you could never be too careful."

"Does he still have an office and lawyer?"

"Not in Edinburgh. He moved his business down to London, and I think his old lawyer followed him a while back. That's not to say he doesn't have friends in Edinburgh—quite the opposite in fact."

"So he could be hiding his documents anywhere," Thomas said, heaving his shoulders.

Leaving the room, Elizabeth took her husband by the elbow. A wicked grin immediately broke on Thomas' face.

"Say no more, hen."

Elizabeth smiled. "I didn't say anything yet."

"But I imagine ye intend to say something about a man in Duddingston."

It was nice when Thomas kept up with her thinking. "More to the point, we need to extend a further degree of friendliness towards the gentleman in question, if we want to receive a sufficient quantity of friendliness back."

"Guess Tytler will have his conversation with Dr Black, then..."

* * *

Interlude
Navan, Ireland—July 1779

It all began with a horse called Job: a plodding fellow with fewer brains than looks, and little of either.

Elizabeth remembered the flash of annoyance when

Catherine Fulham burst into her parlour, because she'd reached a tricky point in her floral embroidery. The flustered look on Catherine's pale and worn face made it clear she'd have to chose between concentrating on sewing and eaves-dropping on gossip.

"Mercy, Catherine!" her mother exclaimed. "What in heaven's name is the matter?"

"The devil take that boy—he's only gone and lost Job in a card game." Catherine wiped her face with the back of her hand. Ma made a few stabs with her finger, and Elizabeth's youngest sister bolted from the room to prepare the teapot.

Heart pounding, Elizabeth furrowed her brow at the green thread she was tugging through the cloth.

"Job?" Ma asked. Elizabeth knew this was the Fulham's farm horse, but it wasn't her place to admit that.

"How could Patrick break my heart?" Catherine was muttering to herself. "I can't believe it..."

Ah, so her eldest son was responsible. Elizabeth allowed herself to relax a little.

Ma was doing what she could to soothe Catherine, and Maggie was back with the emergency tea. It was plain Catherine's distress ran too deep for a cup of tea to fix.

"Of course it all happened the week before rent is due," Catherine continued. "He's ruined the whole family this time, so he has. Cleared out everything. There's nothing we can do..."

"You've suffered so much sorrow over that son of yours, Catherine..."

Elizabeth remained concentrated on her embroidery, though not to the extent it looked like she was blocking out the women's discussion. Ignoring them would be as suspicious as gaping. As far as everyone in the room knew, Catherine Fulham was a woman Elizabeth greeted politely if they encountered each other on the roads because she was a friend of her mother.

They didn't yet know that a few weeks ago in the copse at the edge of the Harristown farmlands she'd become *considerably* more familiar with Catherine's middle son Thomas. A boy a head shorter than her, but with a twinkling eye, disarming grin and self-assured manner. In those days he still spelled his surname 'Fulham' like the rest of his family.

Not for the first time, Elizabeth wished her cousin Lottie was still in Navan. She'd coo, blush and giggle at all the right moments in Elizabeth's tales. Elizabeth's sisters tended to ask too many probing questions that ruined her mood—such as, do you really think father will let you marry him? Most of the time she was glad her sisters shared her practical mind, but the appearance of Thomas in her life was the first time she avoided confiding in them at all.

Catherine Fulham had come to Elizabeth's house to vent, and possibly seek advice. She knew better than to ask them for money —their circumstances weren't much better than the Fulhams.

Ma glanced to the front workshop as she fussed over Catherine, a momentary vigilance concealed.

Elizabeth doubted her father would interfere in sobbing women's business, not even out of curiosity. He would keep to his weaving and pretend not to hear.

A few years' ago she would have called her father uncaring or slovenly. A grizzled bear of a man, he looked more like a journeyman than an affluent merchant, no matter how well he dressed. Not that he could afford to dress well any more. It was as if the bankruptcy of their textile business was an attempt by the Heavens to bring him to back to his proper station in life. Indeed, many guests and customers to Elizabeth's household were surprised by the erudition of the daughters, and their ability to read French and Latin. At fourteen, Elizabeth's own education embarrassed her, because of that surprise. For a few years it became difficult for her parents to persuade her to care for self-improvement.

Now as she approached nineteen, more of her father's bankruptcy—which occurred when she was five and barely understood what was going on—came to light, and helped her understand her father's paradoxical mixture of apathy and social striving. He feared another blow of financial ruin—the weaving business they'd rebuilt in her youth never matched the peaks she vaguely recalled, but nor had they faced destitution on the same magnitude. Her father's unwillingness to expand his business beyond its modest confines of Navan was a way of protecting his family; and his insistence all his daughters master the polite arts a way to ensure they married into a better position in life than this.

Elizabeth assumed her father would approve of Thomas the aspiring physician as a suitor, until this morning's disturbance. The whole Fulham family could be dragged into disrepute within weeks. The exact kind of shame and ruin her father hardened himself against.

"I don't know how he managed it," Thomas sighed, once she appeared at their rendezvous point. "He got into a game of Basset with Lord Tara last night. His lordship must have been as far into his cups as Patrick to think he could win anything of value, or that he failed to recognise Patrick was dressed almost as ragged as a beggar."

Elizabeth couldn't do more than stroke his forearm and mutter soothing nothings. Not that she was in the mood for an amorous encounter now.

"I told Patrick he had no head for Basset. Just as he shouldn't drink wine and gin on the same night. It never ends well when he does that."

Frowning and rubbing his forehead, Thomas looked considerably older than his eighteen years. His father died when Thomas was ten, and his elder brother's dissolute nature meant Thomas bore a lot of responsibility in the Fulham household. This felt like an attractive quality to Elizabeth just a few weeks' ago. Now it seemed like a liability.

Thomas had developed a set of folkloric superstitions surrounding the drinking habits of his erratic sibling: whenever he drunk ale he was liable to lose heavily at gambling, but on nights he stuck with wine he managed to keep a hold onto some of his money. And so on. Elizabeth didn't see the patterns herself—as far as she could tell Patrick tended to lose money on days of the week ending in a 'y'—but the superstitious logic gave Thomas some measure of comfort.

She fingered the brooch in her pocket. It was Thomas' token to her, the promise he saw her as something more than a temporary ego boost, and wanted to keep her in his life. She didn't dare wear it; her father was blissfully ignorant when it came to his daughters' pursuit of suitors, but her mother and sisters missed nothing. The brooch never left her person, though.

"The landlord won't negotiate with you?"

Thomas shrugged. "This isn't the first time Patrick's done something like this. Ol' Finn had some choice words for Mother last time we pleaded with him for leniency. She had some choice words of her own back at him mind...but, well..."

"Have you checked the market? Maybe there's a half-decent gelding..."

It would be harvest time before they knew it. Like most families who worked the land, the Fulham's savings were at their lowest ebb.

"Have ye seen the prices those cutthroats charge? Even with the best of luck, buying a horse now just delays the rent problem until next month. It's the choice between losing our livelihoods and then losing our home, or losing our home and then our livelihoods." Thomas spoke with a detached air, as if this wasn't the first time he'd faced such a bleak situation and was conserving his anxiety.

"Could you take on another boxing match?" she asked.

Thomas shook his head. "Not before rent comes due."

That was a small relief. Thomas fought a few times for money before they began courting, and Elizabeth shuddered to think of him doing it again, or encouraging him to continue.

Elizabeth liked to think she was a few whits smarter than Mavis and Roisin, who'd gotten in the family way and disgraced themselves, because it was as plain as the nose on your face that Conor and Noah were lecherous scoundrels with no intention of treating them honourably.

But thanks to Patrick's stupidity she might be proven just as foolish as the other girls. It was several years before she realised the pox scars on Thomas' face meant such disgrace *couldn't* be in her future—right now she gloated over her superior ability to count compared with the other village girls, while simultaneously fearing ruination.

Marriage would be the furthest thing from Thomas' mind as he contemplated the eviction of his mother from the farmstead, or the gradual destruction of their meagre fortunes. Maybe he'd flee to Dublin or depart for studies in Edinburgh early to escape the mess—she wouldn't entirely blame him.

"My love, have you considered...alternative approaches to get Job back?" She paused meaningfully.

Thomas stared for a moment, then gave an uncertain chuckle.

"One sight of a Fulham lad sauntering towards him, and our Lord of Basset is going to whistle for his hunting dogs. He's not exactly maintaining a friendly attitude towards us."

"Of course nothing that unsubtle would work..."

"Truth be told darling, the sheriff's deputy is looking for any excuse to apprehend Patrick. Suspects him of half the crimes in Navan at this point. He's soured towards the Fulhams as a whole, I fear."

Elizabeth wrinkled her nose. The sheriff deputy was an odious, fat little man who'd started leering at her a few months ago. At the moment he didn't follow when she crossed the street to avoid him, but his new-found interest made her nervous to head outdoors alone. She could well believe he wished ill on the Fulhams.

Elizabeth thought quickly. "But he knows nothing of my connection to you."

Any other Navan boy would wave her silent at this point, insisting they'd sort something out and she mustn't worry. Thomas was different: he looked up from his miserable revere and waited to hear what she'd say.

12

Two things about Margaret Monro-MacDonald were self-apparent. The first was that in childhood she'd been squeezed through a gauntlet of expensive elocution, rhetoric and etiquette lessons. The second was her pristine drawl came about because no man was brave—or rich—enough to tell her to hurry up and get to the point.

She promenaded alongside Elizabeth in a circuit of her New Town garden, her greying hair tinged blue with powder. The atmosphere of strolling among the hedgerows and roses was of peaceful serenity. This gave Elizabeth's deep mortification concerning events of the past hour time to properly crash to the surface.

"Madam, I am so sorry..."

Elizabeth was keen to rectify the errors she displayed unveiling her abilities to Dr Black. The ongoing mess with Monsieur Moreau made it clear: she needed the underhand skills she'd cultivated in Ireland. Setting aside deceptive arts to get ahead in society was naive of her. In fact—getting ahead *relied* on deception, as far as she could tell.

The mistake she made with Black was obvious. Over-preparation and under-confidence. She cringed thinking how she allowed herself to disregard common sense. By rehearsing her lines too closely, she'd been thrown when Black reacted differently.

A simple adornment of the truth would get her through this salon with Monro-MacDonald and her affluent friends. Affecting all the mannerisms, speech patterns and behaviours of the nobility was too tricky to master at short notice, and would look like a conceit on her part. In the same way an inauthentic mantua under genuine diamond accessories would be an easier disguise to see through than an authentic robe encrusted with fake jewels. The authentic adornment of these noble ladies? Ironclad self-confidence of their place in the world. That's all Elizabeth needed to fit in.

Unfortunately, she'd swung her self-confidence too far to the other extreme.

"Elizabeth, darling. I beg you to stop apologising. The error lies entirely with me as the hostess. I neglected to mention our gathering of ladies are not expected to bring a stack of scientific treatises to our afternoon teas."

"Oh, I knew the Stahl treatises were unnecessary, it's just that..."

"You wanted to properly convey your ideas on combustion and avoid misremembering the facts. I quite understand."

Elizabeth wished she still had a glass of sherry in hand.

"I made that poor woman cry!"

"Now darling, Hettie is not a 'poor woman.' I thought her questioning of you was presumptuous—she should know better than to be rude towards my guests—and your impassioned correction of her was no less than she deserves. I must accommodate Hettie because her husband is friendly with my brother, but she deploys sobbing theatrics as a defensive shield against anyone who doesn't know better." Monro-MacDonald shuddered.

"I wish..."

"I'll give you one more circuit of the garden to get your apologising out the way, darling. Then we must consider this self-flagellation over."

"Yes, yes...but madam you must believe me, I didn't realise I'd offended that other lady until she stormed out..."

"Ah. Emilie's late husband was a coarse beast of a man. She was quite like you at your age, dear—very curious and lively. Not to speak ill of the dead, but that brute was very cruel towards his young wife, mocking her incessantly when she spoke and calling her a fool. I don't exaggerate when I say it took a year, maybe more, after joining our little gathering before gentle Emilie dared uttered a word of her own opinion."

"How awful! I...I didn't know."

"How on earth could you have known, darling? You weren't the target of Emilie's ire at all, I think in excusing herself she understood her emotions were misplaced towards you."

"This was my mistake in agreeing to come here," Elizabeth sighed. She had no idea how she'd tell Dr Black.

Monro-MacDonald tapped her elbow. "Right, last apology. We're done with that nonsense now. In truth Elizabeth I admire you tremendously. If you've not already had the misfortune to discover, a lot of men are intimidated by intelligent woman. Not all, but the ones that *are* intimidated have the capacity to get *very* nasty if they think you disturb their place in the world. So that you have gotten this far in pursuit of natural philosophy without being mocked into silence is commendable.

"But today's cosy gathering is for ladies who don't have the time to delve as deep into such chemical enquiries as yourself. I have this shabby pile," Monro-MacDonald gestured to her immaculate garden and spacious townhouse "to keep in order, not to mention the headstrong children within to nurture. Maybe when they're safely married off I can become the eccentric woman who breeds flowers, but until then it's a relegated priority."

Elizabeth understood. No one noticed how much time she spent reading Thomas' books or running dyeing experiments at home, but if they did they'd probably raise the same judgements about frivolous pursuits. The woman she met at Monro-MacDonald's treated science like their embroidery projects, and escaped such scrutiny.

"You remind me of Mademoiselle Lavoisier; I hear that sweet child is quite the talk of the Parisian salons. She also helps her husband record his experiments, I believe."

Elizabeth tried not to groan. "I fear I'm wholly unsuited to hosting salons, madam. I've proven my ineptitude for polite conversation on scientific topics."

"Yet Dr Black spoke highly of you to me—I believe he greatly enjoys your chemistry discussions."

Elizabeth tried to explain Cullen's criticisms. Monro-MacDonald steered her towards the house, making a complicated series of hand gestures towards the waiting servant.

"Well, as you already know, some men will never consider a woman's performance in their domain satisfactory." The servant scurried off, no doubt to prepare more drinks. "The more enlightened ones will scrutinise your argument and form their opinion afterwards. Elizabeth, I fear you will be dissatisfied if you reduce your endeavours to an amusing distraction."

"But I'll get lambasted if I take my hobby to the other extreme," Elizabeth said grimly.

Monro-MacDonald fixed her with a long look. "So I suppose you'll have to decide how important your nature is to you."

* * *

Finding Tytler wasn't difficult, nor did it require another trek to Duddingston. Today, Tytler's whereabouts were proclaimed on the fourth page of the *Caledonian Mercury*.

"It says a lot they'd build the Theatre Royal long before the Register's Office," Thomas noted as the Fulhames traversed North Bridge. "What is the use of the latter? Only necessary to keep the country running."

"I don't imagine it says anything new about human nature or politics," Elizabeth replied. On their left stood the Theatre Royal, guarding the corner where the bridge ended and Princes St began. Crossing the street brought the half-constructed shell of the Register's Office into full view, consuming them with its shadows. "Theatre seduces the masses, or something like that."

Thomas smirked. "Well, if I had eight hours with actress Lavinia Fenton..."

"Eight hours?" Elizabeth's eyebrow rose.

"Ha, ye don't know what I intend to do with her..."

"No, I know *exactly* what you'd want to do...I just don't think it would take you more than eight *minutes*, and that includes time explaining how you spell your name."

Thomas laughed. Despite the Register Office's hollow facade, it loomed over this corner of the new town.

"Was the building works still going on when we arrived in Edinburgh?" Thomas asked.

"If so, it must have been winding down."

Arguments over budget, a change in Town Council allegiances, and general inertia ground the construction of the much-needed Register Office to a halt. As far as Elizabeth could tell, one evening the labourers set down their tools, walked off the site and never came back.

To enter the half-finished building, the Fulhames wove around waist-high piles of gravel and sand left on the unpaved street. They'd been there so long the elements had fossilised them, til they were more midden and stray cat piss than their constituent parts.

They passed a pair of men leaving the site, clasping their notepads and conferring in jovial tones. Elizabeth let out an exhalation of relief, because it told her they were heading in the right direction, and weren't too late. She kept her eyes on where she stepped, avoiding the unglazed windows above, which resembled baleful eyes.

Thomas guided his wife over puddles of rainwater in the entranceway. Most of the interior was in a state of semi-completion, with walls missing. Loose masonry rolled under-foot, and piles of stone almost blocked the passageway. Every surface of the dark tunnel was coated in a layer of dust. A lingering smell of alcohol and dried vomit suggested vagrants managed to sneak in here for shelter, despite the presence of night guards.

They followed the grimy light ahead until they emerged into the main rotunda. Or what would be the rotunda, once the back wall and ceiling were built. As of now, the space was open to the heavens, which provided little freshness on a muggy day like today.

"I wasn't imagining it," Thomas said, mostly to himself. "The place does smell of smoke."

They couldn't get more than a few steps into the rotunda before encountering the massive, smoking linen edifice now crumpled into the space. Here, plenty of footprints disturbed the dusty marble—more black than brown.

In the far corner of the rotunda, Tytler forlornly stared at his semi-ruined creation. He was reeling in the assorted cables and ropes and trying to pack them into a semblance of order.

"What happened?" Thomas asked once they'd skirted the deflated balloon and were close enough to converse. "I hoped we'd get the tail end of yer display."

That was a polite lie. The Fulhames arrived late as possible to avoid paying the sixpence admission fee.

"I think it must have been the soot from the previous inflation." Tytler said, moving as slowly as he could to coil the ropes, as if he wouldn't have to admit defeat until the clear-up was complete. "I wanted to make sure the fire balloon would withstand continuous heating. That's why I tested it yesterday. Then less than ten minutes after I lit the fires today, the envelope caught alight."

"Thank heavens it wasn't a serious blaze," Elizabeth said, surveying the damage. Aside from a few smoking holes, the balloon appeared intact.

"It put the kibosh on the demonstration, though," Tytler replied, too dejected to take offence at her remark. "No one had a chance to see the balloon fully inflated."

"Ye got a good turnout?" Thomas asked, trying to induce enough cheer in Tytler for the Fulhames' request.

"Less than the amount that came to see my prototype last month when I displayed it in Comely Garden." Now finished with his rope, Tytler began dragging in the balloon itself. "I don't understand. That model was only 11 foot tall, I was sure they'd be more excited to see the real thing."

"How big is it?" Thomas pointed at the fire balloon carcass.

"Forty foot. Confirmed because the Register is fifty foot high. I was worried if I displayed this in the Gardens anyone could look over the walls to observe. Here is more secluded."

"How did ye get permission to display the fire balloon in here?" Thomas wondered. "The Register board of trustees hasn't met since last year."

"As you say," replied Tytler, avoiding eye contact and leaving a gap in the conversation as gaping as the sky-light. "I got more newspapermen than subscribers. They were quite *impertinent* with their questions."

Elizabeth thought of the chuckling men she'd seen on the way in.

"Still," Tytler continued. "Important lessons learned. I think a coat of varnish will keep the linen satisfactorily protected from the heat and soot."

"I imagine the finished balloon will look quite spectacular," Elizabeth observed.

Tytler gave her an odd look. Elizabeth looked at the dark stained linen that made up Tytler's fire balloon. It was a network of repair patches, stitched in haphazard fashion over each other.

She'd studied engravings of the French balloons in the broadsheets: gaudy, oversized Rococco baubles painted with celestial bodies, deities and stars; garnished with taffeta and silk. While Elizabeth thought the display slightly tasteless—even for the French—she had to admit they were impressive to look at. Tytler's fire balloon barely had the comeliness of a sackcloth.

There was nothing for it. Pretending she hadn't made that insensitive remark, Elizabeth launched into her plan. "Perhaps you can consult with Dr Black on the most suitable varnish for the task. We need your assistance tracking a man—or club of men—who move through Edinburgh at night unseen…"

* * *

Interlude
Navan, Ireland—July 1779

The valet at Bellinter House considered himself a fair and reasonable man, as long as everything was kept in order. So the appearance of the game seller on a Tuesday morning instead of Thursday put him into a fluster, especially since the lad wasn't their usual one.

"I came round last January when the old man did his back in. I recall speakin' with ye," the lad insisted, tugging his cap with a grin. "Yer looking well, sir."

Richard could only harumph and mumble at the compliment, because it would be rude to admit he couldn't recall the lad's name or dealing with him. He did look vaguely familiar, though—the charming dark curls of hair under his cap and sparkling expression.

"You put us at a bit of disadvantage coming on Tuesday," he muttered, inspecting the proffered pheasants, "But I'm sure Lord Tara will be grateful to feed his guests fresh game."

"Ye've got guests?" the seller asked, looking anxious.

"Not too many, two birds will be sufficient for the table," Richard replied hastily. "They arrive this evening."

"Ah, right ye are," the lad said, fingering the pheasant's limp neck as he spoke. Then he looked around. "How's the fella with the sore leg doing? Spoke to him last time I visited, and wondered if the herbs my mother-in-law swore by worked for him as well as me."

"Who, Logan?" Richard was confused. "I don't recall him having any leg complaints last winter."

"Maybe I'm getting mixed up," the game seller laughed. "It was the fella his lordship spoke so highly of."

"It probably was our Logan, then," Richard admitted. He didn't know what Lord Tara saw in that young stablehand— and why his uncouth disorganisation seemed to endear him to his master.

He was surprised he didn't remember interacting with this game seller before, the lad could talk his ear off! Ol' Ruadhri shuffled about his business with time-honed efficiency, respecting that Richard was a busy man and not one for gossiping like a scullery maid.

"You can take these straight to the kitchen, young sir," he said. "You'll find the cook in the usual place."

"Right, right..." the game seller started towards the entrance, then hesitated. He turned back to Richard, and cautiously eased towards the impatient valet's ear. "To be perfectly honest with ye, sir..."

"What is it?"

"That fair maid with the charming laugh? Is she still in yer service?"

Ah. "How about I escort you to the kitchens, young sir? I recall I have some business to attend to with Cook myself." He wasn't going to let this lecherous rogue weasel into Ellie's petticoats. That girl had been warned about her flirtatious behaviour many times, but it seemed she only half understood his warnings. Finding a competent kitchen maid who wasn't indolent or saucy was a battle he hated fighting—he didn't need Ellie to stray into temptation again.

The annoying encounter with the game seller was almost completely scrubbed from Richard's mind by that afternoon, what with preparing the house for the Earl's cousins. It was why when he heard a knock at the rear door around 3 o'clock he uttered an audible sigh.

It took him aback to find a well-dressed woman at the door, looking deeply apologetic.

Well-dressed for a servant, at least. Her lace fichu was particularly delicate, and she carried herself with aristocratic bearing.

"I beg your pardon for calling without warning, but I have a delicate and sensitive matter I wish to discuss with you. I'm Lady Eleanor's housekeeper, Annabel Meyers, and she sent me...well, I'll get right to the point, sir. She thinks her stolen thoroughbred may have ended up in your stables."

"What?" exclaimed Richard, causing the woman to blush furiously.

"I mean no calumy against your lord or anyone in this household," the woman added as fast as she could get the words out. "Perhaps I can come inside and explain the whole sorry affair from the beginning?"

Out of the corner of his eye Richard saw the butler peer around the pantry door.

"Yes, we can go somewhere more private," he agreed. He cursed as the grandfather clock in the manor entrance chimed —they had barely an hour until the master's cousins arrived. He could only hope this would be a simple mix-up to resolve.

Fifteen minutes later, Richard tiptoed into Lord Tara's study.

His master sat in elegant repose as his desk, a cold cup of tea in hand, engrossed in Locke's *Essay on Human Understanding*. Knowing he was about to cause great agitation where once there was serene leisure, Richard cleared his throat.

"I told you not to disturb me." Lord Tara sighed. "This is the last peaceful hour I'll get before Liam and the others barge through the door." Richard cringed, recalling previous versions of this conversation, for which he always had an excuse to override the master's desires.

"I know, my lord, but I think you should know what is transpiring downstairs..."

Richard filled the master in on the strange servant girl now seated in the front parlour downstairs, drinking tea from the same brew as the master.

"...And she doesn't know you have concerns?" Despite his prior annoyance, the Lord Tara looked thoughtful.

"It's quite a tale, my lord, and she tells it with great conviction and sensitivity for her mistress."

"Yet if the horse she claims was stolen is so valuable, why did the useless drunkard gamble it to a stranger over a game of cards?"

A shame his master hadn't asked these pertinent questions when he sat down to said game.

"That drew my suspicions too," Richard eagerly explained. "But the gentlewoman says it's precisely because the horse is so valuable and noteworthy that the thieves would rid themselves of it..."

"If honest traders could recognise the horse as belonging to the lady in question, then it would be difficult to sell without arousing suspicion." Lord Tara laid Locke's *Essay* on the desk. "Not worth their scoundrel necks."

Richard couldn't tell if he was conceding to his suspicions or casting skepticism on them. It made him more nervous.

"But you see...this maid of Lady Eleanor's is barely more than a child, though she conducts herself with great maturity. She turned up without a letter from her mistress."

"Could she speak to that?"

"Oh, very confidently. The mistress was in such a state she dispatched the girl immediately, too agitated to compose a letter."

"She does not appear troubled by your questioning?"

"No, on the contrary she is delighted to address every concern I raise."

The earl took a sip of his tea, grimaced and set the cup down. "Yet liars are often more polished than an honest man. They take great care over every fact of the story to account for scrutiny, which the good amongst us don't need to do."

"Yes, you see?" Relief wash over the valet.

"So why haven't you thrown her out the house? We don't need to concern ourselves with an opportunistic fraud."

Richard bit his lip, too flummoxed to respond.

Instead of chastising him, his lordship rose with louche grace and buttoned up his waistcoat. "You're right. For a girl as young as you say to lie with such fluency...something is amiss."

13

With Tytler at his elbow, Thomas ducked from the relative order of the college into the cacophony of Nicholson Street.

"Ye found that conversation with Dr Black useful?" Thomas asked, grinning.

Black had proven a gracious host to the awkward Tytler, who fired off questions about the latent heat of air, composition of varnishes and residues of linen bleaching. Once exhausted, Thomas had scooped him up and left, mouthing thanks to his professor for the indulgence.

"Oh, more than you could appreciate. Good sir, you truly..."

"Oi! Tytler!" A short, sturdy woman holding a loaf of bread blocked their path. "Yer wife has been in a world of hurt since ye left 'er and the bairns. Shame on ye." Her body rumbled with indignation.

Tytler floundered. "Good heavens, Mrs, err..."

"Alnwick."

"...Mrs Alnwick. You see, Beth and I..."

"I'm no' talkin' 'bout Beth. I'm talkin' 'bout *Jean*. Sair broke her heart." She fixed Tytler with her filthiest scowl.

Tytler began rattling off a semi-coherent list of excuses, but Mrs Alnwick shoved her way past him, tutting.

"What a craven creature ye are, James. No shame..."

Thomas watched her stomp away as a blushing Tytler wilted into himself.

"Jean and I have been having some difficulties," he mumbled. "She left to stay with her sister for a while."

"No..." Thomas shook his head so his train of thought wouldn't slip away. "Did ye just get confused about which wife that shrew was yelling about?"

"That was a misunderstanding," said Tytler, setting off at a brisk pace.

"Aye..." murmured Thomas, almost jogging to catch up.

As promised, Thomas bought Tytler a brandy in his favourite tavern as thanks for the latest piece of assistance, which promised to yield greater progress than the professors' investigations—such as they were.

The Dancing Bear was located halfway down a narrow wynd off the High Street, and put Thomas uncomfortably to mind of the kind of drinking spots his brother frequented. Still, it was Tytler's pleasure, so he let the man settle onto a communal table in the centre of the room.

"Ahh, Balloon Tytler himself!"

If Tytler was disappointed at the unflattering recognition, he pretended not to show it. Thomas could tell by the liveliness of the other revellers that they wouldn't manage a quiet drink here.

"Did you read the account of the Montgolfier's balloon ascent at Versailles?" the man enthused.

"In fact," interrupted another fellow, pipe jammed in the corner of his mouth. "My friend was there when it happened and shook the elder brothers' hand afterwards. He said the man—Etienne—had the physique of a god. The sun came out as the flight ended, he was like Zeus descending from the heavens." The pipe bounced, spilling ash down the man's waistcoat. He didn't seem to notice.

"Oh, but those two used a balloon filled with hot air," a listener with blackened stumps for teeth tutted. "Vastly inferior to the inflammable air-powered ones, which are said to float like feathers."

Thomas found it hard to believe he'd stumbled into a room filled with aeronauts, but no one wanted to be the first to profess ignorance, and so they hemmed and hewed.

"The Neapolitan Vincenzo Lunardi is the future of aeronautics, that's for sure. His inflammable air balloon is a thing of wonder."

Tytler pressed his head into his hands. "Inflammable air is too expensive and hazardous in large quantities to be used for anything but experimental launches." His words had the appearance of being addressed to the room at large, but no one noticed.

There wasn't a man in this tavern whose waistcoat or breeches wasn't stained with last night's dinner, drink, or mud splatter. Their hands left smears on their beer bottles.

"Ah, I heard that Lunardi intends to attempt an aeronautical flight in London before the summer is out," the first man interjected.

"Really? I heard Kent was his preferred location."

"Nonsense—Lunardi's balloon *has* to launch from St James Park. Where else could the flight possibly take place?"

"Well...Kent..."

Tytler shrank into his chair, looking as if he wanted to melt into the wall. The men continued their furious debate, his presence forgotten.

"I didn't know Lunardi intended to fly in England this

CL JARVIS

year," Tytler whispered. "I thought he would wait until spring."

"Who knows what is true in this third-hand gossip confused with speculation?" Thomas asked. The whole spectacle was ridiculous, but it would be cruel to laugh at how personally Tytler took Lunardi's flight plans. Tytler couldn't seriously consider himself capable of launching a balloon this September?

"Tytler's motivations concern me," Thomas admitted once the two were alone. He told his wife about the strange confrontation near the college.

Elizabeth shrugged. "It's always the men who complain the loudest about their mistresses and wives who seem to acquire the greatest number of both. Though I'm skeptical Tytler could induce more than one woman to marry him."

"If we see that wifey again we might be able to ask her. She was...Tytler's age, I suppose? Very short and fierce. Was carrying a loaf of bread."

"Well." Elizabeth raised an eyebrow. "We better pray to encounter her on a day she's carrying another loaf of bread. Were she carrying a plucked chicken..."

"...or a basket of eels..."

"...why, we'd be totally bamboozled by the sight."

* * *

When Elizabeth set out her dilemma for Tytler, she had no doubt the man would come through with a solution: he relished these problem-solving exercises. Sure enough, she would never in a thousand years have come up with this solution, even though it was true to the spheres its creator operated within. It came in the form of a surprising introduction.

"She's a former woman of pleasure?" Cullen asked with a disapproving arch of his eyebrows when the Fulhames pointed out the woman in question on the street earlier that afternoon. "Did men pay her to rip their heads off? Just goes to show there's a buyer for every seller."

Moira was certainly a formidable woman. She was young for a water caddy—barely forty years old, with some strands of brown hair peeking under her crumpled bicorne hat—but despite the moderate weather was bundled into a thick duffle coat with a thick leather cape on her back. The overall impression was of a physique similar to the water barrels she made her honest living carrying.

Now night descended Elizabeth was enacting the plan itself, which involved waiting with Moira in the queue for the High Street wells, which were turned on at three o'clock in the morning. Elizabeth naively thought her instruction to meet Moira at eleven that night was unwarranted—she'd hoped to get more hours of sleep in before heading out—but by the time she arrived there were twenty water carriers already lined up the hill towards the Tron Kirk, and another twenty filed in shortly after.

She'd braced for a frosty reception, but upon realising Elizabeth wasn't much above her in social standing, Moira grudgingly allowed a conversation to kindle, shifting so Elizabeth could perch beside her on the water barrel.

"Mr Tytler is a disagreeable little wretch, isn't it? No manners, noxious..."

Elizabeth had surreptitiously read *Rangers' Guide* when her husband left the apartment. While the contents failed to shock her, she was surprised how many whores were described as surly, quarrelsome and graceless. Listening to Moira, she wondered if the women's temperaments were more a reaction to Tytler than a reflection of their true natures.

As dusk turned to hovering darkness, Edinburgh traffic

thinned to a trickle and Tytler's plan took on a kind of elegance. It was light enough in late August that any watcher in a close would be quickly spotted, even after midnight. However, no one looked twice at the gaggle of water carriers conducting their usual vigil. Elizabeth fiddled with Thomas' cocked hat, trying to get it to stay on her head.

Moira's manner of speaking was too rough for parlour conversation, but after a few hours' hunched on the High Street Elizabeth understood its true purpose. Moira spoke as a way to pass the time and distract her fellow water carriers from the tedium. The circular discussion about whether Lord so-and-so had got his comely kitchen maid into the family way—who'd seen the girl last, which water carrier heard the oblique remarks his cook made, why it had to be Amanda, not Jackie—initially seemed an inane preoccupation with details Elizabeth didn't consider relevant to the situation, but were designed to spread a two-minute exchange of information over two hours. Once details were hashed out and listener's positions staked—Auld Archie was convinced Amanda had heard the story from Wee Jackie but pretended Lord so-and-so's cook took her into his confidence; Bess fae Dundee disagreed and wouldn't be persuaded otherwise—then they could pick over the juiciest morsels of the story: the maid's culpability in her seduction.

"I heard this wasn't the first maid to fall for his tricks," Elizabeth commented.

There was an intake of breath in the huddle.

"Say?" Moira's eyes popped. In the dim light her cheeks flushed.

"Just a rumour," Elizabeth clarified. "I can't recall who told me, but the Lord's name sounds familiar and I vaguely recall hearing a similar story last year."

None of this was true. But by Elizabeth's estimation it was one o'clock in the morning, her feet and legs were sodden, and her legs were stiff. She needed to throw more wood on the gossip fire to keep herself awake.

The other water carriers nodded and clicked their tongues. Maybe they believed her, maybe they didn't. But in Elizabeth's cynical experience, nobles who took advantage of their servants tended to do so more than once.

She positioned herself so she could look over the other water carriers towards the south side of the street. Identifying everyone who passed by proved impossible. After sunset, a whole class of Edinburgh nightlife were shaken out onto the streets. Cleaners and town guards engaged in semi-honourable business, but other individuals slunk out on nefarious errands, concealing themselves from watchful eyes. Elizabeth suspected the water carrier's inattentiveness to these passersby was mutually beneficial: Moira carried herself with a confidence Elizabeth envied, probably because most of the criminal element was known to her, and vice versa.

The queue became restive, and Elizabeth saw a detachment of town guards approaching the head. The energy in the line rose in anticipation of claiming their water. Was it finally three o'clock? She wondered if it was worth wriggling circulation back into her feet yet.

"Son-of-a bitch Phil!"

A couple of men with barrels walked alongside the queue until they spotted the two women and casually slipped in front of them.

"Good morning, Moira," the queue barger denoted as Phil beamed. "Sure you ladies won't mind if we skip ahead of you? The Earl is an early riser, after all."

"Fuck ye, we do mind," Moira replied, keeping her voice remarkably level. "It's a queue, lard-brains."

"Who is it you're delivering the contents of that barrel to, again? Some tradesmen in the Canongate?" The man beside

Phil matched his cheery demeanour. "Love, we've got to go all the way to Charlotte Square."

"Disnae matter if you're delivering water to sodding King George to bathe in his gold bathtubs, we were here first."

The men were too cheery, and the blank insincerity to their words made Elizabeth nervous. A certain calibre of men knew they could get away with whatever they wanted if they spoke in friendly tones while doing it. Many women struggled to fight back against men forcefully pretending to be civil. She wondered if Moira was angling for compensation to let Phil and his crew ahead of her. But if that was the case the men didn't take the hint.

"You're gonna fuck off to the back of the queue," Moira said. "I'm no' feeling particularly charitable tonight."

Elizabeth expected Moira to shout, gesticulate or shake with rage to chase the men away. Although she was crowding into Phil's personal space and staring him down, she seemed remarkably calm. This made Elizabeth's heart pound. In her experience, dark calm was a predictor of serious violence.

"Fuck off back to your sewing, Moira." Phil and his cronies refused to back down, and sensing Moira's immobility they were trying to force Elizabeth back. Every muscle in her body clenched as Phil's buddy came within a hair's breadth of her, and she feared she'd topple like a doll. The scent of gin and tobacco were equally belligerent. Others in the queue squeezed away and pretended to ignore the looming confrontation.

Last summer, George attempted to teach her the basics of defending herself against assailants. He made a lot of encouraging noises when she attempted to strike him as instructed, but Elizabeth soon realised how slowly the former soldier moved, and how deliberately weak he grasped her wrist. Luckily she and her husband were in George's lodgings with no one to see her sluggish efforts. At this point she gave up:

there was too much of a strength difference between the sexes for her to have a fighting chance at personal defense. She'd be better off running.

Moira shoved Phil. A hard push, enough to cause him to stumble.

There was a frightful pause.

The man on their left surged forward to grab Moira's throat, but she swung her fist at his jaw. He fell with a howl. Noise rushed back into the surroundings.

Phil tried to grab Moira's hair, but she scratched his face. Emboldened, Elizabeth kicked him in the groin as hard as she could. She almost slipped on the wet cobblestones.

A second later her head was jerked back, almost sending her backwards. Elizabeth yelped as a clump of hair tore from her scalp.

The third assailant jerked her forward and tried to push her head down to waist height. In the pause where he debated whether to kick her or throw her on the ground, Elizabeth scrambled a hand to his wrist and concentrated.

She felt the phlogiston-aether crackle through her fingertips. The man dropped like a stone, letting go of her.

Looking around, Elizabeth saw Moira land another kick in Phil's shins. The second assailant was clutching a bleeding nose. Seeing their dazed comrade on the ground Phil—bent double and scuttling like a crab—hauled his dazed comrade from the dirt and tugged them away. Emboldened by her success, the water carriers jeered Phil and his cronies until they were out of projectile range.

Moira grunted at Elizabeth, who was gingerly prodding the side of her head. That was all the sympathy and gratitude she appeared ready to offer.

"Give them an inch, they'll take a yard," she said, huffing. "Fucksters."

All of the female water carriers in the queue, even the

wizened ones, had a meanness about them. Elizabeth imagined the elderly ones would stab a queue-barger with a needle if they were in Moira's position. If she'd let Phil cut ahead of her today, others would do the same to her tomorrow, until the only place for her was at the back of the queue and a few drops from the well, if she got anything at all.

Elizabeth almost missed it, but a clump of lean figures rushed through the shadows on the opposite side of the street while she was assessing her hair loss. Dillon. His timing was so suspicious she wondered if Phil's aggravation had been pre-arranged.

Ignoring the ruckus, Dillon and company slipped into a close a hundred metres down the street. There was a hint of blue to the darkness, suggesting daylight was soon to become a possibility.

"That's Chessel's Court," she remarked to Moira, who watched the disappearing figures with mild interest. With everyone else in the queue dissecting Phil's beating, Moira probably wanted to get her breath back.

With a shrug, Moira permitted Elizabeth to sneak down the street, though a few glances at the well warned her to be back in a minute to help with filling the water barrel.

She didn't need to lurk long, Dillon was entering the large building on the south edge of the close. Now it was clear what his business was.

* * *

Interlude
Navan, Ireland—July 1779

There was a swagger in Lord Tara's steps as he descended to the parlour. Richard recognised his young masters' sometimes arrogant nature overturning his desire for solitude. He wanted to uncover this fraud himself, test his might against a saucy girl.

The girl did not appear intimidated when the lord of the manor strode into the parlour. She rose and bowed with all decorum. Lord Tara eyed the girl, some of his indignation transforming into another one of his proven weaknesses. Richard hung back, uncertain if it was worth intervening to distract the earl's appetites.

"You are in the employ of Lady Eleanor? I hold a great affection for your mistress. It's been six months since I last had the pleasure of her company."

The girl smiled shyly. "It wasn't that long was it, my lord? I recall you called upon her two months ago."

"Well-remembered," Lord Tara rejoined, smiling.

Richard tried not to panic. The dinner hosted by Lady Eleanor at Boyne Hill was a large event, and drew in many tradesmen from the local area to organise. That his lord attended the gathering would be common village knowledge.

"You were not Lady Eleanor's maid then, who did you replace?"

"I was a kitchen maid at the party, that's true. However, Maisie fell ill with influenza shortly after. My aptitude for sewing and hair-dressing lended me for the role while she recovers."

Richard didn't know the names of any of Lady's Eleanors servants, but his master nodded as if the answer was satisfactory.

"You're story is quite an extraordinary one, you must understand..." he said, flinging himself onto the sofa and kicking his legs out. "To implicate a stranger in horse theft, however incidental their role, is quite bold."

"My lady understands this is an honest mistake she is anxious to put right." The girl wrung her hands and made cow-eyes at the earl. "She only desires returning Frederick to his proper owners."

The lord's posture changed. He pulled his legs under him. Seeing him move so abruptly, the girl flinched.

"Did you not tell Richard the horse was called Samson?"

She had, Richard realised with glee.

The girl blinked. "Oh, misspoke. I meant Frederick."

"And if I was to write to Lady Eleanor this very afternoon, asking her about a stolen white horse called Frederick, how do you think she would respond?"

The girl wrinkled her brow. "Why, she would tell you exactly what I've told you now. A letter wouldn't change the particulars."

"What if I were to tell you..." Lord Tara leaned forward, his eyes narrowing. "That a letter has already been dispatched to the estate of Lady Eleanor, asking that very question?"

The girl swallowed, then laughed. It sounded more like a choke. "I would tell you I hadn't heard a sound of a rider dispatched since I arrived?"

"The stables are on the other side of the building," Lord Tara pressed.

The girl must wonder if they were bluffing, but Lord Tara crowed in triumph, her lie about the horses' name proof enough of her duplicity.

"Who did you steal that lace fichu from?" he demanded. "You are no lady's mistress. Was it another poor fool who took you at your word?"

The girl opened her mouth to stutter further excuses, before the parlour door was flung open and a scruffy man in his twenties stumbled through.

"Logan? What in God's name are you doing in here?"

The stablehand ignored the scandalised valet and approached his master directly.

"My lord, I had to warn you. The woman calling herself Annabel Myers is a horse thief."

"I think we concluded that," Lord Tara said, folding his arms.

"Yes, but she's in league with the scoundrel who gambled away the horse in drunken error."

"That ugly fellow?" The lord frowned, glancing at the now-stricken woman.

"All this about Lady Eleanor and her steed Frederick— forgive me for eavesdropping, m'lord," the master waved his hand, "is a complete fabrication to hook your sympathy. That horse is no purebred, plain as the nose on my face."

"But how do you know all this? Were you listening at the keyhole the whole time?" Richard tried to shoo Logan from the parlour, but the earl held up his hand in a signal to continue.

"Didn't need to, my lord. A sheriff deputy from Navan just waylaid me in the stables. He'd overheard some of her private scheming with her *amour* and tracked her here, hoping to catch the bitch in the act." He glanced at the half-open door. "He's had an eye on her unsavoury associates for quite some time."

Lord Tara caught Logan's glance. "The deputy is here?"

"Yes, forgive me. I wanted to bring him to speak with ye, only we realised she'd got to ye first."

The lord cleared his throat. "He's here to apprehend her?"

"Seems the correct thing to do, m'lords," came a guttural voice from the corridor. "I've 'eard enough."

"Come in, sir," Lord Tara replied, rising. "I don't wish to leave you standing out there."

No doubt he has the whole of the servant body for company in the hallway now, Richard thought.

The sheriff deputy was a short, squat man, his thick paunch leading him slowly into the room. He wore a dishevelled periwig under a battered cocked hat. The miasma of alcohol and sweat was so strong Richard recoiled, despite himself. The master was better at controlling his disdain: he simply stared at the deputy with an almost curious expression.

The deputy looked at the young thief, now slumped against her chair, with sleepy bloodshot eyes.

"That's the one. Won't be keepin' ye." He nodded brusquely to the assembled men. "On yer feet, miss."

Richard winced as the deputy hauled the young woman by her arm. She cried and made a show of struggling, but was no match for a heavyset man like this, who barely looked at his resisting prisoner as he marched out the door.

Richard felt a flicker of concern for the girl—young enough to be his daughter—left alone in the care of a brute like this. His only consolation was the alcoholic deputy probably hadn't the manly functions remaining to consummate his lusty impulses.

"Will take the horse in question back to its rightful owners," he grunted, looking to Logan for confirmation.

"Of course," said the master hurriedly. He paused for a moment then rose and approached the deputy, whose hesitated and gnawed his lip.

Lord Tara fumbled in his pocket, and withdrew a small purse. "We can only apologise for troubling you with this business, sir. Please, accept our measure of gratitude for this inconvenience."

The thief-taker eyed the money with unconcealed greed, but to his credit he made a cursory show of hesitation.

"No need, m'lord..."

"Oh, I insist. It's a small token for your trouble, after all."

Lord Tara stood stock-still as the deputy's dirt-encrusted fingernails brushed against his palm. Another guttural grunt and the deputy was out of the room, yanking the limp woman with him.

The smell of gin and body odour hung in the room. Logan, Richard and Lord Tara stared at each other.

"Urgh, Richard. Let's get rid of the foul smell before it sets into the carpet. Heavens deliver us—Wilma and Liam will be almost at the front gates by now."

"Right you are, my lord." Richard spun on his heels. "Logan, tell Etta to bring the lilies from the dining room in here."

Richard was so consumed by indignation and mounting fluster—how dare that filly take him for a mark, I hope she swings for her impertinence, what right did that disgusting oaf of a deputy have to stamp horse shit into his Turkish carpet— that he never stopped to consider why the deputy would make no mention of his own horse or carriage.

14

With the location of Dillon's hidden papers pinpointed, Elizabeth made Thomas swear he wouldn't reveal to the professors how they uncovered the knowledge.

"Fine, love. We'll just say we asked Moira to keep an eye out, and she spotted them."

"I don't want Dr Black or Cullen learning about the street scuffle." Elizabeth pressed on in the hope that if Thomas understood her concerns, he'd be less likely to slip up. "They'll think I'm no better than the water carrying lassies."

When they called upon Black around midday, they found him in a receptive mood.

"The Excise Office makes sense," Black said. "Sir Finney is on friendly terms with its president."

"He'd trust him enough to hide the papers on his behalf?"

"If he wanted to conceal the papers, yes. From your account Miss Lydia believed—or pretended to believe—the papers were in Sir Finney's possession."

Thomas nodded. Elizabeth had to tell him about her altercation, because she needed to know how much hair was torn out on the side of her head. He insisted there was no visible missing patch, but she'd taken pains to sweep her hair back and hide everything under a bonnet.

"We could have got into Sir Finney's house with the water carriers," Elizabeth said. "It would have been easier, I think." Moira had pointed out the water carrier who served Moray House, and the man had nodded to her in a semi-friendly manner. A few coins would have probably made him a lot friendlier.

Black nodded. "Let me speak with Adam. His connections within the Customs House might prove useful."

"This is the man who once tried to butter and eat his teacup?" Elizabeth was filled with the rare energy that came after a sleepless night, but she knew she'd crash within hours.

"I believe he put a buttered roll in his teapot and tried to drink it," Black said with a touch of defensiveness, as if that was a more understandable error. "But when it comes to commercial matters his expertise is unmatched."

Elizabeth decided against pointing out that the buttered teacup and buttered roll in the teapot were two separate incidences. She couldn't argue that Smith's head for theoretical concepts was sound. As it turned out, the man himself arrived at Black's shortly after the Fulhames. Elizabeth decided not to depart immediately—she needed another cup of Black's tea to keep her awake.

That said, her exhaustion from the previous night's vigil was almost pleasant: it gave her a dreamy detachment from the scene in front of her.

"You intend to become a professor?" Smith asked so suddenly Thomas started.

"Err..."

"Because you really shouldn't. Worst decade of my life. Paid a pittance to argue with spoilt weans about moral philosophy. Just when you think you're getting somewhere with them...they graduate and the cycle of ignorance begins anew."

He exhaled and leaned back in his chair. "If you want a stimulating and fulfilling career, might I suggest the realm of customs duty..."

Thomas could only grit his teeth and endure. Black received another caller and took them into his study, leaving the Fulhames with Smith and Moreau in the parlour. Moreau wasn't providing much conversational assistance.

He'd done stellar husband duty that morning by assuring Elizabeth the clump of hair torn from her head wasn't noticeable. Still, she'd swept and piled her hair, then buried it all under a lace bonnet to be sure of its concealment. So far neither Black, Smith nor Moreau had said anything.

Elizabeth wondered why she was so restless. It was beyond question that Sir Finney had stolen the turkey red process—he'd laughed about it to her face—and she had no reason to doubt Smith's deduction that he'd seized control of the British Linen Bank.

"You believe turkey red is one of the most sought-after dye processes in Britain?"

"Without a doubt," Moreau said, with a shade of indignation. "It will make a fortune."

"I didn't mean to question you, monsieur. It's just I feel... uneasy about something."

"You are very knowledgeable about textiles, madam," Smith said from across the room. "Can I surmise you have a family connection to the trade?"

"Well yes—my brother-in-law owns a small factory in Lanarkshire, and my father used to run a business in Dublin —but I mean I'm worried about something in addition to that." Did he really think she couldn't identify her own fears? "Mr Smith, what would you estimate Sir Finney is worth?"

"I would need a bit of time to make the full calculation..."

"Yes, but—"

"As an *estimation*, he's one of the ten wealthiest men in Britain."

Elizabeth took a hard look at Moreau. He was a man who'd done well for himself in France, but thought there was more money to be had selling his process to the British. His clothes were fine—the inner satin lining of his coat was fancier than anything Thomas could afford—but when standing next to Dr Black it was clear the professor dressed in higher quality woollen fabrics, even though his cuts were less ostentatious.

"How much of a fortune could Sir Finney make from turkey red?"

"Two thousand pounds per year," Moreau supplied. "I worked it out."

It was an eye-watering sum to Elizabeth. "But how much would that add to Sir Finney's existing wealth?"

"I see what you're saying, madam." Smith looked keenly at her.

"If he aspires to being the richest man in England," Elizabeth said, aware Smith wasn't going to bother explaining to the others. "Then turkey red is a tidy acquisition, but..."

"Unambitious," finished Thomas. "I suppose the other merchants made their guineas trading gunpowder or wine."

"Some of them. Quite a few have some involvement in textile trade, and make pleasant coin. However when it comes to linen these days," said Smith, "the fortune is in Osnaburg." His lip curled.

Thomas frowned. Elizabeth knew he was about to jokingly ask if that was a town in Denmark. She wasn't in the mood for that witticism.

"It's a kind of unrefined, coarse linen," she explained. "Exported to the plantations in large quantities."

Taking in his wife's and Smith's grim expressions, Thomas recognised this wasn't a jocular matter.

"Oh."

"My brother-in-law knew his small mill couldn't compete with the Osnaburg manufacturers, it's why he decided to specialise in high-quality fabrics."

"The turkey red process would be a boon for them, I imagine," Smith commented.

Elizabeth prodded the questions around her head. "But even if Sir Finney secured a monopoly on turkey red—heaven forbid—you think he would still earn less than if pursued Osnaburg?"

"Obviously there are issues of competitiveness and getting a toehold in the market that might make turkey red a more prudent pursuit. But given Scotland and England have traditionally avoided direct competition in the textile trade by specialisation, a linen manufacturer in England in proximity to Liverpool or Portsmouth could dominate the Atlantic trade." Smith was frowning and tutting.

"So I'm right to question why Sir Finney is interested in turkey red? His takeover of the British Linen Bank suggests a disinclination to step aside for preexisting companies."

"We are missing a piece of the puzzle, madam."

* * *

Thomas had told her a story one night, after he'd come home form the tavern.

"Edward said he heard about a slave on St Kitts who sewed a single line of red thread on the inside of her clothes. She was caught—don't know how—so the master burned her clothes and whipped her. Because the clothes belonged to her owners, didn't they? Then he made her work naked for months afterwards."

This kind of storytelling made Elizabeth angry at her husband, and emotionally-insensitive men in general. Thomas didn't ascribe any meaning to this story beyond its macabre entertainment value, and didn't think to wonder if there was a purpose in its telling from someone to Edward, then Edward to Thomas.

Was the tale a warning about the wilful disobedience of African slaves? Or their stupidity in breaking rules? Was it a condemnation of the master and the evil trade?

"I understand why she did it," Elizabeth whispered to herself. If your entire humanity was stripped from you, and the only material you were given to clothe yourself was coarser than the burlap sacks used to return sugar across the Atlantic—an undisguised mockery of your worth—of course you would risk the whip for a few bright threads concealed next to your heart, marking something meagre as your own.

* * *

Despite the relief knowing Black no longer worked in opposition to them, the speed of his responsiveness disappointed Elizabeth.

However, she waited until they departed Black's home to voice those feelings to her husband.

"The Excise Office is less guarded than Moray House," Elizabeth pointed out. "But we could be waiting for weeks for Dr Black to arrange on the necessary introductions and overtures via Mr Smith, when we have a days at best."

"I'm sure Dr Black understands time is of the essence," Thomas said, stepping around a clump of damp rags.

"Yes, though a theoretical understanding of the urgency doesn't preclude the *application* of haste..."

Instead of turning right, the Fulhames turned left up Nicholson Street in the direction of the modest printing shop 'Bell, Macfarquhar & Smellie.'

"Does Dr Black really think it's beneath him to walk fifty

metres down the street and deliver these papers in person?" Thomas asked, waving the densely annotated sheets.

"Given Mr Tytler's unnerving ability to take a yard when merely proffered an inch, I suppose he hopes to establish a boundary."

A pair of apprentices loitering under the awning waved the Fulhames inside the cramped shop, where Tytler could be found in a side office frowning over page proofs.

Elizabeth declined his offer of a chair, since every surface in the premises were coated in a fine film of ink, and her cream-coloured muslin dress would suffer for it.

"My goodness...I didn't expect so thorough a response from Dr Black," Tytler exclaimed with a beam. "So many references he suggests I consult! The next edition of the Encyclopaedia will be a thing of beauty."

Elizabeth wondered if Black's level of correction implied Tytler's current Encyclopaedic entry on latent heat was defective, but Tytler was too excited to care.

"If you're heading back towards Dr Black I have another draft he might wish to inspect concerning animal respiration..."

"That's not really Dr Black's area of expertise..."

"Oh, I'd just like him to take a quick look over, a common sense check if you will..."

"...Aye, I suppose I can hand it to him when we next call upon him..."

"Not today, you must understand."

"No, Mrs Fulhame is right—Dr Black isn't receiving any more visitors today, I'm afraid."

"Alright." Tytler looked disappointed. "I left the papers next door, so if you'll excuse me..."

With Tytler briefly out of the room, the Fulhames resumed their earlier discussion.

"Let's say that Dr Black and Mr Smith can arrange our

visit to the Excise Office next week—that seems a realistic timeframe, aye? But is that too slow?"

Elizabeth didn't need long to consider. "Far too slow. Smith's enquiries will probably alert Sir Finney to our plan. He can just walk into the Excise Office and pick up his papers, he doesn't even need to greet the excisemen in the process."

Thomas tapped his fingers on the desk in a show of mounting frustration.

"Even better. We've doomed ourselves by asking for assistance, haven't we?"

"Is there a way we can pretend to be on business from Mr Smith and just walk into Chessel's Court during the day?"

"Hmm, Mr Smith seems like a stickler for rules, it might be hard to persuade him to cooperate..."

"Not that I wish to intrude..." began Tytler, taking a half-skip back into the room. "But I am acquainted with a certain gentleman with means to assist you."

"Really?" said Thomas.

"Yes, quite." Tytler glanced down at his feet for reassurance. "We first met over dice..." Thomas folded his arms. "...Where I discovered he worked in the Cowgate as a grocer..." Elizabeth's eyebrows began to ascend. "...And locksmith."

Thomas spun around so fast he almost knocked over Elizabeth.

"If I divine your intentions correctly," added Tytler.

"Aye, ye did."

* * *

The next morning Thomas sat on the edge of Salisbury Crags with a squat, under-shaven fellow calling himself Georgie.

"All there is to know about locks," Georgie was saying, pipe jammed into one corner of his mouth. "Worked ten years in the trade, so I have."

Thomas swung his legs, letting his heels bounce against the rock face. Below him was a drop of several hundred metres to the dingy grasslands below. The morning sun pierced through the night-time mist and city smoke, turning the tenements of Edinburgh a warm yellow colour.

Georgie took another puff of his pipe, sending tobacco smoke billowing around his unshaven face. He took the pipe out of his mouth and gestured towards the Canongate.

"Two ways of doin' it, so I see. First is to head through the gardens under cover of darkness, break in through the back. Might need a man or two to carry in ladders. Second is to go in the front after daytime business is complete, before the night watchman arrives at ten o'clock. Given sunset is back of eight it doesn't leave us much time."

"Ye think the second option is less risky?" Thomas asked.

Georgie gave him a sideways look. "It's robbery we're doing. Get caught and we swing for it."

"Right," conceded Thomas. "It's all risky."

Georgie took a slower inhale of his pipe. "Making a wax cast of the key should take you minutes. Think the Excise Office leave theirs on a hook outside the building like most tradespeople. I can have the key copy ready for you the next day."

Georgie wasn't the kind for braggadocio, but he made it plain to Thomas this wasn't his first nocturnal venture. Thomas thought Georgie would be suspicious, or at least surprised, that a university student wished to orchestrate a night raid on the Excise Office, but he'd shrugged off Thomas' roundabout probing.

"Get all sorts needin' my help. The way I see it, the richest citizens have the darkest secrets. Or at least the most pricey ones."

The sun felt good on Thomas' face. He was turning into a proper scholar: he couldn't remember the last time he'd been outdoors long enough to enjoy a morning as pleasant as this.

"Well, if it pleases ye sir, then it pleases me."

* * *

Interlude
Navan, Ireland—July 1779

The man and woman were a mile down the lane to Navan when the man's hand slid to the woman's arse and squeezed.

"There'll be no *country matters* until we're out of the countryside," Elizabeth retorted, refusing to encourage her companion with eye contact. "We could pass Lord Tara's cousins on the road."

Thomas looked around. Gentle farmland and hedge rows as far as the eye could see.

It was Patrick—passing through one of his rare hours of semi-sobriety—who advised his younger brother to take any maidens to the copse at the edge of their farmland for the purpose of seduction.

"Listen Tom, girls these days need at least three trees sheltering them before they lie down with ye. Two trees for cover: they'll complain about someone catching 'em in the act and start clutching their petticoats. Can't be two trees and a bush, has to be three trees."

It was the only time his older brother had given him good advice.

"Might settle for a roll in a ditch," Thomas replied, ego undented by Elizabeth's reprimand. "I can't end up smelling worse than I already do."

"You doused yourself in a whole bottle of gin?"

"Swilled enough, I hope." Thomas undid the top buttons

of his waistcoat and reached inside. He tugged out a long roll of cloth and tossed it over Job's back.

After duping the valet with his gamekeeper outfit, Thomas had retreated to the woodland on the other side of the house where Elizabeth was waiting with his second costume. She advised him to exert himself until he worked up a sweat; rubbing his eyes until they turned red was his idea.

Job tossed his head and nickered.

"I didn't think they'd be so easy to fool," Thomas admitted, fingering the coin in his hand.

"I told you, people can only focus on a few key things at a time. It's all about directing their attention to the differences, so they overlook the similarities." Elizabeth patted Job's nose. "Your timing was perfect, sweetheart."

Exuberance ran through Thomas. Elizabeth worried he'd start skipping. "I convinced the stableboy to wait in the corridor and listen at the door. He got even more excited knowing he would make a dramatic entrance into the performance."

The giddiness was spreading to Elizabeth, combined with a warm feeling towards her partner in crime. She didn't know Thomas would manage to extract useful information from the valet, or fool him twice. She'd worried Thomas would disregard their plan, lose track of time, or get held up convincing the stablehand to assist.

They'd needed a long enough interval for the household to crescendo from confusion to uncertainty to suspicion in a natural way. By the time the Earl was pointing trembling fingers at Elizabeth accusing her of fraud and theft, he was too distracted to notice the real fraud and theft happening under his nose.

One day I'll have the money and talent to knock on an earl's door and steal something from under his nose without anyone helping me, Elizabeth thought. I'm smart enough to know I'm not there yet.

"Think you're ready to speak with my father, mister?"

Thomas grinned, the first time in days his incorrigible demeanour sprung back.

"Asking yer father's permission for yer hand will be a breeze. Yer mother's another matter, right? She's the one who might curse me."

He laughed, and Elizabeth tried to laugh too.

It wasn't that Thomas had voiced a belief uncommon in Navan—or that he was the first to voice such rumours to her face. Elizabeth's mother had always acted as a healer, and even Thomas professed some respect for her skills—though he viewed her field of expertise as a narrow strait (*"It's not that childbirth and women's pains aren't important, but..."*). It was the way she held such quiet confidence that seemed unnatural, and why women like Catherine Fulham would seek her counsel before consulting their own kin. People joked that the cold never phased her, and she must have oxhide for skin.

The Navan townsfolk couldn't know of tiny flames that floated around her mother like a hundred candles when she thought nobody was looking, or that she could boil a kettle by touch. Elizabeth only saw such displays once when she was too young to make sense of them: her mother dancing alone in the parlour while the rest of the family slept, wreathed in light.

"It's a pretty conjuring, isn't it?" she said, scooping Elizabeth into her arms and carrying her back to bed. "Did a nightmare disturb you again?"

After a few years Elizabeth would wonder why she never saw her mother perform such tricks again. After a few more years, she wondered why her mother never showed joy like that night she danced by herself in her own magical candlelight.

As she contemplated her impending marriage, Elizabeth vowed never to tell Thomas her mother's secret. She didn't deserve to be accused of witchcraft should the knowledge spread.

She never broke that promise. Not even the day Thomas came home from classes at the university with a strange sheen in his eyes. When he sat down at the table and took a number of steadying breaths Elizabeth was more relieved than apprehensive, because Thomas had been acting distant and secretive for several weeks, and refused to tell her what he was doing. Thomas had licked his lips, and fumbled over his words.

"I have to show ye this, Elizabeth...but ye must promise, *please*, promise on the Bible..."

"I swear I won't breathe a word to anyone," Elizabeth had whispered.

Thomas was sweating and stuttering so profusely it felt like several minutes passed before Elizabeth noticed the crimson flame cupped in her husband's palm.

15

As the conversation with Georgie was relayed to Elizabeth shortly thereafter, she assumed the robbery undertaking was in capable hands. The first few minutes of their Hyndford's Close rendezvous made her wonder if Thomas had imagined an idealised discussion.

"Ye didnae tell us 'bout the wummin..." a rat-faced man hissed, jabbing his finger at Thomas.

As much as Elizabeth wanted to swipe at Thomas' head for this crucial omission, she couldn't raise a note of disharmony.

"But I agreed we'd need a lookout," Thomas said, refusing to look at his wife.

"Aye, and ye..."

"A woman's inconspicuous, though," Thomas interrupted. "A strange man loitering in the court after sundown, that'll alert the Town Guards."

There was a pause. Georgie's men exchanged glances. Their ringleader stood for a moment, his lips parted.

Thomas laid a hand on Georgie's arm and smiled warmly.

"Yes?"

Georgie sighed and pulled away. "Aye...suppose."

"That's settled, then," Elizabeth said, extending a brittle smile to the unhappy men, daring them to object. She set off after Georgie, hoping the other men wouldn't have time to rally and raise an objection.

Chessel's Court occupied a secluded square off the Canongate, the central grassy space sheltered by birch trees. The generous winged mansion containing the Excise Office took up its south edge. Built as a lavish set of apartments for visiting nobles, it had lost its lustre in recent years. Hence the rental of one floor to the Excisemen.

Elizabeth arrived first and positioned herself under a tree on the western corner on the square. With her darned dress and tousled hair, she looked like a maid awaiting a sojourn with her lover. While the sight would cause residents to tut, it wouldn't set them on edge.

As Thomas and the other slipped into the building, Elizabeth wondered if she'd made a mistake. She didn't like being alone, even though the courtyard appeared peaceful. Plenty of men assumed that if a woman was publicly expressing interest or availability to a single gentlemen, she would accept attention from them all. To be seen wanting an amorous encounter could stop a passerby in his tracks, and change his immediate plans. Elizabeth tried to shuffle deeper into the shadows under the tree. She didn't think passersby would notice her, but trying to look inconspicuous carried its own danger too.

How long did it take to conduct a robbery? She wasn't familiar with how these things went. But she assumed it would take minutes, and it felt like hours were dragging by.

A hint of candlelight brought a touch of orange to one of the third floor windows. Not that she knew which windows corresponded to the Excise Office, or how large the premises were.

A rough murmur startled her, and she almost exclaimed with fright. Three men crossed the courtyard with purpose, chatting in subdued tones. Heading directly to the Excise building.

How could she been so dull-witted? She'd been so busy staring at the windows for signs Thomas and the crew were finishing up, that she'd neglected to keep an eye on the street. Now there was no way she could overtake them into the building, or cry out a warning. Elizabeth turned back to the building, where the candle had vanished. Odds were, her croaky voice wouldn't carry up to the third floor anyway.

The men didn't pause at the door of the building, they just filed into the main entrance. Unsure what else she could do, Elizabeth crept across the square. They'd left the door ajar.

"Didn't matter..."

"Two minutes..."

"After..."

The snatches of conversation in the stairwell didn't seem focussed on danger or theft. The fact they were talking at all suggested they weren't here to investigate a robbery. But the voices had come to a stop on the third floor, and Elizabeth could hear a key scraping in a lock.

Would George's crew have heard them coming up the stairs and have time to hide? Was there anywhere to hide in the office?

It didn't occur to Elizabeth to do anything other than flit up the stairs. Thomas had warned her to run if something like this occurred—but abdicating her responsibility wouldn't prevent her from hanging along with the rest of them if caught.

Edging up the stairs one at a time, her back against the wall, the landing finally came into view. Two of the men stood conversing in front of the open door. Their relaxed posture wasn't reassuring in the slightest: as soon as the third men uncovered intruders, they'd come running.

Elizabeth tightened the shawl around her head. Rendering the pair unconscious would take seconds, but she couldn't do it without sticking her head to see what she was aiming at. It wasn't dark enough to conceal her appearance completely. And what if one of them had a pistol?

Inspiration had only a second to settle before she moved, hands outstretched. There was a blinding flash of light, and the two guards dropped with little more than a sigh and thud.

She stepped over their bodies and tiptoed into a small antechamber, with doors branching off to other offices. The rooms beyond appeared large and comfortably furnished.

There was a noise on her left.

"Thomas? Are you there?"

"The fuck yer doing up here, lass?" came his immediate reply.

"I saw the men too late, I just..."

"How many?" Elizabeth could feel the sharpness in Thomas' disembodied voice. The creaking in the adjacent room continued.

"Three, but I knocked two out."

"Well, number three is in the other room from us. I suggest ye conceal yerself fast if you don't want to get caught...oh, but he's about to see his two pals knocked out cold on the floor, so I guess we're all still fucked."

"Calm down." Elizabeth tried to concentrate on her proculopathic conversation, listen out for the third men coming back out the other room, and find somewhere to hide in an antechamber lacking suitable hiding places.

"Get in here."

She took a large but careful step to the right. Or at least, tried to.

Crrrrrrk.

"Oh aye, the floorboards creak. Thanks for that."

"Just coming, Will!" Footsteps rose in the adjacent room. "You were right about the files..."

A face appeared in the doorway. And froze.

Elizabeth could only stand there, as startled as the other man.

There was a flash of light from behind her, but the man ducked back into the room, missing it.

Thomas grabbed Elizabeth's arm and tried to steer her towards the door.

"But the others..."

"Fuck 'em."

"No, they'll turn you in as the ringleader when making a plea bargain," Elizabeth tried to explain. Thomas hesitated.

The man peered round the doorway, a new tension to his crouch and glint of metal in his hand.

Not a big enough target for her to hit.

Elizabeth raised her hand.

This time, the blinding beam of light appeared in the palm of her hand, like a miniature sun. She thought she heard a muffled curse from the man in the corner at the blinding light.

Trouble was, he'd squint and overcome that distraction in a second.

Elizabeth started to pulse the light as fast as she could. The effect was instantly nauseating.

Now she just needed to move so the man was in her line of sight...

A pistol shot exploded around her. Elizabeth almost fell to the floor, but it was the man in the corner who slumped forward, his cry mixing with a gurgle.

"Get out!" One of Georgie's man waved the pistol at Elizabeth and Thomas. The other crew members were coming towards them. "Run!"

Thomas yanked Elizabeth's arm, and she staggered after him.

There was nobody to confront them in the stairwell, but Elizabeth fancied several more windows alight in the courtyard as they sprinted towards the main street.

As soon as they got onto the Canongate, Elizabeth was the one tugging Thomas down into a casual walking pace, inhaling furiously to get her breathing under control.

"It wasn't there," Thomas said after a few minutes.

Elizabeth glanced around. The street was almost empty, and no one was watching. "You're sure?"

"There was an empty drawer with a red swatch in it." Thomas held up his hand, demonstrating what Elizabeth assumed was the dye sample, though she didn't care to look at it. "Nothing close to the papers otherwise."

How was that possible?

"Sir Finney *couldn't* know we'd break into the Office tonight." Their feet carried them towards St Ninian's Wynd and the shortcut back to their lodgings. The plan was they'd regroup with Georgie tomorrow morning, and hope everyone avoided arrest.

"Sweetheart, about the intruders…"

"It's alright love, Georgie spotted them through the window."

"What? Why didn't you leave?"

"Georgie thought it would be too suspicious if we met them on the stairs. We all squeezed into a closet in the backroom."

Her husband's tone remained light, but Elizabeth recognised the dark undercurrents that brokered no further discussion. An apology would wipe the veer of calm away instantaneously.

"Was the flashing light trick something Dr Black taught ye?"

162

"No." Elizabeth disliked the layers of presumption and tension in that question. "It was my own conception."

Thomas' snort indicated he didn't believe her, but he kept quiet the rest of the way home.

Would be nice if he thanked me for saving his worthless hide, Elizabeth thought as she pulled the blanket over her head.

16

Black's response to the Fulhame's update was muted. He sighed and grabbed his cane.

"I was supposed to meet with William—Dr Cullen—later today. I suppose we can head in that direction now, if you don't mind a slight detour to drop off a book."

"Not a problem," Thomas said brightly. Elizabeth felt less accommodating. She preferred those sweet spots of time when Cullen wasn't drawn into their business. Still, a walk through Brown Square then back down the High Street would help keep her awake: pulsating tiredness swept through her head.

Three-quarters of the circuit worked an invigorating magic upon her. Until...

"Good morning, gentlemen and madam."

Black froze, his physician cane suspended in midair.

Sir Finney trotted up to the group astride a black horse, its flanks gleaming like polished leather. They'd reached the High Street's Tolbooth bottleneck, there was no path of retreat.

Black inclined his head a fraction of an inch, never breaking eye contact. Thomas and Elizabeth could only mumble salutations.

"Rather pleasant day," Sir Finney continued, smiling. "Seems a waste to be stuck in the city all day. I thought I would take Arion along the coast to stretch his legs."

"Sounds wonderful for you, and yet wholly uninteresting for us," Black replied. Although mostly concealed by his cravat, Elizabeth could see the tendons of his neck coiling.

"Well," Sir Finley said with a laugh, "if you were so inclined you could try and search my dwellings for Monsieur Moreau's papers while I am enjoying the Firth breeze. It would fill your day with as much sport as mine promises."

"It would be a more purposeful day than yours," Elizabeth said, annoyed at being mocked by a man on an expensive, beautiful horse. She'd seen japanned cabinets with less shine than Arion.

"Mrs Fulhame, you have a tongue that would shame a washerwoman. I'm delighted to re-acquaintance myself with your wit."

Dillon's gloved fingers crept into his waistcoat pocket, withdrawing a folded handkerchief. He dabbed at his nose.

Elizabeth's elbow and shoulders were jostled. Fellow pedestrians mumbled curses at the idiots stopping in the middle of the street.

"It's fascinating, Dr Black," he said after a pause. "While your companions' alarm is like the frantic aria of violins, yours thrashes like a bow across a cello. Your emotions are always so deep and layered."

Something jolted across Black's face, quickly repressed. Laughing at the reaction he'd provoked, Dillon spurred his horse round and trotted off down the hill, raising a hand in parting.

"I can only hope Arion reacquaints himself with his father Poseidon in the process of traversing the Midlothian coast," Black muttered at the departing figure. "Preferably from atop a steep cliff." This was uncharacteristically mean of Black—he rode frequently himself—but he was as shaken as Elizabeth by the encounter.

"He knows we broke into the Excise Office last night?" Thomas asked. It was an imbecilic question to pose, but someone had to say it.

"Dillon likes to believe he's the most important man in the city," Black said, tapping his cane on a loose cobblestone. "And stealing the turkey red process plays into that fantasy."

"How could he have known of our plans?" Elizabeth whispered. "You said Georgie's crew wouldn't breathe a word..."

Black motioned for the Fulhames to keep walking before Thomas could launch a rebuttal. "A man with a quarter the sense of Dillon would take great pains to protect an asset like that. If the men you intercepted in the office had a connection to him, word would have reached him. He's smart enough to piece the rest together."

It was true, but it didn't make the revelation any less depressing.

"Was Sir Finney always this obnoxious?" Elizabeth asked.

For a moment Black said nothing, and Elizabeth regretted posing such an impertinent question.

"I was younger and more willing to overlook boorish behaviour when I wasn't the target," Black said eventually, before she could recant. "That doesn't excuse my complacency."

For several minutes they could only trudge in silence. Elizabeth was too shaken to think, and Thomas knew better than to try and lighten the mood. However, once the initial shock wore off, and it became clear Dillon wouldn't return for a second jab, she found herself homing in on every detail of the brief exchange.

Her mind was too jolted to immediately absorb the significance of the individual fragments she'd observed.

"Is Sir Finney consumptive?" she asked, settling on one peculiar detail holding her attention.

Black frowned. "No, no one has ever commented upon the fact. His complexion is always lively." He turned to focus on Elizabeth. "Did something about his appearance struck you as unusual?"

"On his handkerchief, I caught a flash of red. I first thought he was coughing up blood, but it didn't look like a blood splatter." The stain was too vivid. Besides, why dab his nose with a blood-soaked handkerchief?

Black nodded. "An interesting observation."

They continued down the hill in silence for a moment. Clouds passed across Black's eyes.

"The remark he made comparing violin music to fear reminded me of a conversation I had with Sir Finney shortly after we first met." Black's pace slowed. "He'd heard of an Oriental philosopher claiming emotions provoked tastes on his tongue: anger tasted of oranges, sorrow tasted of cucumbers. I told him it might not wholly be a product of Oriental mysticism, for I once met a Fleet Street livery boy who said each person's Christian name provoked a colour in his mind's eye. Apparently 'Joseph' was a soothing dark green."

"So an emotion could theoretically provoke a sound in one's ear?"

"It was a lighthearted conversation," Black said, a note of wistfulness in his voice. "We debated whether we'd choose colours, tastes or sounds to indicate what another person felt." His voice hardened. "The topic came about because we'd been discussing proculopathy. Like many men introduced to the concept, he quizzed me on my ability to read minds. I assured him thoughts had to be directed in my direction to be 'heard' by me. At the time it appeared he was anxious about my reading of unwitting minds."

"It's not possible, though is it?" An uneasy sensation

tingled down Elizabeth's back. "To read inner thoughts with proculopathy?" Secret thoughts. Concealed thoughts.

"They're too subtle to detect. That's why proculopathic communication needs directing." Black's strides lengthened. "I think we need to consult with Dr Cullen."

A flight of stairs led up to the first floor entrance to Cullen's house in South Gray's close. Crumbling King James heraldry above the door denoted it as the former dwelling for the Master of the Royal Mint. While Black rapped on the door Elizabeth surveyed the broad close. Most of the sturdy buildings in the quadrangle were constructed in service to the Scottish Crown several hundred years ago for housing the mint and its artificers. The union of the crowns at the turn of the century put a stop to its operations. This all took place before British architects realised if they wanted a building to look grand they should make it Greco-Roman.

As she was ushered inside for the first time Elizabeth spotted a few traces in Cullen's home of its illustrious past. Faded floral paintings on the oak ceilings, and heavyset, boxy furniture predating the Glorious Revolution. The carpets in Cullen's parlour were threadbare, eroded by tides of visitors. The place smelled of dust and Castile soap. Even the bookspines on Cullen's shelves were bleached from sunlight.

The genteel shabbiness of Cullen's home caused Elizabeth's eyes to momentarily itch, because though she'd lived more shabby dwellings than she could count, this was the shabbiness that grew from living in the same home for decades, letting your possessions wear down alongside you.

She took a few breaths and recomposed herself in time for Cullen to settle himself on the settee and look expectantly at his friend.

"We have a nasty suspicion about Sir Finney's sudden

interest in textile dyeing..." Black began. He told Cullen about the unsettling taunts on the High Street, and the strange stains on Dillon's handkerchief.

Cullen crouched over his desk and tapped the nib of his quill onto the paper. "It's an unusual application, but I suppose under aethereal theory it makes sense." He looked at Thomas. "Have you ever noticed how cloth dyed black will overheat the wearer faster than cloth left white?"

"Yes, I err, suppose so?" Thomas glanced at Elizabeth. She nodded guardedly.

"While white linen seems to dazzle beholders on a bright day, almost like a mirror catching the suns rays."

"Yes," Thomas said with more confidence.

"To Newton, light, heat, noise and electricity are all flavours of aether, the invisible substance that transmits these sensations across the universe. My esteemed colleagues might argue otherwise, but our nervous system operates using another flavour of aether yet. It's through these interconnected forces that proculopathy is possible."

"Newton's experiments with a prism breaking light into a rainbow show us that colour is a component of aethereal light," Black continued, settling into a chair.

"The red substance in his handkerchief had some effect on his ability to sense our emotions," Elizabeth said, attempting to balance polite firmness.

"An enhancement?" Cullen's brows furrowed into themselves. "I did wonder if there were ways to augment man's natural phlogiston-wielding or proculopathic abilities. I experimented with a handful of natural nervous system stimulants over the years, but those didn't lead anywhere."

Elizabeth had expected an impassioned denial; Cullen claiming such a hypothesis was ludicrous. The seriousness of his response made her quasi-victory chilling.

"He inhaled the red powder?" Cullen asked.

"It appeared so."

Cullen's eyebrows arched then dipped. "Nasal tissue is rather delicate. It is a quick way to get volatile compounds into the bloodstream. I suppose it might be faster administration than ingestion."

"If we're correct in what we saw, the enhancement was instantaneous."

"Whatever Sir Finney was self-administering, it wouldn't be proper turkey red," Black said, swinging his walking cane by his side. "Plenty of European and British manufacturers have guessed at the procedure and can create passable imitations from the common ingredients."

"Which means if he gets hold of the proper manufacturing process to create a more lustrous dye, its enhancement properties could be even stronger?" Elizabeth asked, her throat turning dry.

There was silence.

She hadn't prepared for this. Should she? *Could* she?

"Does he intend to sell the dye as a proculopathic enhancement?"

"Why would he give his competitors his true secret?" Black asked. "Sir Finney covets the dye process because it's lucrative, the proculopathic enhancement is a tool for himself."

She'd been right to wonder why Dillon sought out the turkey red manufacturing process: the acquisition of wealth through textiles was only part of his plan.

"The problem with Dillon," Black continued, looking at his lap. "Is that he doesn't care about the consequences of his actions. He betrays friends and family in exchange for the right quantities of wealth. I don't think he realises it's not how everyone treats their loved ones."

Elizabeth didn't suppose men like Sir Finney could be made to care. If empathy hadn't struck him by now, it never would.

"All the same gentlemen, we don't know how much of an advantage pure turkey red would give Sir Finney. Emotions as musical instruments isn't the same as uncovering dark secrets. And if he needed to imbibe the dye moments before using his powers on us, it suggests its effects are short-lived."

"True, madam," Cullen conceded. "But perhaps we have the collective chemical expertise to find out for ourselves?"

"Who would we even test the dye on?" Elizabeth dreaded to think what ill-effects powder consumption might have on the body, given its interference in the users' nervous system.

Black shrugged. "Adam would be an ideal test subject."

"Surely yer joking?" Thomas almost spat out his tea.

"I, um...didn't know Mr Smith possessed the capacity to wield phlogiston?" Elizabeth rephrased her husband's spluttering outburst in more polite tones.

Cullen made an equivocating hand gesture. "If I am honest madam, 'capacity' is stretching its definition in that context. Adam possesses residual aptitude for phlogiston-wielding, but haphazard application. His sole attempt at proculopathy gave everyone in a five metre radius nosebleeds."

Elizabeth found her mouth hanging open. "Then why on earth would you want to..."

"Because I once saw Adam eat an entire quill," Black interrupted. "He spilled pease soup on it and started licking the feathers clean, only to progress to eating the quill itself in the middle of composing a letter." Black ran a hand through his hair. "He suffered precisely zero ill effects doing so. My reasoning is that there's nothing we can put in that man's stomach capable of harming or even mildly inconveniencing him."

17

Elizabeth told herself she needed to clear her head, and maybe call upon Moira, who lived in the shadow of Holyrood Palace and might have acquired gossip since they last met. And if those two urgent tasks took her down the Canongate past Moray House...so be it.

Dillon's temporary residence loomed like a fortress over the street. It lacked street level windows, and the entrance was accessible through a guarded gateway. While not an ostentatious dwelling, it had to be one of the hardest buildings to sneak in to.

Then she noticed a sedan chair seated just inside the gates. Following a small outpouring of servants and guests, the chair was manoeuvred onto the street. A well-dressed periwigged man—portly enough to strain the arms of robust carriers—bade goodbye to someone just inside the gates and waved his hands at the carriers in an instruction to commence onwards.

Before climbing into his chair, the man slid a notebook into his breast pocket.

By the time his chair was lifted off the ground, Elizabeth had crossed the street.

The good thing about tailing a sedan chair was you didn't get out of breath chasing it. She ambled at a distance as the chair turned onto North Bridge.

They weren't going anywhere unexpected. Elizabeth fancied she recognised the man: if correct he dwelled at the far end of Princes Street. His chair made steady pace through the street throng.

As the chair made its way across deeper into the new town, she wondered if she it would be prudent to rush back into town and summon Black or Thomas. If they ran they could probably catch up with the target before he disembarked.

Probably.

There was always a risk she'd miss a subterfuge: what if the notebook was passed to someone else two streets over? She wouldn't have an opportunity this clean and easy for a while.

Besides, whenever she had an idea in the vicinity of Thomas, credit for it always transmuted to her husband. She tightened the strings of her lace bonnet and lowered her gaze, so anybody who spotted her on Princes Street wouldn't notice a fixation on the chair.

When the chair was set down outside its destination, Elizabeth hung back. Blending in wasn't hard: the street hummed with messengers, traders and glossy carriages. Her target emerged from the chair and slipped into conversation with the valet, who'd hurried out the front door to greet his master. The pair stood close together, but she saw something pass from the master to his servant. The valet nodded and withdrew. Instead of heading back in the front door he walked along the street and turned down the steps leading to the basement floor. The master turned back to his carriers, no doubt issuing instructions about their activities for the rest of the day.

Elizabeth had to act fast. She crossed the street, assessing her available tools.

The chair was set down in front of a small mule-drawn cart, laden with sacks and pots. Elizabeth noticed the valet left the stair gate open when he disappeared through, and the harried cart owner was setting a small pile of sacks down near the gate.

As she approached she could hear his grunts and wheezes. The man seemed a few years younger than herself. The master and servants paid him no attention.

"Right ye are," she said gruffly, startling the man so much he almost tripped over a cobblestone. "Let's get this in the usual spot a'fore it starts pissin' it down."

Her Irish brogue, usually under tight control, burst forth. It didn't matter that she was flushed, Irish servants were always red-cheeked and coarse.

"Ah, um, yes." The skinny man looked relieved he wouldn't be the one to take all the sacks into the scullery. "Thank you." He spoke with a faded Borders accent.

A few huffs and Elizabeth hoisted a sack of sugar onto her hip and made for the side steps. She could see the valet in the doorway, talking to an older woman in a stained apron. He clutched the ledger in his hands.

"S'cuse us, good sir and ma'am." Elizabeth leant against the wall for a second to readjust her grip. "Got them sundries off the cart."

The valet and cook nodded. "Right," the valet said, stepping aside. "We'll settle the accounts once you've brought them down."

"God bless ye." Elizabeth let the cook point her towards the storage room. Fortunately, the valet was not in a rush to leave and remained in the doorway as she dropped off her first sack and went for more.

It could all come crashing down in an instant. The deliveryman thought she was with the household, the household thought she was with the deliveryman. A single reference to "your Irish maid" or "your wife" would ruin her. Heaven help her if she was trapped inside the building when that happened.

Back in the street, her unwitting accomplice had unloaded all the sacks and a few genuine servants began to assist. Elizabeth could feel a spit of rain on her face. Before she picked up her second burlap sack, she yanked the top knot loose.

The basement was a hive of activity now, with servants decanting and relocating wares, or yelling questions to the cook about where she wanted this-or-that. The valet migrated inside—almost to the rear stairwell—and stood with folded arms while the cook fielded the delivery into various rooms.

A small step separated the pantry from the corridor. Elizabeth only noticed it on her return.

"Oooft!" Elizabeth bent a knee and let the weight of the sack drag her down and forwards. Once tilted, the flour erupted from the top of the sack. It was an unfeigned scrabble on Elizabeth's part to stop the whole contents from pouring out.

"The devil curse this!" Two servants rushed over to catch her and the bag.

"Are you alright, miss?"

"Yes, yes…Gawd, yer floor bit me." The flour bag was coaxed from her hands.

"Hmm, the sack knot came loose," the valet murmured, now peering over her. The ledger was no longer in his hands.

"Heavens, what a mess! The rats'll have a feast," Elizabeth croaked, frantically dusting the worse of the spillage off her dress, being careful to knock the powder onto the row of silverware beside her.

"Quite…" The valet snapped his fingers and pointed. The servants flinched, before shooting out the room to locate their brooms.

"Right, will just get out yer way…" Elizabeth backed out

of the pantry. She took two massive steps back then ducked into the stairwell. The commotion rose as everyone tried to cram into the pantry to clean out the floor.

As expected, the ledger was set aside on the first step. She dropped onto the stairs and picked it up.

Sir Finney had elegant, expansive handwriting. He clearly enjoyed looping his ys and gs. Only the first twenty pages of the notebook were filled. Trying to leaf through the pages as fast as she could, Elizabeth saw plenty of references to 'Turkey red.'

The book was filled with names, addresses, and accompanying notes.

R. Donahue. North Dunhilly. Proximity to stream? 20-50 workers. Lacework.

M. Lewis and sons. 5 miles west Dunhilly. Good roads. 800 sq ft. Cotton and indigo

This was an account of potential turkey red manufacturers on the west coast of Scotland. Sir Finney had recorded in painstaking detail the strengths and weaknesses of fifty textile works.

But it wasn't in strict alphabetical order. Sir Finney must have grouped the millers by location or size. Elizabeth thumbed faster, trying to concentrate on the noises round the corner. And there it was, in the final cluster of five:

D. O'Neill. Lanarkshire. Warehouse space. River. Roads. 5-10 workers Linen dyes.

Underneath her brother-in-laws' name was a single word: "Probable."

Footsteps on flagstones grew louder. Elizabeth snapped the book shut.

"Oh!"

"Eh!"

"I'm sorry, what are you doing here?" The valet sounded peeved.

"'Scuse ye, sir. Had a funny turn in the head just there and needed to rest m' legs." Elizabeth let her exaggerated Irish accent flow. "A thousand apologies. I think I'm well-rested now, thank youse." She got to her feet, refusing the valet's offer of a hand. Not suspecting a clod-hopper from Dublin could be up to much mischief on a stairwell—could she even read?—he let her scuttle out the way she'd came.

Elizabeth broke into the fresh air like she'd come up from the bottom of a lake. Sir Finney's ledger hadn't told her anything she didn't already know: that was trying to destroy rivals. Knowing Lottie's name was on the list simply confirmed her existing fears. However, she was too tinged with adrenalin to feel the full extent of her disappointment.

As she passed the front door on her way towards the cart, she almost collided with the master of the household in conversation with another waistcoated gentleman.

"The West Bow apothecary makes a fair imitation, though the quantities are meagre," he was saying. "Promised to deliver around eight." Elizabeth kept her head down, hoping her wouldn't notice her.

"Finney's circle of acquaintances never fail to surprise me," chuckled his friend.

Elizabeth sped up. She hoped if the deliveryman happened to see her passing, he'd assume she was heading out on an errand. The familiarity of the old town couldn't engulf her quick enough.

"Do you know of an apothecary on West Bow?" Elizabeth asked Thomas back home, once she'd explained everything else that transpired.

"Hmmm, might be young Tam working there now," Thomas said after some thought. "He sat in on the chemistry course a few years ago. Can't tell ye anything more about the lad, I'm afraid."

"But he has a passing chemical knowledge...and you could recognise the face?"

An impish grin split Thomas' face. "Am I confident enough in his likeness to sneak up behind him in the dark? Separate him from his wares in....say, a couple of hours' time? Is that the direction yer line of enquiry is leading me to?"

"Perhaps." She liked it when Thomas showed creativity like this.

"Phew." Thomas whistled. "That will put Sir Finney in a steaming mood. Do ye think we can cut off his entire supply of phlogistonic enhancement?"

"The disruption might not last more than a few days," Elizabeth mused. "Unless..."

"While Tam is waylaid on route to his appointment someone checks his apothecary cupboards for spare dye?"

"It seems reckless *not* to."

18

Once the Fulhames were coaxed from the room—exhibiting palpable reluctance to depart—Cullen turned to Black, a significant look on his face. Time for the adults to get down to business.

After checking the Fulhames had indeed left the house, Black settled down next to him.

"This is a mess, Joe. We need to act."

"I don't doubt the urgency," Black conceded. "But I'm unclear what we can do."

"Getting the process back from wherever Dillon's stashed it is the most important task. He still has friends in Edinburgh, does he not?"

"They don't tend to stick in his close circle for long," Black admitted, staring into the fire. "Not if their business interests overlap with his."

After a few minutes brain-wracking, Cullen cleared his throat. "What do you make of Archie McIntyre joining him on the Linen Bank board?"

"Adam called it a classic case of overlapping mutual interests. Archibald makes most of his money through madeira imports, while dabbling in silk manufacture."

Cullen swirled the remnants of his claret around the glass. "Exactly. Not in direct competition to the viper, but if Dillon prospers, so does he."

"Even if he isn't hiding the turkey red process for Dillon, I wager he knows who is." Black felt a spark of optimism.

"Exactly!" Cullen slapped his knee. "Let's go to McIntyres house and see what his correspondence turns up."

Black's spark of optimism momentarily snuffed out. "I didn't know you had a connection to the gentleman."

"Of course I don't!"

"Then how...?"

"Under cover of darkness!"

Splendid.

Black knew he operated with limited negotiating capital—unlikely to dissuade his colleague from abandoning an idea once rooted—so he focussed on controlling the narrowest, more important parameters.

"If we're going to McIntyres' house after dark, then we should go there after dinner with the Greys tonight."

Louis Grey and his wife lived at the far end of the New Town, a few streets away from the McIntyres.

Cullen released an exaggerated groan. "Louis never knows when to stop talking. We'll leave his house at two in the morning...if we're lucky."

"We need to avoid detection," Black insisted. "Calling on the Greys gives us an excuse to be in the New Town, and provides a cover if we're later implicated in anything."

"Fine..."

* * *

Despite Cullen's grumblings, Black thought he enjoyed the Grey's hospitality. Not that it took much for Cullen to laugh or trade witticisms, and anyone who didn't know him as well as Black would assume he'd be naturally drawn to the voluble Louis Grey.

As the pair waved goodbye to their hosts sometime after midnight, Cullen didn't wait until the door closed to huff and grumble.

"I don't know how that boy has the energy to talk so long. By all rights he should have worn his throat out hours ago."

"Practice, I suppose," Black said, following Cullen on a shortcut through the mews towards Charlotte Square.

Most of the New Town dinner parties wound down by ten or eleven o'clock, leaving becalmed streets. Apart from a few carriages and sedan chairs returning from the old town, Black and Cullen reached Archibald McIntyre's side of the square without passing another soul.

Black wished for many things over the long evening. That Louis' conviviality would somehow erode Cullen's desire to intrude upon the McIntyre's tonight; that the McIntyre household would be aglow with visitors or the square bursting with onlookers. He had also expected his wishes to be crushed. Yet the sight ahead was both disappointing and concerning.

"How many servants do the McIntyres retain in Edinburgh over the summer?"

This side of the square was cloaked in darkness in contrast to all the others, where faint candlelight winked from the odd window.

Cullen paused and slowed his approach. "It would be the usual handful, wouldn't it? He has the space for a live-in butler and cook."

Black tried to peer into the basement level below the entranceway. Complete darkness and disconcerting quiet.

"You would expect someone to still be awake at this hour. Even if it's just the servants relaxing with a game of cards."

"Well, let's look around the back…"

The rear side of the building was equally dark. However, horses humphed and whinnied in the stables, and a carriage sat in the corner.

"Seems like the owner is in," Cullen muttered, peering at the windows. Black squeezed his forearm and tugged him deeper into the shadows.

Despite the horses fretting at their presence, there were no more signs of human occupancy—lit candles, or noise—round here than at the front.

"Maybe Archibald is dining within walking distance, and the butler snuck out to indulge in the old town," Black said, glancing around. "But it seems more probable the house is occupied."

Cullen didn't hesitate. "Well, it's not as if we need to ask Archie any questions. We can sneak in through the servants' entrance without disturbing anyone, take a look at his papers in the study—or wherever he keeps them—and then sneak out with them none the wiser."

"There is nothing about that stream of ideas that isn't a portent for disaster," Black hissed. "William, neither of us are young men." The McIntyres' residence took up half a side of the square. Black couldn't recall ever stepping inside. It was also pitch black.

The older physician was not to be deterred. "We'll move quick and silent."

Cullen rising from his chair unleashed a creak of bones loud enough to be heard in the adjoining room. Not that Black believed his joints any more discreet.

"Don't forget our situation is urgent, Joe."

Black wished he could protest that a day wouldn't matter.

That they could abandon their quest for tonight and try again in the morning. But the time before Dillon departed for London could be measured in days and hours.

With a sigh, Black pulled out his pocket watch.

"Alright, William. We're giving ourselves twenty minutes, until one o'clock, to get in and out of McIntyres' house. Any longer and someone will wake up and hear us, or come home —I guarantee it."

Cullen brandished his own pocket watch. "That seems over-cautious...but we're using my watch. I don't want you winding your clock forwards, Joe."

"Well, I don't want you winding your clock backwards, *William*."

Black darted from the shadows to the rear entrance. It was now or never.

After his eyes adjusted, Black was able to make out the outlines of the space around him and move through the unfamiliar McIntyre household. Tapping his physician cane along the skirting boards, he found the stairs and navigated to the first floor.

Cullen followed behind. Black could hear his breathing, and the intakes of breath that suggested repressed curses over a stubbed toe, but otherwise he made little noise.

A clock ticked in the front room, which appeared to be the parlour-study, but otherwise the silence felt thick. No snores or floorboard creaks. Maybe a neighbour was making use of the McIntyres stables, and the place truly was empty?

Heart lodged somewhere in his oesophageal tract, Black scanned the rest of the first floor. Next to the parlour desk was a door leading into the back room. He glanced through into what appeared to be the master bedchamber. A faint glow from the hearth illuminated an empty four-poster bed, embroidered curtains tied back. Black couldn't see any more of the room without pushing on the door, but it confirmed the house was in use. It would only take a few hours of neglect before the fire dropped that low, wouldn't it?

Across the landing he found a water closet and reception room with its furniture covered in sheets. The remaining bedchambers must be upstairs.

Satisfied there was nobody on the first floor, Black returned to the study, where Cullen had fumbled his way to the desk by the embers of the hearth. This room too was recently in use.

Black got close enough to nod. Cullen raised his hand and let a faint ball of light form in his palm.

"Give me a moment, Joe—there's quite a few letters here."

Cullen began to finger through McIntyres' letters, all stacked in neat piles.

Black held out his own hand, cradling a similar light, over the letters. Cullen extinguished his own illumination and sped up the examination.

The minutes ticked by, with Cullen's breath striking a discordant note with the clock. Ten minutes remaining.

There wasn't room for them both to read the letters, and crowding Cullen would cast more shadows on the papers.

When he turned to get a better look at his surroundings, Black noticed one of the shutters left wide open. A hazy silver light spilled in from the street.

Now thoroughly involved in his task, Cullen had decided to light a small candle. He'd flitted through enough of the owner's private letters to identify general trends.

"That's the second mention of Sir Finney. Looks like he met with Archie on, what was it, last Wednesday?"

Whoever turned the room down for the night must have

missed the latch. A solitary candle couldn't be visible from the street to a casual passerby, but...

As Black approached the window, Cullen's proculopathic commentary continued.

"He's getting letters from his solicitor and associates sounding like a loved one died. 'Deeply concerning,' 'tragic misfortune,' 'unexpected loss.' Archie's wife and children are all alive, are they not?"

Black leant against the wall and edged as close to the window as he dared, so he could look out without being seen.

"There's a half-drafted letter to his wife here, assuring her that they won't sell the house. Heaven's Joe—what's going on?"

The square was quieter and darker now than it was fifteen minutes ago. Black couldn't see anyone. He craned his neck, hoping to see more of the pavement below.

"Archie left his Perthshire estate to return to Edinburgh early, told his family there was business to attend to. He's urged at least one friend not to tell his wife about their recent conversations. But it's all so vague and euphemistic, I can't make hide nor hair of what this all means..."

"William..." Under a street lamp stood a motionless figure. Only the faintest glimpse of a pale face indicated they were looking towards the McIntyre's house.

Could they be staring straight at this unshuttered window?

"The top letter was drafted this afternoon. It's a garbled mess. The man was in a state of crisis, Joe. Where the Hell is he?"

A burst of crimson light disengaged from the shadowy figure and hurtled towards the building. It took Black only a second to see it was aimed at him.

"William!" All concerns of secrecy vanished as Black dived to the side. For a second the room was bathed in crimson before the window shattered and a ball of fire flew straight at Cullen, frozen with a hand raised protectively in front of him. Shielding his face from flying shards of glass as he stumbled against the wall, Black could only watch in horror.

Then Cullen's hand shot round in a snatching motion and the fireball lurched to the side. Cullen passed his hand behind his back and the fireball arced around his body. Black could see tendrils of flickering crimson connect Cullen's hand to it.

Cullen swapped hands behind his back and shot his right hand out, pointing at the fireplace. There was a second explosion of light and heat as the fireball impacted the back of the hearth, sending flames licking out and causing glowing embers to fly across the room.

The paralysis broke and Black rushed forward to stamp out the embers on the carpet. With a pulling motion, Black snuffed out small fires on the curtains and furnishings, drawing the excess phlogiston into his body and letting it dissipate through his limbs as he worked.

If anyone were in the house, commotion and smoke would have roused them. But there was no feet rushing up the stairs or shouts.

Cullen determinedly swatted at the flames near him, clearing the desk of sparks. A glance back out the window told Black the attacker had vanished.

"There's some blankets in the bedchamber, I think," Black said, eyeing a cluster of blazes in the corner. It wouldn't take long for them to get out of control.

Cullen didn't say anything, too strung on adrenalin.

A faint haze of smoke hung inside the bedchamber. Black tugged a blanket from the bed and was running back to help Cullen when the sight of what was in the corner stopped him in his tracks.

"Providence have mercy," Black whispered.

In a dark, cynical way, he wasn't surprised by what he saw. Every sign tonight already indicated something was terribly wrong in the McIntyre household. A lifeless body slumped in an armchair was perhaps what Black had been expecting to find ever since he crept through the door.

19

"I didn't expect ye here so soon, love."

Elizabeth insides unclenched as the shadowy figure in the close reformed itself into her husband.

"Everything went well?" she asked, nudging him with her elbow.

Melrose Close was barely wide enough for two people to stand abreast without touching the slick green walls. Jettied timber frames blocked out all but a glimmer of moonlight.

Somewhere above them, a baby cried.

"I caught him from behind just past the city walls," Thomas said, lowering his voice. "He never knew what hit him. Left him sleeping it off beside the ironmonger." He was holding a medium-sized sack in front of him, which clinked as he adjusted his stance.

"You had a more bountiful harvest than me," Elizabeth said. Someone—the baby's mother perhaps—was pacing near a first floor window and muttering. She motioned for Thomas to follow her. "I found a decent quantity of the dye's precursor elements, but Tam didn't have many vials stored."

Thomas slowed his walk.

"No one spotted me, love. I picked the lock like you taught me, and burned what I could in the backroom furnace.

"I wasn't worried about that sweetheart. I was more thinking why Sir Finney needs so much powder."

The man had a point.

"Let me see that bag…" Elizabeth tested its weight. "You're right. He only needs a dab at a time, at least from what we've seen. How long would this supply last?"

"Months?"

"I don't like this."

Aware they'd come to a stop, Thomas shrugged and started walking again. They were almost out in the Canongate, and the steepest part of the close. Elizabeth didn't want to know what her feet were slipping through, nor did she want to put her hand out to steady herself.

Whatever Dillon had planned, she hated to think it included this much proculopathic enhancement.

At the end of the close Thomas hopped over a puddle into the Cowgate. A few night soil workers congregated at the next close entrance, but otherwise the pair remained unseen.

"Hold on a minute."

"What are ye doing?"

Elizabeth pulled the glass vials from her purse, unstoppered them and started to pour the red powder into the puddle.

"This seems a quick a way to destroy his cursed dye as any."

Thomas blinked. "We should save some for Drs Black and Cullen. Remember they wanted to test its effects on Mr Smith?"

"I well remember." Elizabeth didn't look up from her pouring. "If you ask me, that's a terrible idea."

"What? Testing the effects of Sir Finney's enhancement to

better understand the threat we're dealing with? Yer calling that a bad idea?"

"I'm calling..." Elizabeth huffed as she pulled out another handful of vials. "...The continued existence of any quantity of Sir Finney's dye a bad idea. Be it in his hands or the good doctors'. He'll suspect our involvement in its theft, even without proof. I don't want to risk him reacquiring any of his supply."

Thomas paused, his hand protectively over the satchel. "I don't disagree. I mean, I assume any vials are safe enough with Dr Black but ye can never be too careful...but I think he'd want us to retain at least one vial of the stuff for testing."

"We know what it does already." Elizabeth shook the last of her vial out. The nightsoil cleaners shuffled down the Cowgate, one glancing back to look for the source of the raised voices. "Even one vial represents a week's worth of mischief for Sir Finney, I imagine."

"But he probably still has a couple in Moray House..."

"Which is why I don't want him to get his hands on any more." Elizabeth tossed the emptied vials into her purse. She could rinse them out and use them for storing her metal scraps. "Come on Thomas soon-to-be-doctor Fulhame. Hand over the booty."

Thomas paused for a moment. Elizabeth saw the flash of his tongue across his lips.

Then he sighed and tugged the bag open.

"Fine. We'll get rid of them all."

Not that Elizabeth felt an absence of guilt at depriving Black of something important, but she wasn't going to let it clash with her principles.

In a few short minutes the puddle shimmered the colour of blood.

"That's all? There's no more in your pockets?"

Thomas chuckled. "Of course not, Elizabeth my dear. They all went in the satchel."

They crossed the street and began the final leg-burning ascent into the High School Yards.

They were almost at the turnpike door when Thomas spoke again. "I should really call upon Dr Black first thing tomorrow."

"Is that really necessary?"

Elizabeth took one last glance at the street to make sure no one was following them, then closed the door.

"He deserves a warning that Sir Finney might go on the rampage. It makes sense to do that as early as possible." Thomas handed Elizabeth the satchel as they climbed the turnpike stairs.

Elizabeth would prefer they stayed home and barred their door, but that was probably an overreaction. Besides, Black deserved a warning. He would have gone to sleep early tonight thinking all was fairly stable with the world.

"Besides," Thomas continued. "If I recall, Dr Black and Moreau are heading out on business this afternoon. They might not return before evening."

20

"You look a little pale, Joseph. Maybe the cook can get you something to eat?"

In the warm light of day, McIntyres' study looked almost normal, aside from the lingering odour of smoke. The emerald carpets barely showed the scorch marks made a few hours' prior. The broken glass had long been swept away and the furniture righted.

The observation of his fatigue only compounded its strength. Black rubbed his eyes.

"That won't be necessary, Andrew. I managed breakfast."

Andrew Duncan shrugged and jerked his head towards the bedchamber, where he'd spent the last fifteen minutes working undisturbed. Stifling a yawn, Black followed the professor, nodding to the red-eyed butler cringing in the doorway.

The fabrications flowed easy enough. Doctors Black and Cullen were walking home from a dinner gathering when they spied a ruffian throw an incendiary object through McIntyre's upstairs window. Anxious to render assistance they'd rushed

195

inside and tackled the blaze, only to find poor Archibald McIntyre bled to death in his bedchamber.

While the selfless heroics of two august physicians raised some eyebrows among the servants and Town Guards who heard the tale, their presence at the Grey's dinner party was corroborated, and Black's willingness to assist the under-staffed, grieving household while the McIntyres were summoned from the country was tearfully seized upon.

Such assistance came in the form of Black's colleague most familiar with the application of medical theory to the law, whose expert opinion might assuage the servants in blame for what occurred.

"Think of it less as a method of physician examination," Duncan explained. "And more as a consideration of the questions one must answer in court that would satisfy a counsel ruling on the cause of death."

He pottered about the chamber, carefully checking the master's body—now laid on the bed awaiting the family's return—and objects in the room.

"Questions like whether there was a sign of a struggle, and how confident are you about the cause of death?" Black asked, watching his colleague work.

It was a good job no one had inspected his hands and face, or they might have wondered why the professor of chemistry was covered in tiny nicks. That might raise the reasonable follow-up question of where Black was standing when the McIntyre's window shattered.

"Quite so." Duncan gestured to the garish lacerations on McIntyre's wrists. "His artery was severed in a single cut, quite cleanly. You can see his blood is concentrated around the chair, indicating the deceased did not move about after the cut was made. The bloody instrument was left on the table, close to the deceased's right hand. There are no signs of physical restraint: bruising, rope burns, what have you. This tells me there wasn't a struggle. While the deceased clearly drank that evening, it wasn't enough to incapacitate him completely."

"You are confident that McIntyre took his own life, then?"

"I would say 'reasonably confident' in legal terms. We have clear evidence of Scenario A, paired with no compelling evidence of competing scenarios."

If the tableau was staged to appear as self-slaughter, they'd have a hard time proving it.

Duncan returned to the front room, where he'd left his belongings.

"That's good to know, Andrew. I appreciate you coming here such at short notice."

Duncan pulled on his hat and coat. "I'm glad I could be of assistance, Joseph. Send word if there's more this humble servant can assist you with, but I'm afraid I have to depart now. We have six initiates at the Beggar's Benison to frig tonight, and I need to make sure the servants put away my rugs."

With that he departed, humming.

"The draw of such public exposure eludes me," Black muttered, mostly to himself. "Are these otherwise judicial men all seized with identical perversions, or do they see the reward —equally unclear at present—as justifying the means?"

Black could affect composure, but his nerves were shot. He'd got no sleep last night, and he needed to be out of bed at five o'clock to deal with the mess left by McIntyre. The butler was only too relieved to let someone else investigate the matter, because it reduced the focus on his whereabouts when his master lay bleeding to death. Black deduced a mistress in the Canongate played some role in his absence.

In the corner of the parlour Adam Smith coughed.

"Are you posing that question to me in my capacity as a moral philosopher, Joe? Or as a consultant for free trade policy?" He pushed another ledger onto the growing pile at his left hand.

Black smiled in spite of himself. "I don't know. I suppose I assumed the answer would be the same in both cases."

"Perhaps." Smith stretched his arms. "The replies only differ in granularity."

Only a thin stack of unread letters and incomplete notebooks lay in front of him.

"It doesn't look like the accounting exercise took you long."

Smith rose, groaning. "The departed gentleman—God rest his soul—employed mostly honest accounting: plain and boring reading. Over the last decade he steadily accumulated wealth without interruption..."

"Until?"

"Yesterday." Smith waved a couple of letters he'd set in a separate pile. "His shipping business collapsed. The devastating blow was that he took out several loans to try and mitigate his crumbling business: the gambit he was trying to play didn't work out, leaving him with the failed business and a catastrophic debt."

Black nodded. The shattered bay window was already boarded up, but sunlight poured through the others. The room was reassuringly bright, and the square outside reassuringly busy.

"Adam, this isn't a case of the ledgers being too good to be true?"

Smith joined Black at the window.

"That's very unlikely, Joe. If this was a deliberate murder, then why not have the assassin knock over a candle to start the fire after they'd completed the killing?"

Black wondered the same thing. But it was nice to hear his friend say it out loud. They lapsed into silence as a carriage trotted past the house, its driver mangling a country ballad.

"Did you find much of Dillon in McIntyres' papers?"

Smith rested his temple against the shutter. "I'm fairly confident the casualty is indirect. McIntyre kept his business enterprises clear of Sir Finney. He's been in trouble for a while, I think: the latest tariffs from Westminister meant the madeira trade is swinging back to Spain, and his exports were drying up.

"The stacked dominoes fell yesterday because a panel of investors reneged on their recent contract with McIntyre. From the language in these letters, McIntyre pinned his flagging fortunes on that deal going through, and he may have taken out additional loans when the contract was first signed last week."

Black closed his eyes, in the hope his headache would fade. Instead the image of Cullen returned from last night: the phlogiston fireball hurtling towards his friend, and for a second it looking like the old professor wasn't going to raise his hand in time.

He shook his head. "What prompted the contract break?"

Smith clicked his tongue. "That's less clear, but I imagine the investors found out how badly McIntyre's business was struggling, or another party came in with a stronger counter-offer..."

"It sounds like Sir Finney uncovered a secret, which he used to his advantage."

Did Dillon pace about this very room, surreptitiously applying red powder to his nostrils as his friend unwittingly revealed the true state of his finances? Or maybe McIntyre's investors were the object of Dillon's experiment, their surprise at McIntyre's destitution a beautiful aria in Dillon's ears?

"Exactly, Joe."

That scenario took the edge off Black's paranoia. He'd worried for hours Dillon's fire attack was directed at himself and Cullen, and what that would mean for everyone's safety.

Instead, it seemed Sir Finney found out McIntyre had ended his life—perhaps an accusatory letter dispatched hours before he committed the deed—and decided to get rid of any evidence.

Not that it made the outcome much better.

"It's economic destabilisation," Smith said on their walk home. "With McIntyre dead, it means another set of businesses consolidated. Prices then rise, either because other companies are disadvantaged by the loss, or to take advantage of reduced competition. Everybody suffers because of Sir Finney's games."

"We need to strike back before he has time to cause any more destruction," Black said. "William is meeting us this evening. Our mission may become the destruction of Moreau's papers, rather than their recovery."

"Better it falls into no one's hands than the wrong one." Smith turned to regard Black. "Will you and Monsieur Moreau be secure until then?"

"As safe as we can be." It would be a while before Dillon was put on alert. Cullen was calling upon patients this morning, and Black was taking Moreau out of town that afternoon. Right now, Dillon would believe his involvement in McIntyre's death had gone unnoticed. But someone would have spotted Black leaving the McIntyre residence with Smith. It was inevitable the servants would talk, revealing Andrew Duncan examined the body at Black's request, and Adam Smith had autopsied their master's correspondence, untouched by the blaze. By then Dillon would know he'd failed to destroy the evidence. Would it be too much to hope he feared for his reputation at the news?

At that point, Black knew Dillon would be at his most deadly. But with any luck, they had a few hours' head-start on the hurricane.

21

Thomas thought if he hurried home along the wide, crowded Infirmary Street he'd be safe from malevolent forces. As soon as four men disengaged from the crowd and blocked his path he realised how stupid that was.

His wife hadn't wanted him to leave the apartment. But he needed to warn Black about what they'd stolen from Dillon, and hoped to catch the professor before he left with Moreau. Upon arrival, Black's manservant told him Dr Black wasn't at home, leaving Thomas confused. Perhaps they'd decided to head out in the morning instead?

The four thugs moved into place—flintlocks and daggers drawn—so fast Thomas didn't have a chance to duck around them.

"Do the smart thing, Mr Fulhame," one of the men said, in tones just edging out of politeness.

Thomas didn't want to argue with the rusty, blood-stained knife waved at his abdomen. Even if he fought the men off, those blades carried a guaranteed death by infection if they touched him.

Thomas raised his hands and allowed them to prod him to

the nearby carriage. As soon as his hand touched the door frame a thick hemp bag dropped over his head.

"Dinnae make a scene," hissed someone before he could react. "If ye ken whit's best fae ye."

* * *

Thomas started awake. He didn't remember falling asleep. An insistent headache and bitter aftertaste in his mouth suggested his kidnappers had administered something to him in the carriage.

His hands were manacled to arms of a surprisingly comfortable chair. His feet sank into a lush Ottoman carpet. He was in the middle a spacious but low-ceiled atrium, with an open balcony in front of him. The translucent curtains rippled in a gentle breeze. It looked out over a vista of the Forth from a considerable height. The tips of trees swayed beyond the balcony, suggesting a steep drop before him.

Glancing around the sumptuous room with its gilded portrait frames and mahogany shelving, Thomas finally noticed the unusual octangonal shape of the room.

"Are ye jesting me? Goosepie Hut?" he muttered.

"Between you and me," an amused voice said behind him. "I don't know what John Ramsay was thinking constructing such a strange shaped dwelling. But it's not for me to judge, I suppose."

Sir Finney sauntered into Thomas' line of sight, hands in the pockets of his embroidered gold waistcoat.

The view made more sense now. Ramsay's Lodge perched next to the castle at the pinnacle of the Lawnmarket. If Thomas stood on the balcony he'd enjoy an uninterrupted view of the Nor Loch basin and New Town.

"The owners are in Italy right now," Finney continued. "I

have use of the space as part of a favour to a friend. You know how these things go."

Sir Finney couldn't possibly think Thomas had experience staying in friends' villas while they sojourned in Italy, so he decided not to bother rebuking. He craned his neck to see if anyone else hid behind him. The room smelled of a sea breeze and furniture polish.

Standing in front of Thomas, Sir Finney pulled a small vial out of his waistcoat pocket and unscrewed the lid.

The manacles almost cut off circulation into Thomas' hands. Someone had put thick leather gloves on them too, the kind blacksmiths might wear, making it impossible to move his fingers. Nor could he clench or angle his arms enough to direct phlogiston at his tormentor. That was if the gloves didn't absorb all the phlogiston, which is what he suspected they were designed to do.

Not that he could see it clearly, but the vial in Sir Finney's hands bore an unfortunate resemblance to the vial of red dye Thomas had secreted in his own waistcoat pocket the previous night in express disobedience of his wife's wishes. He didn't like deceiving Elizabeth, but he was sure she'd wake up the next day and realise how foolish it was to leave no samples for Black. Right now, he couldn't really feel whether his pockets were emptied or not.

Sir Finney leant against the balcony door, annoyingly angled away from Thomas' palms.

"I have half a mind to piss on yer friend's Turkish rugs now."

Sir Finney dipped his pinkie into the vial. "I would simply buy Sir Alan a new rug if that were to occur." His finger came out crimson.

"Since ye don't seem to be in a rush, my lord, I wonder if ye intend to tell me at some point what I'm doing here."

Sir Finney paused with his finger almost touching his upper lip.

"I can understand why you might feel threatened, Mr Fulhame. But rudeness is not in your best interest." His pinkie touched his nose.

There was a flash of yellow light. For a moment it blinded Thomas. A second later he found his head lolling on his chin with no sensation of dropping it there.

"There's a delicate art to rendering a man unconscious with phlogiston and aether," Sir Finney said, position unchanged. "Or killing him, if one is inclined that far. An individual strike with lower power does not do much harm by itself, but a rapid succession of semi-incapacitating strikes can do all sorts of damage to a man's constitution. I understand you're a man of medicine; I'm sure you are familiar with this."

A powerful aetherial strike would kill a man by stopping his heart. Thomas imagined repeated strikes below that threshold could also fatally interfere with the heart beat and nervous system. Death would just be a lot slower.

And more painful.

"Consider me warned, then. What is yer business with me, Dillon?"

Thomas gave an experimental pull of his legs. They were manacled to the chair with the same tightness. Despite jerking his hands back and forth, the bindings stayed where they were.

"You and your illustrious friends have an unseemly interest in my personal property. It is maddening that I would need to explain to an associate of Mr Adam Smith that personal property is an inalienable right...but here we are."

"See, I'd have said the property in question belonged to a Monsieur Philippe Moreau."

"Oh, we're pretending that the Excise Office robbery wasn't anything to do with you? Alright then." Sir Finney pushed himself away from the balcony door, and strode to the adjacent settee, putting him even further from Thomas' hands. "At first it was amusing, watching Dr Black's crude attempts to gleam information about the protocol's whereabouts. I wish he knew when to stop a joke."

Another flash of yellow light caught Thomas unawares. He tried to twist to avoid it, but the light consumed his vision. When it cleared a grey fuzz speckled across his eyes, and his headache deepened.

Sir Finney applied more of the red material under his nose. "Can you wield phlogiston?" he asked.

Thomas scrambled to calm his mind.

"You're lying!" Dillon exclaimed.

"I didn't say anything!"

"Ah, but I saw you formulating the lie in your head."

Thomas didn't know how to respond to that.

"Begrudging admiration," Dillon said, swinging his leg over the side of the settee. "It blends interestingly with your apprehension and anger. I'm not sure if you're familiar with the works of Vivaldi—but your discordant emotions melding together reminds me of his *Four Seasons*."

"Some culture does make it to Ireland," growled Thomas. "Ye'd be surprised."

Sir Finney had to suspect Thomas of possessing phlogiston-wielding ability, or else he wouldn't have tied him up quite so scrupulously. Thomas supposed this question was more a test of Sir Finney's enhanced lie-detection.

"Does Dr Black ever let the industrious Frenchman out his sight?"

"I don't imagine he scrutinises his chamberpot activity or reads him bedtime stories."

Another flash of light broke off the rest of Thomas' remarks. This time the brightness seemed to last longer, and left him sweating.

Thomas had enough time to see Sir Finney frowning at him, then the light flashes recommenced.

As they abated Thomas struggled to breathe through a constriction in his chest, curiously detached from his body and thoughts.

"Do you know where Moreau is at this precise moment?"

Sir Finney dipped his finger back into the vial.

"Ah, it appears you *do* know."

Another storm of light.

Thomas tossed back his head in a futile attempt to get more air. Even though he was lashed to the chair it felt like he was falling.

"University. Tenement. River. Street. Office. Bridge. Wood. Tavern." Sir Finney spoke evenly but quickly. "Friend. River. Sea. Business. Water. Water."

Thomas tried to empty his mind, but it was too late.

"Dr Black and the Frenchman were seen heading west this morning, which is in the opposite direction of the Firth, but will take them to the Water of Leith, where several gentleman physicians tend to gardens. Also a good place to stimulate discussion about mills and waterworks."

Thomas was too relieved that the aetherial onslaught had stopped to panic. He wouldn't have the stamina to commit such a sustained assault, even on someone he hated; the dye must be enhancing Sir Finney's phlogiston-wielding capabilities too.

Sir Finney gestured, and three men entered the room. Thomas hadn't realised the door behind him was open.

"I have dealings to attend to, and I've wasted enough time on this villain." He raised his voice so Thomas could hear every word. "Don't let him move his hands, and deal with him as you see fit. It doesn't matter who learns of my involvement afterwards."

With that he departed. Thomas he heard the click of heels

on a marble staircase.

The first punch caught Thomas in the stomach. He grunted.

A couple of blows glanced his head, and a kick to the shins broke his concentration with sharp pain. One man grabbed Thomas' collar and started to pull the cravat from his neck.

Sir Finney might loiter in the corridor to check that his work was being carried out and Thomas wasn't fighting back. But he had to think fast before the thugs grew bored with a casual beating and moved onto their instructed task.

Whatever warnings the thugs received beforehand, they began to overlook them in the excitement of violence. Which is why they didn't notice he'd wiggled one hand out the leather gloves.

The bindings hadn't shifted, but Thomas' finger brushed against the thigh of the man drawing a blade.

"Ach!" The man hopped to the side as if stung. He should have turned into a pile on the floor. Thomas found his power weakened, a lingering after-affect from the torture no doubt. He clenched his biceps and tried again before the man had time to react.

Second time lucky. The man stumbled, almost toppling the crony next to him. Thomas flapped his wrist in the opposite direction, the binding tearing at his skin. The third thug—waiting his turn to inflict violence—was too busy staring at his colleagues to see Thomas' next strike.

The final thug was still supporting his unconscious colleague, as if preventing him from hitting the floor would reverse his faint. The sound of the other man collapsing on the opposite side of Thomas finally made him re-focus on the prisoner.

Planting his feet on the carpet, Thomas lurched forward and up. As expected, the chair was heavy but not secured to the floor. He pivoted until the chair leg bumped against the fallen body, but that was enough. His calves screamed and cramped, but Thomas pushed his right hand as far forward as it could go and unleashed the final strike, catching the final attacker square in the chest.

He panted as he made the final pivot. There weren't any more footfalls rushing closer, and the atrium descended back into the stillness. The door was still open—unhelpfully, it looked out onto the corridor wall.

The adrenalin rushing through his system wouldn't last long. Thomas had to get out of here while he still had some energy.

The ugliest, least shaven man was probably the ringleader. Dragging his heels along the rug, Thomas shuffled to the body and kicked around his midriff. He was rewarded with the jangle of keys.

Thomas eased a foot out of his shoes, and after a few abortive attempts, hooked the keyring with his toe. Getting that foot free from the rope bindings was easy enough, and before long he'd dropped the key onto his lap and fiddled the shackles open.

Standing up gave Thomas the promised breathtaking view of Edinburgh. He stumbled away from the bodies, clutching his wrists. They were scarlet, swollen and flecked with blood, but not broken.

Thomas had never been inside Ramsay's Lodge. Thinking about it, he doubted anyone ever said anything in his presence concerning the layout of one of the most coveted addresses in the city. He supposed the corridor behind him would lead to the main entrance, but it all depended on who else...

"Callum?"

Great. Thomas backed onto the balcony. Of course someone was coming to check on his friends after the room fell suspiciously silent in the middle of a beating. Thomas wasn't sure he could repeat the disabling exercise, the aether and phlogiston in his body wasn't responding the way he wanted it, which wasn't a problem at close quarters when facing men who didn't notice what he was doing. A pitched battle might be beyond his means.

Stepping out onto the balcony, Thomas was greeted by a vertiginous drop down the side of Castle Rock. Sir Allan would hardly be able to sit in the wild grassland that constituted his garden without sliding all the way down to the Nor Loch.

"Fuck ye, Dillon," Thomas said with feeling, before swinging his legs over the railing.

It was a long way down from the top of the world.

"Wha' the devil?" someone cried. Several voices blurred together.

Thomas didn't face his chances going down. Fortunately a flat rooftop abutted the central pointed octagonal building. Standing on the railing with one hand on the building for support, his fingers brushed the stonework above. Curse his short height.

The voices in the atrium swelled. In a second they'd realise their comrades weren't dead, and would turn their attention to the fluttering curtains and empty veranda, where any halfwit would flee.

The fear of re-capture overwhelmed Thomas' fear of falling. Letting go of the supportive wall, he hopped. His fingers got a grip on the stone lip, and Thomas kicked his legs up the wall until he got one foot over, and clawed onto the flat roof.

"Where'd he go?" Voices now spilled onto the balcony.

"Bastard..."

"What'd he do tae Callum?!"

"He's no' in the gardens?"

"Couldnae crawl far after that fall..."

"He's up there?"

Thomas ran across the rooftop to the front of the building. He had seen the outside of Ramsay's Lodge from the Lawnmarket, and he was considerably closer to the ground on this side of the building than the other.

If the mob had a savvy ringleader, they'd already be splitting up to intercept him on the top floor and at the front of the building. They'd mill around in confusion for a few minutes, tops.

Thomas dropped to a crouch and looked down. His legs were decidedly quivery.

He wondered where Elizabeth was. Had she managed to avoid a similar interrogation? He supposed Sir Finney would have bragged if she hadn't. Should he try and find her? Or run to the Water of Leith and warn Black? Thomas wanted to collapse in his bed, he didn't know what would happen to his body when he stopped moving.

He was two storeys above the earth now. There were a couple of servants milling about outside the lodge, but no carriage or guards. Thomas jumped from the balcony to the triangulated gables over the first floor windows, falling forward to hug the cornice. One tile slipped loose.

He let himself slither down the other side onto the porch roof. The servants at the front door continued their conversation, not noticing the patter of tiles.

Glad no one could see his undignified descent, Thomas slid off the porch, dangled for a moment clutching the gutter, then dropped, smacking onto the dirt.

He wanted to burrow into the earth and doze off, but staggered to his feet. The servants were now staring at him, frozen in the act of a conversation interrupted.

"Sorry, gents..." Thomas swayed past them and started to run. All he could focus on was his legs swinging back and forth beneath his body. They might fall off before he got home. Who could say? If any thugs were yelling in pursuit, he couldn't hear them.

22

From her vantage point at the window Elizabeth spotted Thomas as soon as he rounded the corner in the Yards. She intercepted him at the front door.

"Can't explain, love," Thomas panted. "We've got to hurry."

"I think an explanation is a very necessary part of the procedure," Elizabeth retorted as her husband collapsed against her, damp with sweat to the touch. She noticed discolouration and rashes on his face suggesting bruises were imminent, and when she tried to take his hands he yanked them away with a gasp.

She'd suspected something was wrong when Thomas didn't return home from Dr Black's. While he had the right to head off on errands and not tell her his whereabouts by the minute, with everything Sir Finney was up to, and Black departed on business, she feared the worst.

It therefore was a relief to see her husband appear after only a couple of hours, in a miserable state but alive. He gasped out the necessary explanation.

"We have to warn Dr Black!"

"Well, Sir Finney is probably at the Water of Leith already, I'm under-dressed and you're half-dead, so we may as well take a few minutes proper preparation." Clouds were coming in, putting a chill in the air and threatening rain. At the mimimim she'd need her shawl and purse.

Thomas mumbled in annoyance.

"Humour me and eat a slice of bread, sweetheart? I have a cold pot of tea that is better than drinking nothing."

Her husband was flagging, and barely able to walk unsupported. But he rebuffed her suggestion that he rest and let her warn Black.

"Sir Finney is a remorseless killer, Elizabeth. You mustn't face him alone."

"Yet I fear you're more of a hinderance than a help to me in your current state, sweetheart."

"Nonsense..."

By the time they made the hackney ride to the gardens—an expense Elizabeth begrudgingly dipped into their emergency coins for—the skies were ominous. Thomas had dozed on the ride over, and even though that couldn't have granted him more than a couple of minutes' rest, it seemed to replenish his strength.

The gardens were almost deserted, with the gentleman gardeners dissuaded by the threat of rain.

Only one man could be found knelt resolutely next to a hawthorn bush, stabbing the soil with a smug expression on his face.

"Professor Monro? Have ye seen Dr Black and Monsieur Moreau?" Thomas asked.

This wasn't a welcome development, but unfortunately it wasn't a surprise either. Thomas recalled Black mentioning Monro expected to be at his cottage this afternoon.

"The French gentleman?" Monro dropped his handful of weeds in the corner of the allotment. "He was searching for violets. I pointed him towards where I spied a clump growing last week."

"Dr Black wasn't with him?" Elizabeth's unease grew.

"Is Joseph here? I've not seen him." Monro shrugged. He looked back and forth between the Fulhames. "The flowers were around the river bend."

Monro always struck Elizabeth as a pompous fool, but his demeanour sharpened as he took in the couple's agitation and dishevelled state of Thomas. He rose and set off at a brisk pace. Thomas flashed Elizabeth a look to assure her he could keep up.

It took a couple of minutes to leave behind the manicured allotments and gardens. Rounding a corner, the Water of Leith spread out before them, roaring its way through the rocky valley towards Dean Village and the promise of the ocean.

"Look!" Elizabeth pointed.

A man stood in the middle of the river, gesticulating wildly. Thinking him in distress, the Fulhames broke into a run. A few paces closer and Elizabeth realised he stood next to a second figure, submerged in the water. He wasn't waving to onlookers at all—he was forcing the other man under.

"Stop!" she yelled.

Thomas stumbled to the edge of the bank and raised his hand, but the man had already scrambled up the other bank and dived into the undergrowth.

"Halt and explain yourself," Monro cried behind her, a little belated. The second figure was little more than a bundle of rags in the water. Monro took off downstream towards the nearest bridge as the attacker squeezed through the bracken out of sight.

Thomas waded into the river and grabbed the floating

coattails. Elizabeth stood on the banks, debating whether to wade in and assist. Not worth it: the rocks were slippery and her skirts would drag her under within seconds. Leaning over, she grabbed two fistfuls of Moreau's sodden sleeve and helped Thomas tug him onto land.

She wanted to cry at the sight of Moreau's grey, dulled skin. Moving him was like hauling a sack of flour.

Panting, Monro re-appeared.

"He escaped. I couldn't get a proper look."

"We know who it was," Elizabeth spat. "Or who paid him. Same murderer."

On an intellectual level, Elizabeth recognised the drowning of Moreau meant the lives of her, Lottie and Thomas were also in danger. Right now there wasn't room for anything but rage.

Monro inhaled several times, in a breathy way that made Elizabeth want to strike him. "Not yet a murderer. Come on, Thomas."

Monro gingerly lowered himself onto his knees, grimacing as he touched the sodden ground. The anatomy professor belonged to the traditional school of physicians who wouldn't demean themselves to touch a patient, or otherwise inconvenience themselves in pursuit of their profession.

"Tip him onto his front," he told Thomas. "Clear as much water from his lungs as you can."

Thomas frowned, assuming as Elizabeth had that Monro was only going to pronounce the Frenchman dead, since he surely was.

Monro didn't lift a finger, so Elizabeth helped Thomas tug Moreau by his shoulder and arms. There was no groaning or even a twitch.

"Right, now lay him on his back again. But keep his head slightly raised." Monro fumbled through his coat pockets, glancing around as if checking no one was around to catch him treating a patient.

By the time they'd manipulated Moreau, Monro was rubbing lint off a small wooden tube stowed in his coat.

With a surety that finally convinced Elizabeth the physician was following a standard medical procedure, Monro twisted the pipe into Moreau's nostril, squeezed his jaw and other nostril shut, and puffed into the pipe.

"You saw the patient's lungs expand?" he asked a stunned Thomas.

"Err..."

"Well, they did. Press on his chest —both sides—to expel the air."

After a few cycles of this artificial respiration process, Moreau made a faint noise.

Monro tugged his pipe free and wiped it on Moreau's lapels.

"That's his respiratory system working on its own. We have to warm him up now."

"Blowing into his nose was enough to bring him back to life, professor?" Thomas asked, staring at the patient half propped up on his knee.

"Well," humphed Monro, "Dr Cullen advises blowing tobacco smoke up the drowned person's rectum to revive them. However, I notice none of us here are currently in possession of tobacco or matches. So it seems my method must suffice. Alas. It was only good enough for God and Adam, after all."

"Thank you, Dr Monro," Elizabeth said quietly, tugging her husband's arm to ensure he made the appropriate noises of gratitude.

A few minutes later Black appeared on the other side of the river. Elizabeth almost gasped with relief.

"I thought I saw some ruffians hiding on this side of the

river. I told Monsieur Moreau to stay near the bridge while I investigated."

Monro started and stared at Thomas. Elizabeth realised he was surprised to learn Black communicated proculopathically with them. Then he looked very sharply at Elizabeth.

"Unfortunately, you've learned the same lesson as us, Dr Black," Elizabeth replied as clearly as she could, making sure to project her thoughts in Monro's direction. *"Monsieur Moreau keeps his own counsel."*

"Women learning proculopathy?" Monro muttered. "Something I think you and Dr Cullen only joined this medical school to mock it up close, Joseph."

He spoke too quietly for Black to hear him on the opposite side of the river, but Elizabeth suspected he grasped the gist of what his colleague said. At her feet, Moreau coughed.

"I'll meet you at Dr Monro's cottage," Black continued.

Monro watched Black's retreating form for a moment. Then he harumped and turned to the bedraggled Moreau.

"Normally I'd say this isn't work for ladies, but since Mrs Fulhame seems determined to inveigle herself in Man's domain..." He glared pointedly at the half-conscious body.

"Right, professor," Elizabeth said, stepping up as Thomas draped one of the Frenchman's arms over his shoulder. "Don't trouble yersel'."

By the time the Fulhames dragged Moreau back to Monro's cottage, Black had stoked the hearth and gathered a pile of coats, blankets and curtains. Monro looked like he wanted to complain about her to Black, but kept his mouth shut. If he exchanged any private proculopathic conversation with his colleague Elizabeth didn't notice him doing so.

When Moreau was recovered enough to make his way out the cottage almost unaided, dusk had fallen. Black remained as tight-lipped as Monro, and Elizabeth knew better than to interrupt or speak. At several points Moreau started to say something, then lost his courage.

He had a brief exchange in French with Black that Elizabeth couldn't catch, but it didn't last long.

She wondered if they were safe out here.

Cullen didn't appear surprised by the latest turn of events. In explaining what transpired at the Water of Leith, Elizabeth decided it was best to steer clear of the method Monro used for resuscitation. At least Cullen didn't press for details.

"That man was always malicious when he couldn't get his way," Cullen said. "Would put a pleasant front on it if he saw you as an equal, but after assuming the baronet there was no hope for him."

Moreau couldn't hide his nervousness, he peered into every corner of their living quarters, only settling once he was satisfied no killers lurked in the room, and when he'd positioned himself near the wall with a clear view of the room.

"Still," said Black. "We didn't expect that onslaught of violence. I underestimated the speed news of our business last night would reach him."

Elizabeth spun to confront Thomas. *"You did not..."*

For a moment she was furious: her husband promised he wouldn't let their theft slip, because they didn't need the professors knowing they could have received a satchel full of red powder for experimentation.

Yet her husband's confusion seemed genuine. *"I never breathed a word sweetheart, there was no chance to..."*

Elizabeth tried to return her attention to Black as if she hadn't wordlessly turned on her husband, but the chemistry professor's eyes narrowed in suspicion.

"Madam, what occurred last night?"

"It's best if you tell us everything," Cullen said.

The worst part was Black didn't even lose his temper after Elizabeth—through gritted teeth—caught him up on last night's activities. He simply sighed. A tired, weary sigh. Like he wasn't surprised the Fulhames precipitated this disaster.

"Well, that *would* explain things. Two strikes from different directions. Uncovering his ruination of McIntyre and stealing his proculopathic enhancement on the same night. No wonder two people nearly ended up dead."

Elizabeth knew better than to apologise. Black's demeanour was deadly calm, but a storm could thrash up at any moment.

In the corner Moreau shivered. "What will happen to me?"

"Moreau will be safer staying with Adam," Black said, addressing Cullen and refusing to look at anyone else. "If we smuggle him over there now it should take a few days until Dillon realises he's no longer with me."

Even a man as headstrong as Moreau would think twice about disobeying Smith's mother, a woman less 'diminutive' than 'concentrated.'

Cullen nodded.

"What does this mean for us?" Thomas asked. It was a tentative question, trying to draw the conversation away from the building thunderstorm, and pretending Black wasn't furious. "It was bad enough thinking up ways to recover the papers without needing to keep Mister Moreau alive, too."

"The Board of Manufactures needs them both," Black said. With another stab, Elizabeth realised Black was too tired of the pair to berate them tonight. He just wanted them gone. "Some aspects of the turkey red manufacture only Moreau can answer to because he was present in the room when adaptions were being discussed, others appear only in the procedures themselves. Sir Finney may have copied the papers, but getting rid of Moreau means he doesn't have to worry about competition."

"It's the Scottish weather," Elizabeth interjected. "The turkey red process requires the cloths be laid out in the sun to dry. Which is fine in the south of France, but they'll need a workaround for the average North British summer to produce the same lustre, probably through an additional calcination step."

It was something she'd wondered about as she tried to piece together the manufacturing process for herself.

Black gave Elizabeth a queer look. "I would keep that insight to yourself, madam. I don't think Dillon would react well if he learned of it."

No, he wouldn't. But it was annoying sharing a room with these scholars and being forced to pretend Thomas knew more about textiles than her.

* * *

It was more than pessimism making Elizabeth suspect more bad news was on the way. Dillon acted violently, loosening multiple strikes in quick succession, which implied there were likely more cards to fall.

Once Moreau was secured in Smith's Canongate house, Smith and Cullen offered to walk the Fulhames' home. Elizabeth didn't like to think how much protection those two venerable gentlemen afforded, but by this point Thomas was shivering and close to collapse. Black pointedly refused to accompany them.

The walk was conducted in stony silence.

When she heard her name yelled from the foot of High School Yards, Elizabeth's first inclination was to ignore it, in the hopes the miserable tidings would vanish of its own accord. Instead, the yells got louder until they overtook the Fulhames at their front door.

"Liz—I came as fast as I could," gasped Moira, leaning against the turnpike doorframe. "Thought ye were awa' and nearly headed off, then caught ye coming back. I jist saw Donnie on the Canongate—mind that fella I showed ye?"

The carrier who delivered water to Moray House. Elizabeth gave the slightest nod.

"Well, the cook told him he didnae need to serve the house tomorrow, and was annoyed at paying for his full allotment of water today. Donnie was cursing the dolt from every angle when we spoke; couldnae believe the cook only gave him a penny..."

"You mean the Dillons are leaving today?" Elizabeth asked, knowing a digression on the penny-pinching shiftlessness of cooks was on its way.

"They left a few hours ago I guess—else they'd take the fair share of Donnie's water without fuss."

Thomas swore. Everything hinged upon them retaining Dillon in Edinburgh just a few more days.

"Is his whole household departing?"

Moira nodded. "They were making enough fuss, so it seems. Donnie had to shove through a crowd of Highland ruffians waiting on the master. Said he found the kitchen in uproar."

Elizabeth didn't like the sound of hired Gaelic muscle. It would render the man nigh-untouchable.

"You did us a great favour telling us...can I offer you some tea?" Elizabeth asked, realising she had only a couple of grubby coins to give Moira by way of thanks.

Moira shook her head. "Naw, I've got to deliver the rest of this water to the Canongate. Anyway," she patted her bosom, which clinked. "I took a wee dram 'fore I came up the road."

With that she trotted off, an audible sloshing of water receding behind her.

Cullen watched with bemusement. "She ran over here with a full water barrel on her back?"

"It appears so," Thomas said.

"There goes our attempt to recover the papers," Smith said, having seen the enough of the exchange and the Fulhames crestfallen faces. "He'll be halfway out of the Lothians by now."

"Now that I think about it," Cullen said after a pause. "One of the letters on Archie's desk contained the agenda for the next British Linen Bank meeting. The date struck me as imminent..."

"The second of September, which is next week," Smith added. "I saw that paper too."

"The Bank is based in Glasgow?" That settled the matter. Sir Finney was heading to the west coast.

"Ye saw the contents of Lottie's most recent letter?" Thomas asked his wife, voice dropping to an urgent whisper.

Elizabeth thought she was going to throw up.

"'An opportunity to change our fortunes...please keep Don in your prayers.'"

The bank committee would convene to review petitions and decide on loan applications.

"I told Lottie not to be afraid of debt, that she could trust Don to repay a loan. I wrote all that in my last letter...and she believed me."

She'd believed *Thomas*. He told his wife not to be so skittish around borrowed money. And she'd transcribed it all without question.

"Sir Finney will blacklist Don—he'll never receive money from the Bank again," Thomas muttered.

"Oh, that's not the worst he can do," chirped Smith. "A loan with aggressive rates of interest and strict repayment schedule is a quicker way to ruin someone than denying them payment. Debt, my boy. Debt is control."

Sir Finney was the type to grant a loan with stomach-churning interest rates, then send ruffians to torch her cousin's mill to eradicate any chance of repayment. There were a thousand cruelties the man could perform while waiting to replenish his turkey red supply. Mercy, he could trick Lottie and Don into producing turkey red for him, under the pretence of evaluating the suitability of their mill for larger-scale operations.

Elizabeth's imagination accelerated like a runaway carriage. She couldn't keep track of the awful scenarios rushing into her head.

"Can ye do nothing to stop him?" Thomas asked, a whine creeping into his voice.

Smith drew his walking cane to his shoulder like a rifle. "My boy, the Customs House operates through committee. Contrary to scurrilous ballads, we require a quorum of commissioners to authorise asset seizures and detain suspected wrongdoers. Since John is visiting his mother in Abernethy..."

"Alright!" Elizabeth wished they'd stop talking to give her time to think.

"Besides, Dillon operates a fast carriage. He will outpace all but the most determined horseman. He's gone, madam."

23

Dillon departing Edinburgh was the worst news they could possibly receive, Elizabeth thought as she climbed the turnpike to their rooms.

Then she saw their front door stood ajar.

Or maybe not.

Thomas bunched his fists and glanced at his wife. She moved to the side—out of the line of sight of inside—and nodded. Thomas pressed the door open and tiptoed inside.

Elizabeth gave it a second then decided to follow. There was a stillness in the air which made her decide whoever had forced the door was long departed.

Glass crunched under Elizabeth's heel.

She didn't need to look around their destroyed apartment to know what she was stepping on. Sir Finney's thugs may have scoured the place for valuables—good luck finding spare coins or pretty jewels—or they may have only been told to send their warning and leave.

But the distillation and Nooth apparatus used for her experiments was cleaner than their crockery, and occupied pride of place on the central table. Anyone would notice the attention paid to its set-up and upkeep, even if they didn't understand its purpose.

Her husband staggered past her, a faint glow around his arms. She let him search their rooms, hoping to strike down any concealed intruders. Elizabeth knew better: his message delivered, Dillon was gone.

Thomas returned at a slower pace, perhaps surprised to see his wife immobile and expressionless. He saw her looking at the glass shards, then reached for her hand.

"It's alright, sweetheart. We'll buy new apparatus."

Except they wouldn't. It took years of saving: pennies hidden out of sight and temptation; another round of haggling at the markets even when she was tired and wanting to pay those extra shillings to make the transaction go faster. The laboratory glassware she'd got discounted due to some minor imperfections, through a fortuitous relationship with the glassblower and a cancelled order.

"They destroyed everything," she said. If there was supposed to be emotion in her voice, she couldn't summon it.

Where her prized glassware once stood, Elizabeth found a notebook. She didn't recognise it as one of her own, and it took a minute to understand why it seemed familiar.

The green marble ledger belonged to Dillon, it was the one she'd tracked across town.

Dillon helpfully left a ribbon at the page he wanted her to turn to first, least she misunderstand his intent.

Lottie's name underlined in red ink, the lines etched so fiercely they'd almost stabbed through the paper.

There was new writing too, scrawled diagonally on the blank sheet opposite.

FLOUR ON YOUR HANDS, MRS FULHAME. AN UNSUBTLE MAGPIE.

24

They could have surveyed the wreckage for hours or seconds. Thomas sprang into action first.

"There's nothing for it—we must warn Don and Lottie." Thomas cast around their apartment, mentally building a list of provisions. "I'll get in a carriage to Glasgow this afternoon, I suppose ye can stay here provided Dr Black and the others look out for ye. We've lost several days to Sir Finney, but it'll be a week or so before he can put his retaliation into action, no?"

"There's little I can do if you're out of Edinburgh," she said quietly.

"What is there to be done?" Thomas sounded weary. "Dillon's left with his prize. All we can do is try and protect yer brother-in-law and family from the consequences."

"If we scatter on the four winds then yes, there's nothing that can be done."

Elizabeth knew her husband. He was preparing to rush to Glasgow on behalf of his in-laws because he believed it the honourable thing to do, not because his heart was set on it.

The left side of his face was swollen and bruised, his usually ruddy complexion pale. He couldn't put weight on one ankle.

"Just give me the opportunity to appeal to Dr Black," Elizabeth said. "Give us the chance to agree upon a plan. See if we can do more than save Lottie from bankruptcy."

"We're between a rock and a hard place, Elizabeth," Thomas said, sinking into a chair. "I hate our options as much as ye do. But Professors Cullen and Black—bless the men—are going to do whatever they want to do, regardless of what we say."

Elizabeth refused to believe it. She rejected this. "No, it's better we try to corral the professors, make them listen to me."

Thomas sighed. "It's not that I don't support ye..."

"But that's just it, Thomas—you don't support me."

"Sweetheart!"

"No, you provide the bare minimum tolerance for my chemistry experiments, even though I'm more likely to make a profit off my studies than you, and you always let Dr Cullen insult me." Elizabeth was dimly aware the words coming out of her mouth were more serious than she'd planned, but it was a relief to let them rush out.

"That's ridiculous, Elizabeth." Thomas' agitation rose. "I defended ye against Dr Cullen a few days ago, and ye were there when I admonished the boys in our first lodgings..."

"I hate it when you do this." Her husband would seize upon a careless 'always' or 'never' like it were driftwood in a storm and she could never separate him from it. "You know what I mean and you're distracting me with semantics."

Thomas tried to pat her hand. He both understood and didn't understand what he did during arguments. "It's not fair that ye say I *always* abandon ye to mockery, when there are plenty of times when I didn't."

"You know what I mean," Elizabeth repeated. The words came out of her mouth faster than she could control them.

Belatedly she realised this wasn't good. She took a breath and tried again. "I feel like it's a chore for you to show your support, that you do it when I remind you, or you feel it convenient. When it should be instinctive."

"Sweetheart, Dr Cullen is a genius, but we all know he's old and set in his ways. Of course he's going to object to yer involvement in natural philosophy; that doesn't mean anything."

"It means a lot. The Royal and Philosophical Societies of Britain are filled with men like Dr Cullen."

Thomas wordlessly exclaimed and broke away from his wife, stomping towards the window.

"Why do ye now care about those societies? Just last week ye were telling me about Mrs Monro-MacDonald's *salon* and how excited ye were to talk about natural philosophy with other ladies. Then ye told me it was all a mistake and ye wouldn't go back. Why are ye suddenly worrying about the Royal Society?" He sounded wounded and frustrated, as if Elizabeth changed her mind to keep him in the dark.

"I was mistaken, all right?" Elizabeth's voice rose. "I thought I'd be happy sipping tea and talking about kitchen chemistry with other ladies, but I realised I'm not. I *want* to make contributions to chemistry that natural philosophers will respect, I *want* to prove Dr Cullen wrong and that I'm not some...some...silly girl with her head full of frilly fancies."

"Elizabeth..." Thomas drew towards her again. "These natural philosophers are going to laugh at ye. They're going to see "Mrs Fulhame" and think yer a joke. I know it hurts when Dr Cullen says something stupid about yer experiments—I'm sorry if ye think I don't care when he says that sort of thing—but you'll get bores who've never met ye, and some women too I imagine, acting in even worse ways."

Elizabeth wiped her eyes with the back of her hand and sniffed. She stared out the window. "So that means I must become even better. Run my experiments in triplicate or quadruplicate, keep a record of where the sun is in the sky and what I had for supper on the day I run a reaction. Give them no chink of weakness to question my methodology. I just..." she wiped her eyes again. "I just want to know you're not... embarrassed by me."

"Elizabeth!" Thomas wrapped his arms around her. Hair curls brushed against her nose. "Yer a force of nature. I dunno, like a goddess from the heavens walking around Edinburgh making witty remarks about fruit-sellers. How could I be ashamed of ye? If you can make those metallic dyeing experiments work—I worry it will be very difficult, ye know I've told ye that already—then of course ye can tell the Royal Society what you achieved."

"We just need the money," Elizabeth mumbled, not trusting herself to respond directly.

Thomas laughed. "We'll get the money, wifey. Don't ye worry."

* * *

Until the moment Cullen shuffled into their ruined apartment, Elizabeth feared her summons wouldn't work.

"Hmm, that's a lot of destruction," he said. The Fulhames did their best to tidy up the mess, but Cullen couldn't miss the damaged furniture and ripped clothing piled in the bed chamber.

"We'll manage, Dr Cullen," Elizabeth said stiffly. Cullen didn't argue.

A few minutes later Black came.

"Will this be all?" Cullen asked, with a trace of sarcasm.

"Yes." Elizabeth decided against inviting Tytler for this very reason, and she didn't feel close enough to Smith to send a message requesting his presence. Besides, too many august, bickering gentlemen would hamper her shot at persuasion.

"I understand your distress, Mrs Fulhame," Cullen began. "Sir Finney has behaved in an abhorrent fashion. Dr Black and myself will do everything to ensure neither of you come to harm."

"I did not doubt that for one minute, dear doctor. I hoped we could use this opportunity to discuss the recovery of Monsieur Moreau's papers."

Black's mouth tightened, as if he suspected this is what would happen.

Elizabeth needed care to thread this needle. "Part of the reason we're in this mess is because the left hand didn't know what the right was doing. Sir Finney reacted strongly to our simultaneous actions, and I believe with better coordination we'll be able to bet him."

Cullen's expression was harder to read. "The sense of lost control and helpless is very familiar to me, madam. I dislike the sensation as much as you do. However, it is better we channel that energy into the productive options available to us now he's disappeared westwards."

Thomas had expressed surprised at Elizabeth's intention to invite Cullen, given her outburst over his intransigent behaviour. To her, it was a disdainful yet necessary gamble. Black was the cautious pragmatist; Cullen was the hot-head. Right now the former would be repressing his grudge against Dillon as strongly as the latter would be stoking it.

"Hope is far from lost." She took care to speak as calmly as possible, least the gathering dismiss her argument as womanly theatrics. "Sir Finney has kept the turkey red process close to him ever since he stole it. The papers are travelling west with him, they won't arrive before he does. Whatever he's set into motion can still be halted."

Cullen heaved a hearty sigh, summarising his views of the

229

situation without resorting to syllables. "But Dillon is well away from Edinburgh; and must have covered a day's distance by now."

She had to remind herself this wasn't personal for Black and Cullen the way it was for her. Black would get the Board of Manufacturer's consultancy money regardless; Dillon had gone out of his way to avoid attacking him directly. It was her husband and Lottie who stood to lose the most from Dillon riding into the sunset.

"Then let's force him back to Edinburgh." Elizabeth looked at the older men across from her. "Or do you think we have a chance at catching up with him in Perthshire?"

Cullen grimaced, no doubt hating the thought of how bumpy *that* coach ride would be.

"It appears you were a victim of your own success, madam," he said. "Dillon must have felt you had a shot at getting the turkey red papers back, which prompted his exit from the game."

It was a small detail, but it annoyed Elizabeth Cullen said 'felt' instead of 'realised'. She wouldn't be distracted at this critical juncture, though.

"Once Sir Finney grows bored with the objects of his attention, he is quick to discard them," Black added. His dark, contained anger had faded today. Maybe he'd decided Moreau's assassination attempt would have happened regardless, or he'd decided little could be gained from red dye experimentation. That didn't mean it wouldn't return, just that the Fulhame's apartment wouldn't be its venue.

Elizabeth had used the past hour to ponder how to motivate these philosophers to action. Pride, rather than altruism, appeared the strongest lever. She needed to convince them that luring Dillon back to Edinburgh was do-able. If that was fixed, Cullen's ego in particular should leap to bridge the gap.

"Well, we need to transmute his attention onto something

else." Elizabeth splayed her hand across the sheets of paper she'd amassed. "The only language Sir Finney speaks is that of commerce, the only thing he cares about is his own enrichment. Does he have any lawyers in Glasgow?" Cullen and Black shock their heads. "Right, his Scottish legal and business affairs remain concentrated in Edinburgh, as do the people who attend to Sir Finney's wealth in his absence. A crisis in his businesses or sudden asset loss would be enough to warrant his return to Edinburgh."

Elizabeth could sense a tremor of apprehension in Black's posture, suggesting he wished to object to the way the conversation was going. Cullen, on the other hand, avoiding looking his direction lest he spot his colleague's distress signals.

"Actually, it's safer for Monsieur Moreau when Sir Finney isn't in the same city as him. We have the opportunity—albeit not without risk—to get him on a ship to Germany, London or the Americas."

Elizabeth had worried about that. But she wasn't going to let Cullen wheedle her off track.

"However, if Sir Finney returns to Edinburgh to deal with our manufactured crisis, it clears the road for Moreau to head west unmolested."

Men got away with bold proclamations like this all the time.

"It'll take an army to empty Moray House of his valuables, Mrs Fulhame," Cullen said. "Since our inability to gain access to that facility has led us to this mess I'm not sure we are any closer to our goals."

"I'm not talking about those trifles." Elizabeth wondered if Cullen was being deliberately disingenuous. "You know well as I do news of that on the Glasgow road wouldn't so much as delay his breakfast. I'm talking about the complete destruction of Dillon's entire business folio."

"Fanciful! We have days to act, not six months."

"A company's worth can be destroyed in a day on the Exchange," Elizabeth snapped. "Heavens, an industry can be ruined within the hour."

The lines on Cullen's face deepened. "Not through any fair means *I* know of, madam. You're suggesting the use of... discouraged business practices to devalue Sir Finney's stock?"

"Does my beloved husband need to repeat everything I say for you to understand the import of my delicate, feminine words? Of course that's what I'm talking about."

She wondered a little too late if Cullen would be outraged by her suggestion of illegal stock manipulation. By the way Cullen shrugged and flushed in annoyance, it did not seem morality was a contention. Thomas had already heard some of her ideas so didn't react. Black's expression remained wreathed in shadow.

"All the same, I'm not convinced you've thought through the practicalities of what you're suggesting, Mrs Fulhame. For a start, we aren't targeting a solitary company in Sir Finney's name."

"No, Sir Finney's assets are spreading across five registered companies and as many shell organisations...that we know of. That's a wretched mess of threads to unravel."

Cullen huffed. "I already drew up a list of Sir Finney's concealed assets, madam. I counted a total of fifteen."

"But are you sure you counted *these* companies, Dr Cullen?" Elizabeth slid a torn sheet of paper across the desk. "The provenance of some of these shell companies were well-hidden."

Cullen looked at the list and grunted, then set it down next to his own.

"It doesn't change the impossibility of the task."

Elizabeth could see Black edging into the centre of the room, no doubt intending to physically position himself between the pair.

"I've given the matter some thought and I wouldn't call the task impossible." She set her chin an inch higher. "With respect to the good doctor. It only requires three actors in an interplay of seemingly unconnected events within the Royal Exchange, with the objective of sowing a convincing bed of pecuniary doubt."

"Nonsense!" Cullen shot to his feet and began pacing. Black—a few steps away from securing his blockade—looked dismayed.

"William..."

"Mrs Fulhame's endeavours to assist are greatly appreciated..."

"William..." Black's tone took a despairing inflection.

"...but the task can be accomplished with only *one* person and she needs to cease with this meddling."

Elizabeth wracked her brains to see if she'd missed an obvious trick. She knew she'd riled Cullen up, but hadn't expected this pivot from denying her proposal to one-upping it. "It can't be done alone."

"Of course it can be done alone." Cullen wheeled past Black, his finger coming to rest an inch before her face. "Provided the actor at its centre keeps the coolest comportment, under stress that would crush an amateur."

"William, I know Mrs Fulhame is not casting aspersions upon your intelligence..."

"Quite the contrary," Elizabeth managed, too curious to retain her indignation. "But Sir Finney's activities are spread across multiple sectors, and I imagine the merchants who do business with him don't know the full extent of his holdings. Our attempts to undermine him therefore run the risk of fulfilling his agenda for him, namely wiping out the Scottish economy. That's why it needs a subtle approach from multiple angles."

"I am well aware of the facts, madam." Cullen allowed

Black to lower his waging finger and guide him away from Elizabeth. "You are a woman of rare intelligence, Mrs Fulhame, but you have only been on this Earth a third of the time I have, and I think there's a trick or two I could teach you."

Elizabeth thought for a moment. "I will accept Dr Cullen's scheme to fulfil the first stage of the plan—inducement—provided he supports my plan for the evacuation of Monsieur Moreau."

"An acceptable compromise," Black said hastily, though Cullen didn't look inclined to disagree. Elizabeth supposed his ego had already been satisfied.

"Agreed." Cullen straightened. Then he paused and coughed.

"Err, Joe? If you don't mind, there's a couple of things I need to pick your brains about..."

25

The Edinburgh Royal Exchange enjoyed pride of place on the High Street. Its construction several years prior involved the gleeful trampling of the lands between the street and Nor Loch basin, displacing hundreds of families into an already overcrowded city. If confronted with the displacement, the architects and city planners would most likely shrug. There was life, and there was Commerce. One of those things was cheap, the other priceless.

In contrast to the rickety, bulging tenements on either side, the grandiose Exchange—set behind a large quadrangle—swept visitors into its heart. Fragrant wares spilled out from the booths set into the outer arcade. Enter through the main archway from the High Street and you were transported to the Caribbean, with sweet whispers of sugar and cardamon. By the time you'd crossed the square and entered the covered piazza, clean pine notes and sawdust drew you deep into a Bavarian forest.

Merchants, jobbers and speculators packed the colon-naded piazza fronting the main building, preferring to mingle outdoors rather than occupy the coffeeshops behind them, because it allowed them greater freedom to gesticulate.

That said, a merchant from London would consider the Edinburgh Exchange as sedate as a library, for although it approached noon on a Wednesday, a man could stand in the piazza and still hear himself think.

It was why the click of heels and cane on flagstone from an old figure in a billowing academic gown was audible as he crossed the quadrangle with barely a glance at his surroundings, before stepping into the King's Head coffeehouse on the left. The figure took his time fussing to find a table and ordering a frothy capuchin, paying scant heed to the merchants dispersed around the room. The traders who gravitated to this coffeehouse were more solitary and cautious by nature than the ones outdoors, and they tutted at the disruption.

Once settled, the new arrival focused on the clerk seated next to him, who up until that moment wasn't sure the visitor noticed his presence, let alone intended to consult with him.

"The name's Dr William Cullen. I have some business with shares that must be seen to." He waved a scratchy list under the clerk's nose.

The clerk wanted to object that he knew he looked young for his age, but he wasn't an errant schoolboy needing brought to heel. Then he looked properly at the man's face.

"Are you keeping well, Dr Cullen?" The clerk hesitated. "You look a little pale."

"Quite alright, young lad." The physician bristled. "Venerability doesn't bring out the best in people."

The clerk tried to maintain normal conversation as he went through his ledgers, asking which shares Cullen wished to buy.

As the clerk worked, his client waved a messenger boy over, sliding him a note and coin. He sipped his capuchin, seemingly with relish. The clerk's heart rate pounded with nerves as he tried to decide if his instincts should prompt him to action.

"I'm afraid I'm missing the pertinent ledger Dr Cullen. If you can excuse me for a few minutes?" The doctor grumbled at this minor inconvenience, but shooed the clerk away.

Once back in the piazza, the clerk scanned the crowd for his supervisor, Isaac, glancing to the coffeehouse window to make sure he wasn't being observed. Finally, he tugged at his supervisor's sleeve.

"Stewart?"

The clerk hopped behind a pillar out of sight of the coffee-house window, and wrung his hands until Isaac followed.

"What on earth has gotten in to you, Stewart?"

"Well, there's a gentleman calling himself Dr Cullen asking to re-invest his shares into sherry importation compa-nies as well as..."

Isaac glanced around the pillar with obvious irritation.

"Dr Cullen is the most celebrated physician in Scotland, addle pate!"

"But—" Stewart protested. "But sir, I don't think it actu-ally *is* Dr Cullen."

"I beg your pardon?" The supervisor looked again. They were far enough away to be out of earshot, but there was no missing the black gown, tumbling physician wig and long, doleful face.

"He's acting strange, sir." Stewart started speaking faster, trying to get ahead of the next interruption. "He has too much powder on his face, those clothes aren't quite the right size..."

"Well, even if it's a crank—which is mighty peculiar not to say improbable—he won't get very far with any transaction."

Stewart was practically skipping on the spot. "But that's the queerest part, sir. His paperwork is perfect. He recounted his previous transaction details from memory—corroborating our account records—the handwriting on the order is a perfect match for the handwriting we have in our files."

"Stewart, I don't understand what's gotten in to you. The man says he's William Cullen, he looks like William Cullen, his paperwork is in order. Get back to serving the good doctor."

"But sir..." Stewart looked desperate. "How familiar are you with Dr Cullen?"

"Never met the man in person." Isaac felt uneasy. Stewart had been a model clerk for all the years he'd worked here. He'd never wasted anyone's time on flights of fancies like this before. "Who usually attends to Dr Cullen's accounts? Is it Rob?"

"Rob is still recuperating from his infection, sir." Stewart paused. "Actually, the man calling himself Dr Cullen asked about Rob as soon as he came in. Now I recall, he seemed slightly relieved when I told him he wasn't here today."

"Are you sure?"

Isaac laid a hand on the clerk trying to squeeze past them. "Jeffrey—a moment. Look at that fellow seated at Stewart's table and tell me who that is?"

"Why, it's Dr Cullen, is it not?"

"How sure are you?"

"Would swear on my ma's Bible, sir. I see Dr Cullen around town all the time."

Stewart was not to be deterred. "His countenance doesn't strike you as unusual?"

"Goodness...what has he got on his face?"

At this exclamation, nearby jobbers looked up from their conversations with a frown. The ones deep in negotiations scowled and took a few steps away from the noise, but the younger jobbers slacking from proper work edged closer.

"Of all the facades you could don, why choose Dr Cullen?" Issac continued. "He's a man well-known in Edinburgh. If an ill-intentioned confidence man came in here claiming he were a Jewish merchant from London wishing to take advantage of our rates, no one would know better."

"Nonsense!" said a silver-haired merchant leaning on his cane, who'd clearly been waiting for Issac to finish talking with Stewart so he could ask his questions. "An affluent stranger would arise curiosity at best, suspicion at worst. Onlookers would scrutinise his presence and transactions. Who among us even noticed this supposed Dr Cullen cross the Piazza and make his requests? And if we did, don't we usually give the venerable professor the benefit of the doubt and suppose a sensibility to his investment decisions?"

Several of Isaac's colleagues nodded. He'd abandoned them to deal with Stewart and they'd grown impatient enough to follow him along the piazza in a bid to attract his attention. Now a handful of speculators were elbowing closer into the forming knot, having made the assumption that an important discussion was taking place.

"I heard a similar scam took place in London last winter…" Piped one of those speculators.

"There's no scam here…" Isaac insisted, trying to mute the excited whispers.

The speculator was undeterred. "Like I said, a company selling timber for warships was shorted on the Exchange before news of the peace treaty was made public. The first individual collected the timber shares, and the act of shorting —betting the timber stock value would fall—was performed by the accomplice. That must be what's happening here: the confidence man is collecting the necessary shares without attracting suspicion."

"But this isn't a confidence man…" Issac realised he was saying this to quell the agitation among the crowd around him, not because he knew it was really Dr Cullen. "Besides, manipulations that sophisticated never take place in Edinburgh."

"Dr Cullen!" The cry sent the gathering crowd twitching apart with guilty expressions. A tall noble with fur-lined teal coat approached the seated doctor, beaming.

"He knows Dr Cullen," Isaac whispered. The two figures clasped hands and settled into a lively conversation.

"So he does..." muttered Stewart, his lip drooping. Isaac wanted to reprimand Stewart for his time-wasting fancies, but he too felt a tug of disappointment as the conversation concluded after a few minutes, with no sign of anything amiss.

But as the noble walked across the piazza towards the huddle, an odd series of expressions passed across his face. He was staring at the ground, chewing his lower lip and frowning as if there was an itch on his person he couldn't locate.

The second Isaac caught the nobleman glancing backwards at the doctor—now settled back into his cup—boldness overtook him.

"My lord...sorry to trouble you..."

Beckoning the confused noble, who identified himself as Advocate Henry Gorgie, behind a pillar, a breathless Isaac got through his explanation without cringing.

Advocate Gorgie did not immediately brush aside the merchants.

"You are correct in supposing a peculiar reaction on my part to the exchange, but I struggle to identify the cause. Dr Cullen seemed in fine spirits—I congratulated him on the latest edition of his Materia Medica treatise and we spoke about the revisions—but his manner of speaking seemed odd, and when I mentioned "Clarice" he didn't seem to realise I was talking about my nephew. Which doesn't make sense because Clarice is a frequent topic of conversation between us."

"Could that not be the infirmities of old age?"

"I suppose, but on the topic of his treatise he has never been more lucid. We'd corresponded privately about some of his proposed updates, and I wager his motivation for some of these changes is not common knowledge."

Isaac's confidence in the charade was growing, which gave him the courage to sound the note of caution.

"Looking at him again, my lord—careful you aren't spotted!—and tell me if anything further strikes you amiss."

Advocate Gorgie squinted and hemmed. Then he blinked rapidly.

"That's not Dr Cullen's cane!" The crowd shushed his exclamation. Another pair of merchants wandered over. All other business in the vicinity had ceased.

"Dr Cullen's cane is light Malacca with a golden handle. See how that one is mahogany with a carved snake running down its side?"

"Heavens! Are you certain?"

"Deathly. Dr Cullen is never without his cane. He's had that one ever since he came to Edinburgh."

"This is serious..." muttered Isaac, aware he sounded more excited than dismayed. "We should bring Mr Smith over from the Customs office." Smith was the man in the Exchange closest to Cullen, who could tell without a doubt if the man in front of them was an imposter.

He gestured to a clump of messenger boys. "You! Send for Mr Smith."

"He just departed," one of them piped up. "Two minutes ago, while ye were gabbin'."

"Where?"

"Dinnae ken. He received a letter an' immediately pelted out the door."

A few minutes ago, the Cullen imposter had beckoned a messenger boy to Stewart's table and handed him a note. Isaac couldn't see the boy nearby, but he had a nasty suspicion the two events were connected.

"And Mr Smith didn't say how long he'd be, or where he was going?" The boys looked blank, and Isaac admitted there was no reason they'd know.

"This is truly a remarkable mimic," Advocate Gorgie breathed, leaning his forearm against the pillar. "He completely fooled me: were it not for you gentlemen's intervention I would have left the Exchange convinced I'd spoken intimately with Dr Cullen this morning."

"This is no street hustler," muttered a lawyer at his elbow. "I wager this criminal has taken months to perfect his art."

An uneasy silence descended upon the group. An opportunistic crook looking to empty a notable physician's accounts was one thing, but the level of deceit here suggested a different scale of theft and forgery.

The fact that Adam Smith was temporarily—conveniently—lured out of the building was worrying indeed.

"The shares he wants, is there anything of note?"

"It appears no more than a grocer's list," Stewart said, puffing with self-import. Isaac cursed himself for not taking the document off the boy sooner. "I see no connection here."

"Well obviously he wouldn't make his intentions obvious," Isaac scoffed. "I imagine half or a two-thirds of those are decoys thrown in to blind the casual observer to his true machinations."

"Marcus, can you see any patterns or connections here?"

Marcus squinted at the list. "Not immediately, but I can take it back to my office…"

"We don't have all day," Isaac hissed. "The imposter is sitting there drinking his ridiculous frothy beverage."

"Should we summon the Town Guards? Who knows how much mischief this actor will do."

"An actor?" Grumbled a middle-aged clerk, elbowing into the centre of the ring.

"Yes," Stewart tried to explain. "We noticed…"

"Well, you better wind down your *noticing* and get back to serving your clients." The new arrival glared at Stewart. "While you were chitter-chattering Stewart, the great Dr Cullen himself started complaining about the hold-up. He said he'd been waiting for over fifteen minutes. Scalded the ears of everyone unfortunate enough to be in the coffeeshop."

Stewart's eyes widened. "Well, if you go back in and, err, tell him…"

"I won't be telling him anything," snapped the older clerk. "Because I completed the requested share purchases, grovelled like a underling and sent him on his way with a thousand apologies, none of which dented his disappointment."

There was a collective gasp in the circle.

"Neil, please tell me you didn't…"

"Tell you I didn't do my job? Of course not, I completed the bloody transaction as fast as I bloody could." Resentment dripped off Neil, having borne the brunt of a client's displeasure meant for his junior colleague. He didn't notice the rising agitation around him. "Whatever could warrant a hold up for such a simple transaction?"

"Where…where is this man now?" Isaac croaked, trying to shove a hole in the swirling crowd of clerks and jobbers so he could see out.

"Where is Dr Cullen? How am I supposed to know? He walked out the door just now." The knot of people twisted, but no one could spot the floating black robes.

Neil finally absorbed the mood of his colleagues. "What the devil is going on?"

"He got the shares…" Isaac breathed, his heart pounding. He needed to lean against something, before his legs gave out. "The lord have mercy."

CL JARVIS

"Do you have paper and a quill, boy?" a blanching lawyer asked the weakest-looking clerk, not taking his eye off Stewart's list.

"Here, my lord."

"Good. If you'll hand me the list..." He proceeded to copy out the company names into a ruby pocketbook.

Seeing him, the gathering erupted.

"Actually I might need a copy too..."

"My secretary should appraise the list..."

"Same here, old friend. Better safe than sorry, right?"

As the wealthy men of Edinburgh rushed off to check their portfolios didn't contain any investments on the list, the man calling himself William Cullen sauntered away from the unfolding chaos, licking the last trace of capuchin from his lips and smiling.

* * *

Anna Cullen was the fastest on her feet. As soon as her husband walked in the door she was handing him a damp cloth and pointing towards the washing bowl.

"Thank you, dear." Cullen wiped his face. "Get this wretched gown off me, I tripped over the hem about eight times."

Black stepped forward and helped Cullen out of his robe as if he were a manservant.

"Thanks, Joe. I heard it rip, sorry about that."

"Not a problem," Black replied, folding the gown over his arm. Head still buried in the washcloth, Cullen handed Black his physician cane.

"May no man live long enough to see himself become his own parody," Cullen sighed, letting his wife dab the remnants of powder from his hairline and neck.

"Everything worked?" Black asked.

244

"Yes," said Cullen. "It was beautiful to behold."

Strangely, Black took what Elizabeth recognised as defensive positioning between Cullen and the front door. She didn't have time to wonder why, because at that moment Adam Smith burst into the Cullen house and resolved her confusion.

Smith quivered with indignation in the parlour doorway. "It cannot be a coincidence that this morning I receive an urgent missive requesting I call upon Dr James Hutton of all people, find him not at home, and then upon my return to the Exchange I discover eighteen bankrupt companies, twice as many hyperventilating lawyers, and wild rumours of a *bearish* William Cullen imposter short selling stock?"

"I know you exert a stabilising influence over the Customs and Exchange floor, Adam. But I don't think your sudden absence is *that* destabilising."

Smith glowered. "A cursory glance at the list of tainted enterprises was enough to tell me you were the mastermind of this scheme, William. Though by that point the damage to Sir Finney's wealth was already done."

Cullen massaged his temples in a show of minimal concern towards his outraged friend.

"You know I disprove of such craven, underhand market manipulations..."

"Underhand, or an invisible hand?"

"I can see the hands behind this well enough!"

"I apologise for not taking you into our confidence on this one, Adam." Black's low voice spread across the room, cooling everything it touched like a cloud on a scorching day. "I think you perceive our reasons."

"And Sir Finney's shares haven't recovered their value?"

"They haven't and they won't, madam." Smith ignored Anna Cullen's attempts to hand him a glass of claret. "They're worthless until someone unspools your game."

"Which won't be yourself?"

Smith snorted. "I deplore Sir Finney, and I deplore market manipulations in either direction: up or down. The incentive for me to point out the scheme remains low."

Elizabeth made eye contact with Thomas, who smiled.

"How long do we have?"

"I suspect a rider has already been dispatched west," Cullen said, settling onto the settee. "He'll catch Sir Finney by the evening."

"Which means we can expect him back in Edinburgh tomorrow."

Following her elation at Cullen's success, Elizabeth's nerves returned.

"Good," she said, hoping her voice wasn't trembling. "We can commence the next stage of the plan." Would the venerable physician walk back on his agreement?

Cullen's piercing gaze returned to her. "Out with it, madam. Remember that we need to get poor Monsieur Moreau out of Edinburgh once we've secured his papers."

"I can assure you, Dr Cullen, every desired outcome is already interlaced into my course of action..."

* * *

Elizabeth found Lydia in her boudoir. She coughed in what she hoped was a mildly threatening manner.

Lydia tried to pretend the appearance of this intruder was barely worth her attention. She didn't quite succeed.

"As you can imagine," Elizabeth said, walking further into the room, "the *bonnie monde* of Edinburgh were quite scandalised to learn Sir Finney Dillon brought his mistress to the George Square Assembly, and during our subsequent chit chatter a noblewoman admitted she knew you were kept in St James Square."

Thank you, Mrs Monro-MacDonald, and your discerning lady philosophers.

Lydia flicked a ringlet off her shoulder. "The gentlewomen affect disdain for me, and snub me in public. So isn't it surprising they nonetheless know my exact whereabouts and appointment calendar better than myself? Yet that doesn't explain how you got into my private residence."

"Friends in low places, as well as high."

Moira knew to ask Sheila, who knew to ask Harry. No one hesitated to let a water carrier into the building.

What did Lydia know of her master's ulterior motives for acquiring the turkey red dye? Had she any inkling of phlogiston-wielding?

"Did you master warn you about me?" Elizabeth asked, letting her hands fall by her sides.

Lydia set down her comb, freeing her hands. "He spoke about you and your husband in derogatory terms, going on about you at surprising length one evening while I tried to enjoy the opera. Does that answer your question?"

It was unlikely Lydia knew about phlogiston-wielding, but she was a smart woman. Though she remained seated, Elizabeth watched her pale hands rest on the toilette. A weapon—improvised or not—could easily be within her grasp.

"Is this all you want from life? Being some man's whore-in-a-box?" Lydia's apartment was tastefully furnished, but not much bigger than the Fulhame's lodgings. "Sir Finney discards people all the time, once they stop being useful to him."

"I wonder if you believe you're the first person to ask me such an *insightful* question?" Lydia gave a dainty snort. "Rich men discard young lovers once their beauty fades? Gosh, I never noticed. Do you know what I saw in that disgusting Leith tavern, m'lady? Ladies of pleasure in a far worse condition than me. Yet I wager I was the oldest plying the trade there that night. Their looks deserted them—or were beaten out of them—at a far younger age than me. Most of them will be dead of the pox before they reached two and thirty. Every month I live in comfortable surroundings is a gift others didn't receive, and I intend to enjoy it while I can." She looked at Elizabeth, a faint blush spreading over her cheeks. "Not all of us have your opportunities and the luxury of an indulgent husband."

In a sense it didn't matter what Lydia said, or how she justified her existence. Elizabeth supposed she fancied herself better than this courtesan, but misplaced superiority wouldn't help her accomplish the task in hand.

"Well," she said, stepping forward and flexing her hands. "Forgive me Lydia, but I'm about to do something that's not lady-like at all..."

26

With that business conducted, Elizabeth returned to Cullen's house. She knew there was no feasible way Dillon could reach Edinburgh before mid-morning tomorrow, but she still glanced around South Gray's Close warily, fearful of another confrontation before she felt ready.

The men in the room gave her quizzical looks, but Elizabeth did nothing more than confirm her success with a nod.

Smith sat next to Black, keeping space between himself and Cullen, who he still appeared disgruntled with. Despite Black's culpability in the Exchange scheme, Smith evidently forgave his friend quicker.

Elizabeth cleared his throat.

"Sir Finney will be expecting us to waylay him on the outskirts of Edinburgh, or possibly when he disembarks at his living quarters. Onlookers and pedestrians will give him a sense of security, so will be more vulnerable to ambush en route."

"Which way do you expect him to return by?" Smith asked.

"From the west," she said. "He was taking the usual route

to Glasgow before we forced him to turn back. He'll come back through the New Town." Consultation with Moira and her water-carriers suggested this was the route Dillon left by. The streets of New Town were wide and scrubbed by copious sunlight. He'd prefer them to the narrow, twisting route through Grassmarket or Cowgate.

"So let's catch him on North Bridge!" Thomas said, slapping his thighs.

Cullen looked sideways at Thomas. "Unless you're waiting at the ends, there's no quick avenues for rescue or escape."

"Well, exactly. That's the same fact Sir Finney and his cronies will observe, so they won't suspect an ambush."

"Until they see us standing there waiting for them." Smith pointed out.

Elizabeth looked at her husband. Then she looked at Cullen. He better hold up his end of their bargain during the next few minutes, she thought.

"But perhaps there is a way to strike from a position of concealment..."

* * *

Black and the Fulhames huddled under the central arch of the North Bridge in swampy grassland that was once the Nor Loch. Buildings clustered on both sides of the valley: on the right, stiff rows of New Town houses marched almost out of sight. On the left an uneven scramble of city tenements, looking ready to slip off the precarious ledge they were constructed on.

Black grimaced to himself, but said nothing. He avoided looking at the Fulhames, and concentrated instead on a distant figure standing on the Princes Street embankment several hundred metres away.

"Do we know Mr Smith can see onto the bridge from there?" Elizabeth asked.

"His spyglass is powerful enough," Black said, still watching his friend.

"But he's high enough that he can see who is coming onto the bridge?"

Elizabeth tucked a stray strand of hair behind her ear. It was windier out here than in the confines of the High Street.

"Won't passersby think it queer Smith is watching the street with a spyglass?" Thomas asked, rubbing his hands together.

"Queerer than anything else Adam does? Probably not." Black's bicorne hat was snugly pulled down to his ears. Having talked through Elizabeth's plan, Thomas elected to forgo his hat and wig.

Elizabeth wondered how she could have missed the poor weather coming in from the North Sea. The only blessing was casual pedestrians avoided the North Bridge in blustery weather. The balustrades didn't offer much comfort or protection.

Thomas cracked a grin and wiggled his brows at her. She knew he was pretending to be unafraid: he was still rubbing his hands together, unable to control them.

Even Black appeared discomposed. Cullen—who couldn't move as fast as the others anyway—would come onto the bridge from the High Street end. His role was to protect Thomas in his escape.

Elizabeth jammed her fists into her armpits to conceal their shaking. They'd been standing in the frigid shadows for only a few minutes, but sunlight rarely warmed the basin.

She almost jumped when Smith made his first signal: one arm vertical, the other outstretched.

Dillon's convoy had just passed him.

"Best get ready for the run-up, eh?" Thomas said, his grin

a little too wide and glassy. Without waiting for a response from his wife, he sauntered away from the bridge.

Elizabeth tried making eye contact with Black, but her nerve failed her and she looked away. The thin lines around his mouth were set, his eyes especially dark.

"It's not a question of reflex," Black said, still focused on Smith. "But the sustained power necessary near the end."

He was lying to them. It was a question of the wind, timing, Thomas' position. Looking up at the stone arch above them, Elizabeth didn't know how to begin calculating what was needed from them or how long the ordeal would last. She was sure Black knew better than her—how could he not—but he'd barely glanced up.

"It should work, though?" Elizabeth could hear the pleading in her voice.

Black finally looked at her, but only for a second. "Alternate then synchronise, madam. Do your best to react fast."

Elizabeth nodded quickly. Out of the corner of her eye she could see Thomas jumping up and down on the spot, but she couldn't bring herself to acknowledge him.

Just then the distant figure of Adam Smith split in two; a white curl peeling away from his dark silhouette. The flag fluttered twice and was then snatched out the sky.

Signal number two.

Black grabbed Elizabeth by both wrists, and moved her a few steps away from the arch.

"They're on the bridge." Elizabeth tried to yank herself free from Black's grip, for his skin was burning. Black only tightened his grip. *"Thomas—RUN."*

Thomas didn't hesitate. He broke into a sprint, hurtling towards them.

Elizabeth could only stare at her husband in horror.

"Kneel, madam."

Black pulled her downwards, nearly causing Elizabeth to

trip over her ankle. She sank into a crouch, kicking the muddy skirt hem away from her feet.

Thomas picked up speed, his strides lengthening.

Black focussed on Elizabeth, unblinking. The crush of his grip blended with the scalding heat from his skin. The phlogiston within her own body bubbled to the surface, rushing into her arms and face.

Reaching a slight rise in the grassland only a metre from them, Thomas leapt as if he were skipping over them.

Elizabeth felt the first blast of force leave Black's hands as the word *"Now"* passed through her mind. Thomas was buffeted in the air barely a foot from their heads, his legs kicking.

As soon as she saw her flailing husband fall towards the arch, Elizabeth concentrated. The second blast must have caught Thomas, because he pitched forwards into the wall, nearly scraping his face scraping on the stone. But then Black fired another blast and his hands pawed upwards.

It was working.

She concentrated harder, not giving gravity a time to catch up with her husband. Black's grip of her wrists pulsed in waves. When his grip relaxed, she let her phlogstonic force loose.

"Halfway up," Black whispered, the faintest voice under the roar of the wind and Thomas' cries.

It didn't occur to Elizabeth to feel exhausted. She concentrated in on the flailing sole of her husband's shoe, the occasion flash of their silver buckle, vanishing into the sky.

When he dropped a metre and nearly knocked his head against the stone, Elizabeth matched her blasts of phlogiston to Black's. Thomas continued to rise. The pair shuffled left and right, occasionally colliding with the wall, for what felt like an eternity.

Then Thomas' arm shot out and he half-rolled, half scrambled over the balustrade and out of sight.

Black immediately let go.

"You're alright, Elizabeth?" he asked.

"Yes..." Elizabeth studied her wrists. They were scratched bright red, but she'd had worse scalds doing the laundry. Trembling uncontrollably, all she wanted was to sink into the loamy earth. It was exhaustion, but also a kind of giddy relief.

It was working. It had worked.

Black ventured a smile. He dabbed away the trickles of blood from his nose. "Adam should be almost at the other end of the bridge by now. William can probably get into position faster than him, though." He pointed to the Theatre Royal and clustered buildings abutting the bridge. "I think we can cut through there onto Princes Street."

A flicker caught Elizabeth's eye further down Princes Street. She squinted, unsure of the significance of what her eyes told her.

"...So why is Mr Smith running towards *us*?"

Black's face was pale at the best of times. Yet it surprised her how much colour he was capable of losing.

A force that wasn't her own compelled Elizabeth's chin up to the sky.

"Oh no..."

27

TEN SECONDS EARLIER

The North Bridge seemed quieter than usual, though it might be that the wind swept all the pedestrians to the edges of the paving.

The convoy—Sir Finney's carriage, protected by an armed rider in every corner—moved quickly across the bridge, but it slowed in the middle, as if recognising something was amiss. One of the horses whinnied in objection. The most grizzled of the riders glanced around, sliding a flintlock from his waistband. Perhaps he saw Adam Smith's signal out the corner of his eye, or maybe he sensed the atmosphere change as phlogiston built up nearby.

Thomas rolled over the balustrade and scrambled to his feet. A second later he was bent double against the wall, almost on all fours. His stomach thrashed inside him. The experience of being buffeted up the side of North Bridge was vaguely akin to their voyage from Dublin as a storm picked up. Thomas had adequate sea legs, but once ashore in Glasgow he wondered if his body would ever lose the sensation of being at sea.

The bridge was quiet, with the slowed convoy a few metres

to his left. If the hired soldiers spotted him at this very moment, they'd assume he was a drunkard. Looking at the scarred, ugly Gaels thumbing their pistol butts, Thomas briefly wondered if it could stay that way.

But no. He needed what was in Sir Dillon's carriage, and if he hesitated any longer he'd miss his opportunity.

Two of the mercenaries glanced at the third man, one with a particularly ferocious scowl. He was probably their ring-leader. The rider nearest to Thomas had a pistol drawn, but he wasn't looking in his direction.

Keeping his eye on the convoy while trying not to stare, Thomas reached both hands into his coat pockets and clenched fistfuls of the fine powder his wife stuffed them with. He'd feared only a sprinkling would remain; now he had to hope his sweaty palms wouldn't ruin what came next.

Cullen should be coming onto the bridge at any minute, but up here Thomas was aware of how long North Bridge was, and that Cullen would need to get into firing range to be of assistance.

Nothing for it.

He dropped his head and pelted towards the nearest rider.

Take down the man most likely to shoot first. Then the mercenary ringleader. Sort the immediate and long-term threats.

"On the right!"

Thomas tossed the fistfuls of finely-ground sawdust into the air, letting phlogiston spark out his fingertips.

Instant ignition.

The horses howled and twisted out of formation. It was like a firework exploded just above Thomas' head height. Noise and smoke consumed the bridge.

The rear-most rider stared at Thomas through the smoke, gulping in shock. Thomas didn't see a pistol in this man's hand, so he ducked around and made for the carriage.

The one leading the formation had already fired his pistol, and was partially concealed in a cloud of smoke. Raising his hand, Thomas sent the furthest rider tumbling with an immobilising blast of yellow light. The men may or not know what phlogiston was, but they'd want to kill Thomas all the same.

Ducking in front of the dark horse before it kicked out, Thomas had a clear run to the carriage, where he could make out a dismayed Sir Finney peering from within.

A gleaming black stallion? Hold on a minute...

The smell of phlogiston tore through Thomas' airways. Not allowing himself time to question or think, he dived to the right. An instant later, a blast of phlogistonic fire collided with the cobblestones where he'd been.

Too high on his own nervous energy to register the pain properly, Thomas rolled over and leapt to his feet, turning around to look Sir Finney in the eye.

How could he have missed the mounted noble? He was dressed in the same nondescript clothes as the other hired mercenaries, but the haughty sneer and pristine curls of hair under the cap couldn't be concealed.

Did that mean the papers were with the decoy in the carriage, or on Sir Finney's person?

Sir Finney was steadying his spooked horse with one hand on the reins, and trying to bear the other on Thomas.

He was ready for the second attack, and flicked a phlogiston blast of his own at the same time. Arion reared into the air and screamed with fright, embers catching in his mane. Sir Finney was a competent rider—he'd not fallen off yet—but this wasn't a war horse.

As Sir Finney brought Arion back onto all fours, his free hand brushed his waistcoat for a fraction of second. That was all the proof Thomas needed. He ran towards Sir Finney, dodging the whip of the carriage driver.

Thomas was no jumper, but he used a blast of force to

propel him eighteen hands into the air, one arm catching Sir Finney's neck.

He just had time to wonder if this was a stupid idea, when Sir Finney's foot caught in the stirrup and after a few seconds of tussle Thomas tumbled head over heel to the ground on the other side. Arion lashed out, but Thomas managed to land on his feet and stumble clear.

Sir Finney's eyes narrowed to slits, and he bared his teeth. The other horseman encircled him, pistols pointed at his heart.

The hired men were hesitating to see if their leader would say anything, or if he expected them to fire of their own accord. There was only one direction Thomas could run, and he did so.

The smell of phlogiston mingled with that of gunpowder. Thomas tossed another fistful of sawdust behind him as a distraction, but embers blew back into his face. He heard the crack of a pistol, but didn't have time to wonder if he felt the bullet. His coattails flapped in the breeze, rising to his shoulder. He only had to cross a few metres, but to Thomas it felt like sprinting across a field. He could no longer hear if another pistol had discharged. Two steps to go.

Thomas vaulted the balustrades, twisting mid-jump to look back at his pursuers. For a moment he felt suspended in the air, staring into Dillon's wide eyes inches from his own. But then gravity tore through his stomach and Thomas allowed paralysing terror to claim him in darkness.

His wife gave him enough time to come to before slapping him.

"You useless fuckster! What were you thinking?" She demanded.

His body ached, but the most pertinent stinging pain

came from his cheek. Damp earth seeped into his clothes, but it didn't appear blood was seeping out.

"Hmm..." came the level voice of Black somewhere out of sight.

"Is Thomas alive? I thought he was dead for sure." Smith hurried up, sounding slightly disappointed that he wasn't approaching a crushed body.

Elizabeth was crying. Thomas tried to ease himself upright, but multiple hands pushed him down.

Thomas suspected nothing he could say right now would calm Elizabeth down, so he didn't even try. "Got the papers," he muttered in the direction of Black and Smith. "Not sure where they are now—think I dropped them."

"They're on my person," Black replied.

"You nearly died," Elizabeth howled, wiping her face. "You didn't tell us you were going to jump back *down*."

"No, it was rather a last-minute decision." Thomas fought free of his restraints and sat up. He tried to take Elizabeth's hand, but she swatted him away. "Sir Finney used a decoy and fought back, giving his guards enough time to grab their second pistols."

"You bastard, you didn't even check to see if Dr Black and I were below you. This wasn't part of the plan. What if we weren't there to slow your fall? What if we'd worn ourselves out getting you *up* and couldn't muster the energy a second time to repeat the procedure in reverse?"

"He jumped backwards, I believe," Smith commented, seemingly committed to saying the least helpful things.

"If I'd looked, I also certainly would have lost my courage," Thomas said. He'd tracked the bulk of the ache to his legs and lower back. "Thought it better to keep my eyes closed."

"We need to get away from the bridge," Black said, coming into view and offering Thomas his hand. There were tracts of blood running from his nose to his mouth and chin. Seeing Thomas stare, Black tried to wipe the worst of it off. "I suspect the guards are coming this way now."

Hauling himself up with Black's aid, Thomas realised the professor's hand was slick with sweat. Knowing that he'd frightened Black as much as his wife caused a flush of guilt inside Thomas; that Elizabeth would over-react was inevitable, but it took a lot to shake Black.

28

Cullen appeared in South Gray's close a few minutes after the others.

"Thomas is alive?" he asked as soon as his front door opened. "Oh, good. I wasn't sure if he was shot or jumped."

"Where were you?" Elizabeth demanded.

Cullen glared for a moment. Out of the corner of her eye, Elizabeth saw Black rush forward.

"I saved your husband's life from one of the guardsmen, madam. Then I distracted the convoy long enough for you to escape. At considerable risk to myself, I might add."

Elizabeth spun around to look at Thomas, presently reclined like an invalid on the settee awaiting Anna Cullen's legendary barley bone broth.

"Is this true, Thomas?"

For a moment, Thomas appeared to regret the fact his life was saved.

"I'm not sure, love. I couldn't see past the end of my nose. It all happened in a blur."

Black laid a restraining hand on Cullen's arm, and tried to

nudge him around Elizabeth into the parlour. Cullen allowed himself to be led, but his eyes hung on a glowering Elizabeth for a moment.

Black eventually dragged Cullen's attention to him, and they locked into a brief proculopathic debate. Elizabeth supposed Black was making some entreaty about the volatile, senseless agitation of women and how Cullen shouldn't take it personally.

In truth, Elizabeth knew she was struggling with her composure. Even if Cullen admitted he endangered her husband's life it wouldn't change what happened, or that Thomas was shaken but alive.

Cullen mumbled something and stalked off in the direction of his study. Black closed the front door, trying to use the action to mask his sigh of exasperation.

"Dr Cullen says he understands your distress, Elizabeth, and that he was also shaken to see Thomas jump off the bridge. But from his vantage point he missed Thomas' appearance, and it was only the first pistol shot that alerted him to the ambush underway."

Elizabeth's eyes narrowed. "He said *all* of that to you just now, Dr Black? In a span of one second?"

"No," Black admitted, sounding more tired than guilty. "But knowing Dr Cullen that's what he *meant* to say, were it not for his pride."

"A kind of proculopathy, in itself," Elizabeth said wryly.

"He'll join us in a moment, I'm sure," Black said.

From the corner, Smith coughed.

"That was a rather excellent display of phlogiston-wielding, madam. I was quite impressed."

Not that she depended on Smith's approval, but Elizabeth allowed the glow of pride to kindle.

"You and Dr Black judged the timing and power of the

phlogiston very well. A fascinating application of your talents."

Elizabeth glanced at her husband, but his eyes were closed and if he heard the exchange it didn't provoke a reaction.

"Thank you, sir."

Grunting, Smith retreated back into the book he'd plucked from Cullen's shelf.

Sitting in the chair opposite the prone Thomas, Black smoothed out the Turkey red papers.

"I'll aspect Monsieur Moreau to inspect these and ensure nothing is missing...but it appears we have the pertinent materials. The Board of Manufactures will be delighted."

Some time passed before a stern-faced Anna Cullen reappeared, ushering a bashful Tytler into the parlour. Tytler almost tripped over himself to drop the papers he was holding in front of Black.

"It's as I told you on, erm, Thursday...no! Wednesday..."

Rubbing his temples, Black waved Tytler's excuses away.

"We recovered the turkey red papers, as you no doubted surmised," Elizabeth said.

"Complaints of fire and grapeshot on North Bridge reached me at the bottom of Nicholson Street," Tytler remarked. "Did you enlist an army?"

"The hue and cry came from the convoy guards," Thomas said, eyes still closed.

If rumours of a phlogiston battle were in circulation, Tytler didn't think them credible enough to mention. He looked at Thomas long enough to determine he wasn't at death's door, then returned to spreading his papers in front of Black, a measure of calm settling now he'd passed the gauntlet that was Cullen's wife.

Anna stood in the doorway watching Tytler from behind, not offering him refreshments. She probably recalled Tytler from when he was a student. No doubt Cullen invited him to dinner at one point. Given Tytler's ragged form, he probably received his fair share of Anna's charity cooking.

"We need to get Moreau out of Edinburgh," Thomas said. "Sir Finney won't stop until he's caught."

Tytler swallowed. Any confusion about his expected involvement was evaporating.

"I mean...I think I've, err, overcome the last round of obstacles and um, patched up the fabric, but, you see..." His unease grew when it became clear the other people in the room did *not* see. "Um...I've never managed to get the contraption more than a few feet off the ground."

They'd foreseen this reaction, which was why Elizabeth requested Tytler bring his blueprints.

"What's the dimensions of your Fire Balloon?"

"Forty foot by twenty five," Tytler replied.

Elizabeth stared at the scribblings until she found the sums she was looking for.

"Well, that's your problem, sir. You're missing half the cubic volume necessary to get a person off the ground."

Tytler spluttered. "Excuse me, madam?" It was as if she'd slapped his mother.

Black rose to his feet. "I told him he needs one hundred and forty cubic feet per kilogram of weight."

"Well, he's either miscopied his own numbers—"

"Impossible!"

"—Or he intends to launch a basket of kittens into the heavens."

"Kittens would make terrible aeronauts," Thomas muttered. "They'd get distracted by a fly and fall out the basket."

Tytler was turning puce. "Madam I can assure you I've checked my calculations four-fold times..."

"And your numbers are wrong," Black said, leaning over Elizabeth's shoulder and tracing the lines of arithmetic. "Mrs Fulhame is correct."

Elizabeth bit her lip and tried not to smile.

She waited until her teacup was drained before rising and following the throat-clearing sounds of Cullen to his upstairs study. The old professor appeared settled following their earlier argument—he was reading patient correspondence and scribbling notes.

"Before Mr Fulhame and I depart, I wanted to inform you we've arranged the next steps of the plan..." She filled Cullen in on the details, ignoring his skeptical expression.

Once she'd finished there was a pause.

"I'm not without my reservations, madam." Cullen blotted his quill dry. "You seem fixated on throwing yourself into the lines of danger."

"But can you do what I ask?" Cullen hadn't proposed any alternative plans since his performance at the Exchange; if he remained doubtful he hadn't criticised her.

"Your proposals have been audacious and risky, but it's clear you've considered most of the key variables and are thinking through challenges in a logical manner."

Perhaps that was why Cullen hadn't undermined her: he thought his unsolicited pedagogy underpinned her recent successes.

Well, if it helped her to have Cullen believe that, she wasn't going to challenge his pride to bolster her own.

"It is enough that I know what I'm doing," replied Elizabeth, resisting the urge to fold her arms. "While your confidence in my abilities is welcome, Dr Cullen, it is not necessary to achieving my goals."

Cullen harrumphed. "My respect for young Thomas Fulhame grows the more I learn about his formidable wife."

"I can assure you, I am his better half." Elizabeth permitted herself a smile.

"If he knows what's good for him, he'll concede that assessment," Cullen said. "Do what you will with your chemical experiments, madam. I'm sure your basic methodology is sound."

Elizabeth sighed. "Unfortunately Sir Finney put a stop to that." They would be uncovering tiny shards of glass in their armoire drawers and beneath the furniture for months to come, each one a painful reminder.

Cullen frowned, then grunted as he remembered the destruction he'd seen for himself. "You should ask Joe if he's got spare distillation apparatus in the university cellar. I'm sure he'd give you what he can."

"I'm afraid we're not able to compensate Dr Black..."

"Nonsense, Joe would happily hand over equipment gratis. If you don't mind it being a bit dirty or perhaps missing a valve. Neither Joe nor myself were ones for throwing away laboratory supplies, I'm sure he'll be glad to clear some space..."

Would it be that easy? Elizabeth wondered. She supposed a polished, affluent student wouldn't hesitate to request their professors' cast-off apparatus. That thought stiffened her resolve. She inclined her head. "That is a sensible suggestion. As soon as Monsieur Moreau is safe I'll raise the issue with Dr Black."

"Sorry to interrupt, dear..." Anna slipped into the room and made straight for Cullen. She whispered in her husband's ear. Cullen frowned, then grunted an acknowledgment.

"Let's go downstairs, madam. We need to confer with the others."

Anna chewed on her lower lip.

Downstairs, Black and Thomas looked up from the papers.

"Anna tells me there are gentleman congregating in the close," Cullen announced. "Refrain from looking for yourself, we don't want them to know who is inside the house."

Anna went to the window and peered again.

"There's five of them now, though two might be stopping by to confer. I can't see much in this light."

"Do they not know Sir Finney just lost his entire fortune?" Thomas said bitingly.

"I suppose he still possesses his sizeable purse," Elizabeth said, watching Anna's expression. Then she looked round the room. "Where is Tytler?"

"He left while you were upstairs with Dr Cullen," Black said.

"Departed a good few minutes before these rogues appeared," Anna added. "I think they missed him."

"We can only hope." Elizabeth's plan rested on Tytler getting around Edinburgh unmolested. "He isn't returning to Duddingston, is he?"

"He's sleeping *locally*, no doubt." Cullen's sarcastic inflection made it obvious what kind of local establishment he believed Tytler would spend the night at.

"Do you suppose those men will stay here all night?"

Black pushed away the papers. "It is likely Dillon expects some to-ing and fro-ing from us. His men may well conceal themselves to give us the impression they're no longer spying. Hopefully this is less about violent retribution than tracking down Moreau and the papers. At this point."

"We're not changing the plan." Elizabeth folded her arms. "Parts of it are already in motion."

"Yes, we know." Black picked at a clean sheet of paper. "While all of us together could overpower five hostile sentries, we risk alerting Dillon to our intentions."

Anna re-appeared in the room. "They've not yet filled into Todrick's wynd, as far as I can see. But if you want to take advantage of that fact you better hurry."

"There's an entranceway on the other side of the building?" Elizabeth hadn't noticed.

"Not to our dwellings," Anna said. "Only to the mint factory ground floor. Well, it's been bricked up a good few years now. We have two first floor windows overlooking the wynd."

"I fear you and Mrs Fulhame will have to enact the plan without us," Black said. "I can distract Sir Finney's men by departing in the opposite direction."

It was a sensible, pragmatic decision. Elizabeth's insides still turned cold at the thought.

"Are you sure?"

"They'll follow me home, but I'm doubtful they'll attack. I can try to lose them tomorrow morning, but I worry about drawing them back to you." Black looked calm.

"You think that Adam will..."

"He can protect Monsieur Moreau in adequate fashion, and I know he's alert to the possibility of being tracked."

It would have to do. Anna had brought the Fulhames their cloaks and hats.

"You don't fear an attack, Dr Cullen?" Elizabeth knew what happened to the physicians in McIntyre's house, and the thought of being trapped in a burning building filled her with terror.

Cullen look amused. "Don't forget madam, this building was conceived as fortress to protect Scotland's fortunes. The stone walls are the thickest in the city. I would like to see Sir Finney try to force his way in."

268

Elizabeth supposed the windows *were* rather small. Not that Cullen's hubris mattered much to her—she and Thomas were the ones who needed to sneak out.

Thomas held out his hand. "Let us venture forth, my lady."

"Good luck," Black said. "Stay safe."

29

25 AUGUST 1784

The 25th of August was a typical underwhelming Scottish morning, though Tytler enthused these were perfect atmospheric conditions for a balloon flight. Elizabeth couldn't deny the strong breeze in the air, and the promise of sunshine and warmth when it came time for launch.

At 5 o'clock in the morning, Comely Gardens still bore traces of the nights' festivities. Empty lanterns hung on the trees. To get to the fire balloon Elizabeth walked over a trail of spent firework shells, bottles and dancers' ribbons.

A few sweepers and cleaners poked the debris across the lawns, but otherwise a grey stillness hung over the place. "It's fine for us to do this," Tytler insisted. "I have a standing arrangement with the owners."

It wasn't as though they had a choice: Tytler stored his Fire Balloon in the gardens, and the walled grounds was one of the few places in Edinburgh offering some secrecy for the launch.

Tytler couldn't have got much sleep—Elizabeth wouldn't under those circumstances—and he fluttered around the balloon with useless agitation. Once inflated, the fire balloon would stand as tall as a two storey house. Tyler called the construction that hung below it a 'basket', but to the Fulhames it looked more like a slat of wood with naught but ropes to grip onto.

"The original basket was destroyed the last time I tried to launch the Fire Balloon here," Tytler explained. "Drunken onlookers smashed it."

No one could accuse the Edinburgh mobs of circumspection.

She watched—initially from a safe distance—as the balloon filled with hot air. First he'd hung the empty sheets on a crane above the furnace so the linen wouldn't burn, removing the crane once the balloon lazily bobbed upright of its own accord. Despite its overnight dissection and re-sewing, and despite the conflagration of the Register Office attempt, the flame retardant varnish worked and the balloon held its air.

Elizabeth dared not enquire after the time, in case it raised her heart rate to intolerable levels. She had to believe the inflation would occur without incidence, everything proceeding according to schedule.

"It needs half an hour of heating," Tytler yelled. "Else it deflates the second we remove the furnace."

Elizabeth edged around the tethered balloon to examine it further. Despite its tattered appearance, barely any smoke escaped the fabric. She hoped the trees still concealed it from general view outside the Gardens.

"Maybe stay away from that side..." Thomas called out. He hung close to Tytler, watching with polite interest as the man manipulated the laws of heat and air.

Elizabeth was going to make a sharp retort, but a sound on the edge of her hearing finally made itself noticed.

It was impossible to place at first, and Tytler's merry bustling made her wonder if it came from the Fire Balloon itself.

The roar of the furnace muffled the noise, but it spread around the perimeter and grew more defined.

Thomas tensed. His hands rose from his sides.

"Sweetheart, I..." He began. Then he froze.

"What?" Elizabeth tried to ask, before a blow between her shoulder blades sent her stumbling forward. Before she had time to recover, a hand grabbed her shoulder and forced her head back into a sharp metal object that almost crushed her windpipe.

"Think *very* carefully before you act, gentlemen. Good morning to you, Mrs Fulhame."

Dillon jammed a pistol muzzle into the cartilage of her neck. The loaded weapon wasn't necessary—he would have the same effect with the tips of his fingers—but Tytler and the other onlookers wouldn't recognise the threat otherwise.

She could see the faintest glow around the fists of her husband, though his face betrayed an impotent rage. Dillon's grip on her arm was strong enough to stop her being able to jerk free. He backed away.

Elizabeth could hear Dillon's accomplices step forward, intending to get between them and the men.

"Do us a favour sir, and move away from the balloon. Then we can talk."

It wasn't an abduction yet. Dillon was trying to protect himself while he made his proper threats.

"Remove the stove from the fire balloon," Dillon instructed. "It's not going anywhere."

She heard the sound of compliance. There were a lot more lackeys here in the gardens than she first thought. The balloon —now fully inflated—strained against its tethering. Without the heavy stove weighing it down, it seemed determined to break free. It would be some time before the hot air inside the balloon dissipated, though.

"Tytler forgot to lock the gate," Elizabeth said, mostly to herself.

"I assure you..." Dillon's voice dripped with satisfaction. "...James' oversight was intentional."

A nasty suspicion settled over Elizabeth that she could predict how the rest of the conversation would unfold.

"Do I sense a personal connection to the aeronaut, my lord?"

Dillon made an exclamation of delight. "You know how to cut through social niceties to the heart of the matter, Mrs Fulhame. I first made an acquaintance of Mr Tytler earlier in the summer, when he was seeking sponsors for his Fire Balloon project."

Thomas glowered at his wife. "This was a fact the gentleman neglected to mention."

"However, I admit at the time I was hesitant to invest. Like you, I harboured scepticism about Balloon Tytler's capability of flight. Naturally, I conducted a few enquiries of my own into the gentleman's character..."

"My lord!"

Dillon glanced at Tytler, who'd stepped away from the balloon and was surrounded by flintlock-wielding Gaels. He'd re-adopted a cowering posture.

"What you may not know about our adventurous *Ranger,*" Dillon began, "Is that though his wide-ranging assignations with Edinburgh's ladies might suggest a broad palate..."

"I beseech you, my lord!"

"...Is in fact Mr Tytler is preoccupied with a very specific act of pleasure. In fact, so rare and peculiar a preference that only one lady of Edinburgh offers to fulfil such services. And tragically for Mr Tytler she refuses to accept his visitations."

Tytler looked ready to curl up on the ground.

Dillon ignored his pitiful display. "Fortunately, the misunderstanding that led to such a painful estrangement between the lady and Mr Tytler can be smoothed other by thoughtful compensation."

"It must have been Jean Fordyce - the whore who dresses in men's breeches." Elizabeth exclaimed. "You useless turncoat, Tytler!"

Dillon smirked. "No, in fact the service in question is one even Mr Tytler blushes to mention in the pages of his guide. But I must compliment you Mrs Fulhame for your commitment to diverse reading interests."

"That breeches lady caught my attention too..." Thomas mused.

Why are men like this? Elizabeth raged to herself. They'd sell their souls—and the souls of their friends—for a hour with a raggedy whore who hated their guts. Dillon must have been pleased he didn't have to reach into twice his purse to seal that miserable promise of cooperation.

"He threatened to kill both my wives!" Tytler blurted out.

"Our charming French guest will be waiting at Mr Smith's for the balloon to ready? Mrs Fulhame and myself will call upon them next." Another tug sent Elizabeth backwards. Dillon was moving again, glancing over his shoulder to check he wasn't about to tumble into the balloon.

"Do what's necessary to survive, love," whispered Thomas' voice in her head. *"But if ye inconvenience Sir Finney by killing the bastard I wouldn't be too upset."*

Elizabeth let Sir Finney jerk her back, keeping himself between her and Thomas. He needed to edge around the balloon to reach his remaining entourage.

Now!

Elizabeth dropped her weight down and sideways, as if in a faint, driving her elbow backwards. Sir Finney stumbled, then toppled against the basket, having collided with a guy line. Elizabeth tried to scramble up using the basket ropes for support, but the air balloon basket swung underneath them, straining to lift from the ground. Sir Finney grabbed the back of her gown and with his other hand he reached towards her husband...

Elizabeth sent a blast of white-hot phlogiston through the guy line, incinerating it within seconds. The basket jerked up a metre.

Then the basket jerked upwards again. The other mooring pegs popped loose once the first was freed. The hot air balloon basket lurched under her. With a shriek, Elizabeth grabbed onto a rope and flailed for purchase under her feet. Either a rope was loose, or Tytler hadn't thought to check the basket ropes were of even length.

For a second Elizabeth intended to slide off, but the ground shrank below her at a terrifying rate, and she now faced a fall of several metres onto the packed mud of the park. Her grip on the rope tightened.

Elizabeth jammed the instep of her heel over the rope in the lowest corner of the basket. She could feel coarse fibres tearing at her palm. The basket was almost tipped vertically, but at least the ropes held.

Every muscle in Elizabeth's body trembled with tension. She hardly dared breathe for fear of pitching to her death.

Less than a hands' reach from her, Dillon was experiencing a similar reaction. He was breathing through his nose, holding on to the rope with both hands and balancing his foot on a knot. Elizabeth dared not look down to see how far above the ground they were.

A minute ago she'd assumed Sir Finney wouldn't hesitate to blast her, but now he dared not let go of the rope with even one hand, for fear the basket would upend him. Right now, there was a measure of balance to the basket from the pair of them keeping stock still.

"I'm sick of stupid women like you!" Sir Finney snarled.

"Never thinking before they act. Never caring about the consequences of their actions."

Bit rich coming from him. She could feel Sir Finney's fear, impotence and fury meld together. That was the most dangerous combination for her, so she kept her mouth pressed shut.

Some of the fear was ebbing away, simply because her body and mind couldn't tolerate being this terrified for a chronic length of time. Without moving her head, she could see Calton Hill receding into the distance. They were flying west over the city, which she supposed was a better outcome than drifting into the Firth of Forth. She didn't dare look down—that would cause her body weight to shift anyway—so she didn't know how high above the ground they were.

"You'll pay for your gall, madam." Sir Finney's eyes were slits. "Nothing will give me greater pleasure."

"Are you sure?" Elizabeth asked. Her voice was shaking as she raised it over the roar of air in her ears, but the words had to come out. "Or did you not notice what your cherished mistress is doing?"

* * *

It was the misdirection con. The target was so sure he'd spotted the first deception that he overlooked the second one playing out underneath his nose.

Two nights previous, Lydia had frowned once Elizabeth finished the explanation in her boudoir. "I don't understand what's unladylike about proposing to run off with large sums of money."

Elizabeth sat down on the corner of Lydia's bed, with less tension in her body than she held a moment ago. "Some ladies dislike admitting an interest in that."

Lydia folded her hands on her knee. She looked relieved, as if she'd been waiting for someone to ask her to do this.

"You speak with a refined air, but I detect a west coast inflection in some of your words, do I not?"

"Quite so," Lydia agreed. "I spent my childhood in Glasgow, my mother moved to Edinburgh when I was twelve."

"And you are already acquainted with Monsieur Moreau."

This was the tricky part.

"He's a fool. I could have demanded ten guineas for my services that night and he would have emptied his moneybags without hesitation. Then he would still leave bragging he'd secured my affections through charm." Lydia looked at Elizabeth shrewdly, predicting the flow of the conversation. "Fools like that are easy to manage."

It was a calculation like every other one Lydia made. Was it profitable to remain the kept mistress of Sir Finney Dillon, lately ruined on the Edinburgh Exchange? Or were there safer ways to retain her comfortable lifestyle?

"I imagine there are plenty of harried Glasgow merchants who crave a resourceful business partner," Elizabeth said. "I won't pretend it would be a life of finery like you enjoy here, but perhaps..."

"Finney doesn't keep me for my intelligence," Lydia finished. "His class of men only seek my adornment. I've given up expecting love...but maybe there's a practical bachelor out there with the capacity to respect his wife."

* * *

Sir Finney grimaced. "Bitch."

Elizabeth couldn't help noticing the balloon seemed to be dropping. It was a slow descent—for now—but without someone to supervise the flight and combustion, the balloon was running out of hot air.

Elizabeth recognised the spacious look in Sir Finney's eyes —similar to Moira's before she struck watercarrier Phil in the face. It was the look of a man deciding that the closer to the ground the balloon got, the more willing he was to risk injury if it meant punishing the woman who ruined his fortunes.

There it was.

Sir Finney let go of the rope with one hand. The open palm hovered above the rope for a second, seeking the reassurance of proximity while he recalibrated his balance.

Do it!

Elizabeth launched herself forward, swinging off her ropes and kicking her legs out. Her heels jabbed Sir Finney in the stomach. Not expecting her to perform such a risky move, he folded and his foot lost the support of the rope.

Sir Finney's eyes widened. He fell backwards, clutching onto the rope and the side of the basket for a second, before slipping down and out of sight.

Elizabeth slithered down the tilted basket, allowing herself to fall over the bottom rope of the basket, which caught under her rib cage.

The basket pitched down at a steeper angle, and the rope swayed below her, but by now Elizabeth had got her hands around the rope and folded herself tighter around it. She was like a child again, hanging upside-down on a branch with Lottie, trying to see how long they could last before they got too dizzy to continue. The rope dug into the softest flesh of her stomach, but she wasn't slipping.

Elizabeth saw the ground wasn't too far away from her. Sir Finney might have survived the fall, but she couldn't see where he landed. She thought she could hear shouts from the fields, but maybe that was just dismayed livestock.

She preferred not to let go, but Elizabeth realised if she didn't she might get buried under a deflating balloon and smouldering linens.

Nothing for it.

She wriggled and let herself slide off the rope, until she was only holding on with her sweaty, stinging palms. There was no use holding on at that point—she had no strength left to do so.

With a squawk, Elizabeth dropped onto a freshly-ploughed field, letting herself crumple and roll.

For a moment she was submerged in the damp soil. Dirt covered her eyes, nose and mouth. Then she spluttered up for air.

In the distance, gulls cawed.

Spreadeagled on her back, Elizabeth wasn't sure she wanted to part from the earth again. But her stomach was agony, and the tug of danger from a vengeful Sir Finney meant she didn't want to stay here indefinitely.

A handful of farm workers now pursued the fire balloon across the ploughed field, hopping up and down to catch a trailing guy line rope. Freed of its passenger, the balloon rose slightly out of grasp, but the balloon itself looked shrunken. It would give up within minutes.

An older farmhand—clearly too old for chasing balloons—hobbled towards her. At two metres distance he halted and leant on his walking stick.

Elizabeth staggered to her feet. It took a couple of false starts, with her clinging onto the ground until her legs steadied themselves. By this point, the farmhand decided this strange, mud-caked woman wasn't a threat to him, so ambled forward with a hand outstretched.

"Missy?"

"Forgive me," Elizabeth gasped. She clung onto his smock, because the ground was rocking alarmingly underfoot. "But where am I?"

"Eastern-most edge of the Hopetoun estate."

"You mean, the property of the Earl of Hopetoun?"

"The very same."

"Good." Elizabeth cautiously planted one foot in front of the other, hoping the ground wouldn't play any more tricks on her. "We have a mutual philosophical friend in common. If he is receiving visitors I think I can afford a satisfactory explanation for this intrusion."

"If you say so, madam," the farmhand replied with a frown, still trying to discern if Elizabeth was a madwoman, victim or escaped convict. It was nice in a way—until he learned more, he wasn't thinking of her as someone's wife.

30

The group made a miserable sight in the Nicholson's Tavern. Elizabeth decided to join her husband in drinking as briskly as she could, swatting off Black and Cullen's attempts to inspect her for injuries or shock. The two professors sat in the booth, clutching their drinks and keeping an eye on the surroundings.

"Rest yersel', good doctors," Thomas protested. "They won't be finding us here."

"I suppose not," conceded Black, his claret remaining unsipped. He kept glancing around.

"Admirable work, Mrs Fulhame," Cullen said. A frown crossed his face as Elizabeth drained her glass. "You showed much courage under fire."

"You high esteem of me has always been a great comfort," Elizabeth loudly said. "Even though my resemblance to Russian nobility is meagre at best." Cullen had the decency to look embarrassed.

Sir Finney had not yet been recovered. Elizabeth wasn't sure what height she'd knocked him from the Fire Balloon, which frustrated Cullen.

"Depending on the drop he might retain the use of his

lower limbs," Cullen had commented as he gave up his inter-rogation. "I won't volunteer to treat him, though." Elizabeth found she didn't much care whether he lived. It was unlikely Sir Finney would recuperate in Edinburgh. Black had shushed Thomas and Cullen's attempts to speculate further on the subject, but thanks to Lydia there wasn't much for him left in Scotland, if he survived.

"Dr Black, he's not going to come barging through the door." She was tired and shaken. The Earl of Hopetoun dispatched one of his carriages to get her back to Edinburgh. For most of the journey she'd been numb. It was only when she returned to her husband and saw how the others reacted to her—their agitation and relief—that her own emotions awoke.

"I'm here because I know I couldn't wrestle you indoors in your current state, not for any length of time, so the least I can do is make sure you're safe," Black said quietly.

Elizabeth turned her beckoning of the barmaid into a dismissal. The previous drinks hadn't helped her, and she doubted the subsequent ones would either.

"You can drink a few more cups," Cullen added. "I think you're owed that. After that we might have to intervene."

Thomas looked like he wanted to call the barmaid back over, but hesitated for his wife's sake. Or maybe Black's words struck a chord of guilt in him too. He'd been muted all evening. Elizabeth didn't want to know—yet—what he'd felt as she floated into the sky with Sir Finney.

"With any luck Moreau will be safe. I hope he doesn't tarry."

While Tytler inflated his balloon and Dillon's associates were amassing nearby, Smith handed Moreau over to Lydia, who smuggled him out of Edinburgh. Smith reported the men had rushed after the Fire Balloon, so he directed the pair towards the borders. It would take him longer to reach the west coast, but no one was likely to catch him and Lydia claimed she knew safe routes.

"Does your cousin speak French?" Black asked.

Elizabeth laughed. "Not a word. But I'm sure Moreau can make himself understood." It was too early to allow herself much hope—she'd wondered how long it would take for profits from the turkey red process to trickle back to Meath, or if the business venture would collapse before she and Thomas saw Moreau's promised "token of gratitude."

Dillon was right in his calculations: Lottie and Don's mill was the ideal place to adapt turkey red dyeing to Scotland.

It would be several hours before word from Tytler could reach them. As far as anybody knew, he'd gone to ground once Dillon's men fled Comely Gardens. Dillon's associates might retaliate if they caught him, but Elizabeth knew there was a slimy endurance to Tytler. He'd survive.

"I couldn't help but notice that some of your outrage at Mr Tytler's betrayal seemed...feigned." Black said carefully.

"I may have anticipated the general turn of events, albeit not the specifics," Elizabeth replied with equal care. "I thought it likely Dillon would catch wind of the Fire Balloon launch."

Black nodded. "Very good, madam."

"We should be heading home soon," Thomas said, putting an arm on his wife's shoulder. "We can take care of ourselves, good doctors."

"...But thank you for the company," Elizabeth added.

"Think nothing of it. I had to send my apologies to my friend Dr James Hutton." Black rotated his claret glass as he stared into the candle. "He doesn't like it when our evening plans unexpectedly change, but I know he'll understand."

"Is he still playing around with those geological theories?" Thomas asked. "It seems like he hasn't spoken about them in a while."

Black's face brightened. "Ah, the silence speaks to the nearness of completion. He's too intent on fine-tuning his ideas to talk about them."

Hutton's geological pet project was something Elizabeth often heard mentioned, but the philosophers were so familiar with their friend's ideas they never saw it fit to explain the details.

"It's quite a significant discovery, I understand?"

"Quite." In the candlelight Black's eyes shone. "If you'll pardon the pun madam, it could even be considered...Earth-shattering."

HISTORICAL NOTE

Some of this actually happened. Sort of.

In 1794 a woman called Mrs Elizabeth Fulhame published *An Essay On Combustion with a View to a New Art of Dying and Painting, wherein the Phlogistic and Antiphlogistic Hypotheses are Proved Erroneous.* In it, she described over a decade's painstaking chemical research developing metallic fabrics dyes. Thanks to her observations, she was able to describe the act of catalysis—water speeding up a chemical reaction without itself being consumed—forty years before it was "discovered" and named by Bergus. A few of her metallic salts proved to be light sensitive, and she was credited by William Herschel as laying the groundwork for photography.

Despite these achievements, for all we know of the real woman, Elizabeth Fulhame *may* have been a magic-wielding, horse-stealing crime fighter. We know more about her husband Thomas—a medical student at the University of Edinburgh—than the chemistry pioneer herself. We don't know her maiden name, when she married Thomas Fulhame, or even if she was Irish. Her fiery, feminist *Essay* is all we have of her voice.

I created this fictionalised heroine from the bones of the historical record. We know Thomas Fulham(e) came from Navan in Meath county, where he had a complicated relationship with his brother Patrick. We know Thomas enjoyed unusual stature with Joseph Black: he took Black's chemistry course several years in a row, and Black's correspondence shows Thomas carrying out business on Black's behalf in London, and Black recommending Thomas' own chemical projects to his government contacts. Reaction to Elizabeth the chemist was mixed even in her own time: it is clear from the introduction to her *Essay* that she corresponded with and was encouraged by numerous philosophers, even though her husband considered her goals "improbable." Some reviewers lauded her *Essay*, some found it more titillating than edifying, and others called it "frivolous and womanish." It is guesswork on my part that Black supported her...though I'll note he was one of the few men in Britain to acquire a lump of platina (platinum), and Elizabeth recorded trying platina as one of her metallic dyes. Given that she was the wife of a not-very-successful doctor, I'm not sure she could have afforded to buy the metal on her own.

Two real events depicted in this book have been brought closer together than they occurred in reality. The first British air balloon flight did take place in Edinburgh in August 1784. Its pilot James Tytler was every bit as complicated and extraordinary as I've depicted him here, and he also failed to achieve widespread recognition for his accomplishments.

Several years later, the Board of Trades asked Black to evaluate a lucrative turkey red dyeing procedure smuggled off the Continent by an opportunistic Frenchman. Moreau is a fictionalised version of the real individual. Black's chemical consultancy work took up a lot of his time throughout his teaching career, and Adam Smith was one of his closest friends.

Ramsay Gardens remains a striking feature on the Edinburgh skyline, though its brightly-coloured houses are a remake and extension of the original buildings that sat on this site in the 18th century. The original Ramsay Lodge had one less floor, making Thomas' escape slightly more plausible. I relied on watercolours and sketches from the Edinburgh Capital Collections to imagine how the building would look in the 1780s.

Lastly, the grocer-cum-locksmith "Georgie" made a second attempt to break into the Excise Office in 1788...only this time he and his crew weren't so lucky. George Smith is less well-known today than the gang's ringleader Deacon William Brodie, whose duplicitous life as a gambler, thief and reputable townsperson inspired RL Stevenson to write *The Strange Case of Dr Jekyll and Mr Hyde*.

Through such tales, legends are made.

AFTERWORD

Thank you so much for reading *A Treatise of Air*. With so many awesome books out there, I'm grateful you chose to pick up mine.

If you enjoyed reading this story, please consider leaving a review on Amazon or Goodreads, even if it's just a sentence to say you liked it. Indie authors like myself depend on your honest reviews to help us find our audience.

George Stephens and the professors will return in book three of The Edinburgh Doctrines series, *The Chronicles of Earth*.

The Fulhames will return in book four, *A Philosophy of Metal*.

Acknowledgments

My first foray into the world of Elizabeth Fulhame came while writing a feature about her for *Physics Today*. Thanks to Andy for taking an early punt on her. Extra gratitude to Pete and Jack who shared with me the results of their independent research into the life of Mrs Fulhame, and whose findings inform some of the narrative decisions made in my novel. All inaccuracies are my own.

Getting your second novel airborne is a tricky feat: I'm not alone in struggling with my sophomore book. I must therefore thank the hosts, administrators and fellow participants of Shut up And Write! and Writers HQ, whose numerous writing sprinting sessions helped kick *Treatise's* word count up to a respectable level.

Early drafts of this story were shared with my historical fantasy critique group. Thanks to Anna, John and Angela for your insight.

To everyone who bought, reviewed or otherwise championed *The Doctrines of Fire*: your support means the world to me. I cannot thank you enough.

ABOUT THE AUTHOR

CL Jarvis holds a PhD in chemistry and worked as a science journalist, healthcare copywriter, and medical writer before sitting down to write her first novel. She's held together by cat hair and double espressos, and lives in Philadelphia, USA.

You can learn more about her at: www.clairejarvis.com.

 facebook.com/cljarvisauthor
instagram.com/cljarvisauthor

www.ingramcontent.com/pod-product-compliance
Lightning Source LLC
Chambersburg PA
CBHW011032190726
48290CB00011B/2814